BITE THE WOMAN THAT FEEDS

DIRTY BLOOD
BOOK 1

PENELOPE BARSETTI

HARTWICK PUBLISHING

Hartwick Publishing

Bite The Woman That Feeds

Copyright © 2023 by Penelope Barsetti

All rights reserved.

For My Readers,

You're the reason I get to do this every day.

And I can't thank you enough.

ACKNOWLEDGMENTS

Special thanks to these readers who made this book a reality:

Katy DiPrima

Julia

Shelby Andrews

Alicia Scott

Stacey Gonzalez

Athena Rain

Christal Bolotte

CONTENTS

1

LARISA

I wrung out the cloth soaked in herbs in my hands and squeezed the excess warm water from the fabric. Once the linen was damp and not saturated, I applied it to the woman's forehead, her skin gray as storm clouds. Only a few seconds of silence followed, and then the coughs returned, racking her body as she jerked in unnatural directions.

I returned the cloth to the pail and repeated, applying the damp towel once her coughs had subsided. She wasn't the only patient in the room. The hall was full of sick and dying people, and those who cared for them took all precautions to dodge the sickness, but they would eventually succumb to it as well.

But not me.

The plague had killed thousands, tens of thousands, and those who survived retained permanent disabilities, such as decreased lung capacity, heart complications, and other diseases. It struck our lands six weeks ago, and it continued to hit us in waves. I was a maid in the castle, not a healer, but I'd been assigned the task simply because I remained healthy while others perished from the disease.

I was immune.

Someone else might rejoice at the gift, but not me.

Not after I'd lost everyone I loved.

The door opened. "Larisa, King Elias wishes to speak with you."

My heart sank like an anchor from a galleon. It struck the bottom then tilted over, locked in the darkness of the abyss. I stared into the eyes of the dying woman, her eyes cloudy from the slow spread of death, and then returned the cloth to the bucket. I'd done nothing for her except ease her passing, but she was so far gone she didn't even know I was there.

Nothing. Neither suffering nor pain.

I followed the guard back to the castle and waited for the doors to open. Strict precautions were in place to protect the royal family, their constituents, and their staff. Messages were relayed through written missives slipped underneath doors and windows. Once the guard who escorted me had stepped back, the doors were opened and I was allowed passage into the castle.

The doors were shut behind me, and I was in a different world. Luxurious rugs, crystal chandeliers, goblets made of pure gold, paintings by the finest artists from our history were all displayed throughout the castle. It was also quiet, no coughs echoing down the corridor, and it smelled like fresh flowers instead of death.

"Come with me." The guard escorted me upstairs and down various hallways. I already knew where we were going—and why we took the longer route to get there. We eventually arrived at his study, a large room with a grand hearth, plush rugs strewn across the stone floor, and an imposing desk made of cherry wood.

The guard let me inside and immediately departed.

King Elias stood behind his desk, his eyes locked upon me the moment I entered his presence. Young, handsome, a man who never should have been king. A heavy stare ensued, the two of us thinking about moments that were now locked in the past.

I was the first one to speak. "What duties do you have for me, my lord?" It was easy to keep a straight face because my heart had touched the void. I didn't dare look at his left hand—where the ring of gold reflected the flames in the hearth. It was a cold day, and that only exasperated the sickness.

He came around the desk, his cloak of grandeur trailing behind him, the crest of his house on the handstitched vest that fit snugly over his strong chest. He stopped directly in front of me, standing far too close to someone infinitely inferior. "I've never been so unhappy in all my life."

A rock tossed into the abyss, going deeper and deeper, the pit bottomless. Bursts of agony like shooting stars. A throb. A writhe.

The confession failed to tug on my heartstrings. "My lord, if you stepped into your city, you would see you have no reason to feel so."

He took a slight breath. "Don't do that—"

"This plague has already decimated the population by thirty percent—"

"Call me by my name, the name you used to scream in my ear."

I flinched as if his gloved palm had just struck my face. "I can't do that, my lord."

He released another breath, clearly annoyed by my formality. "You know I didn't want this."

"But you still agreed."

"I didn't have a choice—"

"You're the king, Elias. You're the *only* one who does have a choice."

The window behind him showed the overcast skies. The large flames in his grand hearth weren't strong enough to chase away the harshest winter in living memory. With the posture of a king, he stared at me, clearly at a loss for words.

A pot of simmering water, hot enough to boil if his emotions deepened.

"You made your choice, and now we both have to live with it. So, please...leave me be."

He swallowed, his throat shifting. "I meant what I said to you. I intended to leave my royal ties to settle for the life of a commoner with you. But then my father died...and then my older brother died...leaving the crown to me. To deny the crown in a time of need would be to spit on the graves of all my forefathers."

My eyes dropped. "But you didn't have to marry her..."

Now he looked away too, ashamed. *Curling into a ball, tight around his own body, adopting a fetal position. Withdrawing his mind, body, and soul.* "Yes, I did. I need an heir—"

"And I couldn't birth your sons?" I raised my chin, my anger hotter than the flames in the hearth. "Because I have dirty blood?"

His eyes remained averted. "Even if I wanted to, it wouldn't have been allowed—"

"Then, as King of Raventower, you make it *allowed*."

"I'm a pawn in an institution, Larisa—"

"That's an excuse. You just wanted to ensure the legitimacy of your heirs, which means power is more important than love. At least be a man and be straight about it. A man should never tell a woman he loves her unless he's willing to burn the world for her."

"I do love you."

"Then where are the ashes?"

He stared, locked into silence. Pain. *The kind that throbs. The kind that writhes.*

I stared back, my breaths so deep they were painful. "You're a married man, Elias. You shouldn't speak to a lesser woman this way."

He turned quiet, letting the seconds trickle by until a painful minute had passed. But he remained in front of me, as if he had more to say. "I don't love her. She doesn't love me."

"But you're attracted to her."

Slightly taken aback, he paused as he lost his ground. "I'm not attracted—"

"Yes, you are." I'd seen it. I'd felt it.

He went quiet, his eyes locked on me. When enough tension had passed, he continued. "There's no reason our relationship can't continue."

"So you'll fuck her like a mare to breed and make love to me later? That's romantic."

"I still want to be with you, and yes, I think that is romantic."

The knife was already between my ribs—but now it twisted. "I'll never be a man's secret, only his oath. From this moment on, I'm a servant to Raventower and the royal family—nothing else."

———

Raventower was a ghost town.

Two months ago, it was a booming city of trade and commerce, laughing children playing in the streets and fields, vases of flowers in every window to welcome visitors inside. The pubs were full of men after a long day of work, and the shops were full of women ready to sell their selection of cheeses and perfumes.

Now...there wasn't a person in sight.

I walked home in the dark, the biting cold sweeping down the cobblestone roads and freezing my fingertips. Sometimes I heard a cough down an alley—but I wasn't sure if it was real or just a morbid product of my imagination.

By the time I made it home, my body was weary—and so was my heart.

Before the plague swept across our lands, I was wrapped up in a passionate affair with a man who was willing to leave his royal ties to be with me. My mother was still with me, picking the fruits from our garden to feed ourselves as well as the citizens of Raventower. Now, the man I loved was married to someone else, slept beside her every night, fucked her every night.

And my mother was dead.

I was immune to this plague, but I felt sick nonetheless.

2

KINGSNAKE

Knock. Knock. Knock.

I had been dead asleep moments ago, but now I was wide awake. I jerked the sheets off me and swung my legs over the edge of the bed. "Yes?"

The door cracked, and the servant of my house appeared. "General Viper needs to speak with you. It's urgent."

"I'll be there momentarily."

Prior shut the door.

I threw on my attire, my cloak, and secured my sword to my hip and my dagger to my belt. I stormed through my great halls, passed the bonfires that warmed the stone, and reached the foyer.

The general's eyes were locked on me the second I appeared at the top of the stairs. With his hands behind his back and his body decorated in his armor, he watched me descend, hardly blinking.

We came face-to-face. "What is it, Viper?"

His eyes shifted back and forth between mine. "It's Rose... She's dead."

————

My prey lay there upon the ground, puncture marks all over her fair skin. She was so pale, paler than snow. The blood reserved for me had been feasted upon by lesser vampires. Her eyes were open and lidless, staring at the ceiling she couldn't see. "Who did this?"

Stoic as ever, General Viper seemed unconcerned with Rose's death. "Does it matter?" He lifted his gaze and locked it upon me. "Food grows scarcer every day. We lost a few of our kind—inconsequential numbers, but now we're losing some every single day. This isn't an act of betrayal to their king. It's an act of desperation."

The plague that had swept across the kingdoms was destroying our numbers as much as theirs. We couldn't feed on the sick without dying, and those who remained healthy never left their homes. Few humans offered themselves to us to be prey in return for liberation from the plague through immortality, but we were so hungry we never kept our word. Whether human or vampire, there was no escape from this sickness.

Two months had come and gone, and the sickness showed no signs of slowing. It wouldn't only decimate their population, but also ours. "We're officially in desperate times. We'll need to storm Raventower and feed on the healthy."

"There's no way to be certain who's sick and who's healthy. If our vampires feed on infected blood, they'll die themselves."

We didn't contract the plague the way humans did, simply because we didn't need to breathe. Many of us, myself included, still performed the action unconsciously. But if we ingested infected blood, it would kill us that way, a slow and painful death. "The royal family has isolated themselves from their people. We'll storm the castle and demand a donation if they wish to spare their lives—*for the moment*."

General Viper gave a nod. "If they give us enough, and we control our hunger, we should survive until this comes to pass."

———

We made the trek from Grayson on horseback, through the mountain pass, and approached Raventower from the north. Since it was the kingdom closest to ours, their army was responsible for keeping us at bay, but the plague had now made it impossible to defend themselves from any attack.

We approached their front gate and observed the men on the watchtower turn frantic. Horns blared, but no soldiers came. We'd fought battles at this very gate, but they failed to understand we never wished to conquer them. We just needed to feed, and feeding on fallen soldiers was the equivalent to dining out.

"I seek an audience with King Reginald." I guided my horse forward and stared at the frightened soldier who barely looked old enough to be a man. Their army had been replaced by their sons, sons who'd never been properly trained in the blade.

"King Reginald is dead."

No surprise there. "Then I wish to speak to King Edward."

"He's dead too. King Elias, the second son, now leads us."

His reign would be short-lived like his predecessors. "Then open your gates, and I will speak with him."

The soldier disappeared, and minutes later, he returned. "What is this regarding?"

I couldn't control my impatience, not even for a child. "That is a matter between kings."

He left again, and this time when he came back, he looked frightened. "I can't let you pass."

"Then I'll break down this feeble gate and claim these lands for my own." I gestured to General Viper, my second-in-command.

He immediately moved forward with the other soldiers, prepared to remove the gate from its hinges.

"Wait!" The boy left, returned, and then finally opened the gates. "You may pass."

My heels tapped into the flank of my horse, and I entered Raventower, a once-flourishing kingdom now quiet as if it'd been abandoned by its people. There were no citizens in the streets, all hiding in their homes or dying at the infirmary. I rode my horse down the main cobblestone road, my small army of a dozen soldiers behind me. The hooves from our beasts echoed with every step because the only other sound was that of the wind.

We left the cluster of homes and shops then crossed the open landscape as we approached the castle at the top of the slight hill. The message of my arrival had preceded me because the new king was already past his gates to greet me. He stood there with the other lords of the castle, along with the queen, who wore a jeweled crown upon her brow.

I dismounted my horse and approached.

King Elias raised his hand to stop me. "That's far enough."

I cracked a smile. "Don't worry, King Elias. I wasn't expecting to stay for dinner."

He lowered his hand, but he looked even more uneasy. "What do you want, Kingsnake?"

My eyes narrowed. "I know you're new to lordship, but that is not how you address a king."

He swallowed, his eyes trained on me so hard, like he was afraid I'd attack him if he blinked. "Kingsnake, King of Vampires, how can I assist you?"

"That's better." I stepped forward, and I enjoyed the way he immediately stepped back. "This illness continues to ravage your people, and therefore, it ravages my own. You will donate a dozen or so of your healthiest citizens to feed us—or we'll feed on you."

They were all so still, it was as if they'd turned to stone. King Elias swallowed and instantly breathed harder than he did before. He even looked to his wife, as if she should be able to guide him through this difficult time. "You can survive off the blood of animals. It would only be right to spare us."

"A king doesn't feed on animals. A king feeds on the strong. My prey was killed—and you will replace her with someone worthy of my bite. The others will be given to my people, vampires who are worthy of a feast."

King Elias was quiet, clearly having no solution to this problem. His empire had been destroyed by an unseen enemy, and now he was unable to oppose me and protect the few people he had left. His armies had been wiped out, and he had taken a position that he was never supposed to inherit. He was ill-suited for it, judging by the way his skin turned gray and sweaty.

"Nominate those you'll sacrifice, or we'll take you instead."

King Elias turned left and right, as if searching for his father and brother to ask for advice, but then the harsh reality set in—that he was entirely alone.

His wife reached for his hand. "Larisa."

He noticeably stilled at the name.

"We give her to him—and spare the rest." She lowered her voice to a whisper so I wouldn't hear, but I could hear every word as if she stood directly beside me.

King Elias somehow looked paler than he ever had, like that was a path he would only take if he had no other choice.

"If we offer her, he'll never return," she continued.

My interest was officially piqued. "What qualities does Larisa possess that make her so valuable?"

They both looked at me, surprised that I'd overheard their conversation from fifteen feet away.

King Elias didn't speak, but his queen did. "Larisa is immune—"

"*Victoria.*" He grabbed her arm and steadied her.

"It's the only way to protect us and our people," she hissed. "There is no other option."

I grew tired of this immature quarrel. A righteous king wouldn't need another to speak on his behalf—especially not a woman. "Speak."

King Elias wouldn't speak. Wouldn't meet my gaze.

Victoria continued. "Larisa is the only one who's immune to the disease. She's cared for the sick and the dying every day and has never showed the slightest symptoms. She's the only one of her kind."

"Why is she immune?"

"We don't know. But we're willing to give her to you if you spare everyone else. If you never return to Raventower and ask for more prey. If you leave us in peace forevermore. You asked for the strongest prey—and you can have it for a strong price."

With every passing week, my strength had waned. Rose had belonged to me exclusively, but feeding on the same blood repeatedly had dulled my senses. When my people began to starve, I offered to share her, despite her protests. But they'd become so hungry, they sucked her dry and accidentally killed her. I could pursue the culprit and decapitate them, but I knew that wouldn't be right, not when I was the one at fault. As King of Vampires, King of Grayson, it was my duty to protect and provide for my people—and I'd failed. Instead of punishing them, I should punish myself. Knowing prey with magical blood existed not only increased my appetite, but it made my skin crawl with excitement. To have the perfect prey was every vampire's dream, blood so powerful it made you more powerful. "I will take Larisa, but I will also take others because one woman is not enough to feed us all. But in return, I won't come back to your lands to ask for more. I will travel past Raventower to the other kingdoms."

King Elias looked ill. Not ill with the sickness, but ill with a stomach bug.

Victoria turned to her king, waiting for his decision.

But the man was too weak to give it. "Fetch Larisa and the others. I will depart your lands immediately."

3

LARISA

I heard a scream.

I'd been sitting at the dining table where my family used to have dinner, looking through my mother's books of herbs and spices, when I heard the sound from the street. I moved to the window and drew back the curtain to find the king's soldiers outside my neighbor's home. They dragged Angela into the street then secured her wrists together with rope.

"What's happening...?" With the curtain pulled slightly to the side, I peered into the darkness, seeing the others standing with the guards, hands bound behind their backs. They were being treated like prisoners. I moved to another window closer to the action and pulled back the curtain.

"Why are they taking us?" Angela yelled at Doris, a seamstress.

"They're going to sacrifice us to Kingsnake so the vampires will leave."

The blood drained from my face as quickly as Angela's. Every prisoner in that group was healthy, and I knew that because I took care of all the sick and dying. The vampires had grown desperate for food and made their demands, knowing Raventower was too weak to oppose their dominance. Even at our strongest, Kingsnake and his army were too much for us, and the battle ended up a sacrifice anyway.

The guard moved for my door next. "No..." I released the curtains, threw a pail of water on the open fire in the fireplace, and took off to the next room. My pack was in the pantry, and I immediately stuffed it with my supplies.

Knock. Knock. Knock. "King Elias requests your presence."

I halted my actions because the truth hit me over the head like a brick. Kingsnake had asked for the healthy to feed— and King Elias offered me. He could have excluded me from the list, but he didn't.

I wanted to cry, but there was no time for that. The only emotion my heart could hold was rage, and I used that to spur into action and finish packing.

Knock. Knock. Knock. "Open the door, in the name of the king."

I threw the pack over my shoulder, sheathed my dagger on my belt, and grabbed my sword where it sat in the corner. I'd never served in the army, but every student in Raventower went through military training, men and women, in case we were faced with a battle that required every able-bodied individual to take up arms. I'd taken to sword fighting easier than others, but women weren't allowed in the military unless under dire circumstances, so I ended up a maid at the castle—a very uneventful career.

Bedding the king's son had been the only exciting part.

I left out the back door and ran down the alleyway. With my pack over my shoulder, I headed to the southern gate, knowing Kingsnake and his army would have come through the northern gate. When I reached the main road, I sprinted across it to avoid being seen and then disappeared into another labyrinth of alleyways among the houses.

I circumvented the homes and approached the southern gate, but not before I felt it.

Power.

That was the only way to describe it. An existence larger than others. A being that could project its strength in an unfathomable diameter. It was distinct, hard like metal, cold like steel. Beings were complicated, so sometimes multiple emotions lined up simultaneously, and that caused an array of sensations that were difficult to interpret. But this...wasn't like anything I'd ever felt.

I looked toward the castle, seeing the mass of shadows as the king and queen met with Kingsnake and his army. The torches showed their distant outlines, but they were too far away to be distinct.

Then I saw the guards march toward the castle, eight prisoners in tow. Once they reached the king, they would inform them that I couldn't be found. They would know I'd fled before being captured—and they would hunt me in the countryside.

I sprinted to the southern gate—and didn't look back.

———

Vampires had vision far more powerful than my own, so instead of taking the path to our neighboring kingdom Crowswell, I headed toward the mountains. I hoped the uneven terrain and dense groves of pines and oaks would shield my passage away from the village where I was born and raised.

I knew it was a dangerous decision to go running in the dark in a place I'd never been before, but it was less dangerous than being fed upon by a malicious creature with fangs. Even if I successfully evaded their pursuit, I'd have to hide in the wilderness long enough for them to leave, and then I would need to find a new place to live. I'd have to start over completely with nothing more than the things I'd stowed in my pack.

I moved farther up the mountain, practically blind except for the moonlight that reflected off the blades of grass. It was my savior, but it was also my curse, because that light made it easier for them to see as well.

I knew what lived in the mountain passes, creatures that chose to hide in their caves and leave men in peace as their numbers dwindled from past battles. But they still wandered in the darkness, still claimed the lives of those who were stupid enough to come too close to their mountain. It was the last place someone like me would go—which meant they might not come this way.

I hiked up the side of the mountain until I could go no farther. I collapsed to the ground and heaved to catch my breath. In the far distance, I could see the torches of Raventower, looking like twinkling stars in the valley. When my gaze looked down over the hills on the path I'd taken, I didn't see anything. Not a single torch. No sign of pursuit.

Maybe they went west. Or maybe I wasn't worth looking for.

The man who had wanted to marry me had married someone else—and then sold me to the enemy. I'd never felt hatred in my veins, but I certainly felt it now. Not just toward him—but toward myself.

How could I have been so stupid?

How could I have given my heart to someone so unworthy?

I drank from my canteen and felt the chill start to creep in. The adrenaline had kept me warm up until this point because of the way I pushed my body as I hiked up the side of that mountain, but now that I was idle, I felt the sting of the cold.

And damn, it was cold. I knew snow lay higher up the mountain, but I was close enough to feel the numbness that spread through my extremities. In my haste, I hadn't thought to grab my heavier coat, so I wasn't prepared to weather the elements, let alone in the darkness.

But it was still better than being eaten by a vampire.

———

A fire would be a tremendous help, but it would also be a shining beacon to my location. Day or night, anyone would see it. I shivered through the night, my knees pulled to my chest, my back against a mighty oak to block the howling wind.

"Are you lost?"

I jumped to my feet and nearly fell over when I heard the voice. "Fuck." My hand automatically reached for my sword, and I unsheathed it from the scabbard. My heart went from a calm stillness to an overload of blood, and my hands shook because I was so terrified that someone had snuck up on me so easily.

It was a man, close to my age, with long brown hair and lightly colored eyes. He was dressed similarly, in just breeches and a tunic, not the right apparel to explore the mountainside in the dead of winter.

And that made me uneasy.

He raised his hands slightly. "Didn't mean to startle you."

"What are you doing out here in the middle of the night?"

"I live up here."

"You have a home on the mountainside? Away from the kingdoms? Close to the entrances of the caves?"

"I'm not interested in subjugation to a king. Would rather live and die by my own rules." His hands still remained up, and he glanced down at my sword. "Are you going to put that away?"

"I'm not sure."

He lowered his hands and stepped back. "Then freeze out here." He turned around and began his departure, and quickly, the darkness swallowed his figure.

"Wait." The cold made me desperate for a respite. It'd only been a few hours, and I felt how dry my lips had become already. I resheathed my sword. "I'm sorry for my rudeness. You just caught me off guard."

I heard a twig snap as he made his return, but I couldn't see him yet. "Then would you like to join me?"

"Yes. Thank you very much."

He came closer, and once he was out of the darkness, he was different.

At least a foot taller.

Covered in fur.

And had fangs.

A quiet growl escaped his open snout. He was a beast that stood upon its hind legs, saliva dripping from the iridescent fangs that reflected the moonlight.

"How did you do that...?" Werewolves came out at the full moon, but he'd changed from man to beast willingly. It was probably a stupid question to ask in my current circumstance, but I had to understand how he managed to fool me.

"Now you know fairy tales are lies." He lunged, his enormous body moving with a speed that belied his size.

I only managed to dodge because I jumped and fell on a decline, my body automatically rolling out of the way and missing his claws by inches.

His heavy body slammed into the pine—and knocked it over.

"Oh shit." I got to my feet and unsheathed my sword again, but it was like a toothpick against this beast.

It took a moment for him to rise because he'd struck the tree harder than he'd anticipated. I could have run, but I knew that was pointless when I couldn't match his speed. I held the sword in my hands and prepared to strike him down—even though I knew it was hopeless.

I made my choice—to be the dinner of a werewolf rather than a vampire.

He made a mighty roar then slammed his enormous paws into the ground.

I swore the ground actually shook.

He lunged at me again, and all I could do was jump out of the way and strike my sword down.

I got lucky a second time, and my sword drew blood.

He swung his paw at me, and he hit me so hard I flew across the clearing.

I landed at the roots of a tree, and the world spun for a moment. *Get up. Get up. Come on, Larisa.* I reached for the sword that had landed a few feet away. As my fingers tightened around the hilt, I heard the cry of an injured animal.

I turned to see the werewolf engaged by a new foe.

Their sword gleamed as it spun through the air, slicing through flesh before it came around again and struck another body part. The swordsman had the speed of the werewolf, taking on his opponent with an agility that I'd never seen.

The werewolf tried to run away, but the man wouldn't let him go.

He threw his sword directly at the back of his head—and impaled the animal through the skull.

His body went limp.

I couldn't believe what I'd just seen.

The man paused as he looked at the carcass, and then he walked over to the body to retrieve the sword from its tomb in the werewolf's skull. It took a hard pull to release it, and then he wiped the blood on the animal's fur.

He turned his attention on me then stepped closer.

I saw his armor, black and engraved with serpents. His cloak hung at his back, also black, but red at the edges. Fair skin like snow, with slitted eyes like a snake, a jawline so sharp it rivaled his sword. A handsome face that would forever be preserved in timeless beauty. He gazed upon me with an empty expression. "Rise."

Kingsnake. I pushed to my feet—and ran for it. I left my bag behind. Even my sword. It was a stupid decision when I couldn't possibly outrun a vampire, but it was better to die fighting than submit weakly.

Something tripped me—and I fell.

I crashed to the earth and tried to push to my feet, but my ankles were bound. I kicked hard, and then the tension grew stronger. Every time I tried to move, I found less give. I felt the rope tightening around my thighs and then my torso, some kind of magic.

Hissssssss.

I realized it was no magic.

A giant serpent had its powerful body wrapped around me, pinning me in place, locking its yellow eyes on me. His tongue emerged every few seconds, just inches from my face.

I reached for the dagger at my belt.

"I wouldn't do that if I were you."

The snake had widened its mouth and exposed its large fangs, ready to stab me with his venom the moment my dagger pierced its scales. *Hisssssssss.*

"A small drop of his venom will paralyze you. The poison will spread, and once it reaches your heart, you'll suffer a gruesome death that will leave you writhing in pain—only you won't be able to move."

Hisssssssss.

I tossed the dagger aside.

The snake closed its mouth and swallowed its fangs.

"Good choice." Kingsnake appeared above me, his cloak blowing in the wind, his slitted eyes locked on my face. *A bonfire that had been doused with alcohol. Rage more powerful than the howling winds that swept across the frozen lands. Anger. Raw, unbridled anger.* "Can you walk? Or shall Fang carry you?"

My eyes shifted to the snake. "The name suits you..."

Hisssssss.

Kingsnake made a slight gesture with his hands.

The snake released me, and I could finally draw a full breath.

"*Rise.*" He turned away, his large snake sliding through the grass as he followed.

He left me there, and I could run again, but we both knew that would be pointless. I got to my feet and followed, grabbing my fallen pack and sword along the way. He kept his back to me, like there was nothing I could possibly do to hurt him.

He would quickly learn not to underestimate me.

He didn't wear a helmet, so his neckline was exposed. If I could swipe my sword with enough strength, I could sever his head from his shoulders and kill this ancient vampire who had haunted our kingdom for too long.

I made my move, swinging the sword unexpectedly and with all my strength.

As if the asshole had eyes in the back of his head, he spun around and met my blade with his black steel. *White-hot fury. Rage more scorching than the hottest forge. Hunger for violence.* He pushed his sword into mine and forced me back, his height dominating mine, his fury written all over his handsome face.

I stumbled back, scared for the first time.

"I eviscerated the werewolf with a few swipes of my sword —and you think you can match me?" He gave me a hard shove then sheathed his blade.

I stumbled back and landed on my ass. "You think you can take me prisoner and I'll just cooperate?"

"Yes."

Hisssssss. His giant snake perched at his side, his yellow eyes focused on me.

"Then this is going to be a long journey." His narrowed pupils were absent of emotion. He'd shoved a woman to the ground and slayed a werewolf, but it was just another unremarkable day. "I suggest you conserve your energy."

"You mean you suggest I stop fighting."

He stared.

"That's never going to happen." I pushed myself to my feet. "If you think I'm a pain in the ass now, you're in for a reckoning."

"Never met a woman who prided herself in such a way." He turned around and continued his descent down the hill with his pet snake in tow, his muscular back turned to me, his cloak swirling in the wind.

I considered running again.

He halted but didn't turn around. "Would you rather I drain your blood until you're too weak to fight?"

My blood went cold when I imagined his fangs marking my skin. To have a vampire bite me...was worse than death. I hated their kind, neither living nor dead, horrendous creatures that had been corralling us like sheep for as long as I could remember.

"Then move."

————

We maneuvered in the pitch darkness to the bottom of the mountain. I couldn't see more than a few feet in front of me, but he moved like it was midday. After tripping more than once, I followed close behind him. The snake was gone, slithering through the glass elsewhere. When we reached the bottom, I expected to see his army and the prisoners, but it was just us.

"Where's your army?"

"On their return journey to Grayson." He approached his horse, which had been tied to a tree branch in his absence.

"You came for me personally?" He could have deployed a small group of soldiers to fetch me. That was what Elias would have done.

He mounted the midnight-black horse, its mane perfectly combed, its flank muscular. "The people don't serve their king. A king serves his people." He extended his hand to pull me into the saddle.

I hesitated. "What about the snake? Will he cozy up right between us?" I'd always hated snakes ever since I was a little girl. A day of exploration in the fields had led to a bite. It was just a harmless snake, so I'd escaped without poison in my veins.

"His name is Fang, and you don't need to fear him."

"Right..." I glanced at him, his head perched above the grass, so still he could be mistaken for a branch in the darkness. "He seems harmless..."

Impatient, he grabbed my wrist and forced me up onto the horse.

Behind him in the saddle, I wasn't sure what to do with my hands because the last thing I wanted to do was touch him.

He didn't wait for me to get a hold before he kicked the horse and set off at a dead run.

I started to slip backward, so I immediately grabbed on to him and steadied myself. It felt like my palms had touched a mountain because he was so hard. His waist didn't have the softness mine did. He was straight and solid, just muscle covered in skin.

He pushed the horse to its breaking point, sprinting across the flatlands toward the north. We rode like someone was hot on our heels. Daylight broke across the sky when we'd traveled past Raventower, and we entered the hills that separated the humans from the vampires.

When we reached the forest, he brought the horse to a stop.

They called these woods the Dead Woods because it was considered vampire territory, but vampires weren't the worst things to reside there. Dark creatures thrived under the branches, protecting Grayson from anyone who wanted to oppose it. If you marched an army through it, you would lose half the soldiers before they even arrived. If the monsters didn't get them first, it would be the hidden quicksand, the poisonous fruit, or the unsuspecting sinkholes.

"We're not camping here, are we?" I did my best to keep my voice strong, but the fear slipped out in my tone.

He dismounted the horse without waiting for me to get off first, swinging his leg over the horse's neck and dropping down on the other side. The snake appeared a moment later, slicing through the grass until he climbed a tree and made himself at home on one of the branches. The end of his long body hung down, and he rested his head on the branch and immediately closed his eyes.

I stayed on the horse because the last thing I wanted to do was nap in these woods. Never thought I'd prefer the vampire kingdom over some trees. "We finally have daylight. We should continue forward."

He ignored me, taking the pack off the horse and dropping it on the ground.

How could I be so stupid? "That's right...vampires hate daylight."

"Get off the horse." He spoke to me like I was one of his soldiers, and he let the annoyance escape in his tone. He hardly looked at me, and whenever he did, his slitted pupils were full of rage.

I dismounted the horse and let my boots dig into the earth.

He removed rope from his bag then approached me.

"Whoa, what are you doing?" I backed up, keeping the distance between us.

"I need to rest."

"Then rest." I eyed the rope in his hands.

"You expect me to sleep when you've tried to kill me twice?"

"You know where we are, right? These woods are dangerous—"

"For your kind. Not mine." He grabbed me by the shoulder and, with force I couldn't resist, secured the rope around my wrists with a biting tension.

I fought him hard, but it was like fighting a tidal wave. I threw my hands into his stomach then butted him in the head. "You fucking asshole—"

"*Enough.*" He grabbed me by the neck and slammed me down into the dirt. The force was so immense it felt like a tree had fallen on top of me. His fingers squeezed into my skin like he wanted to choke me. Tighter and tighter they became, and exhibiting resistance, he didn't cut off my air supply altogether. But I could feel his desire to end my life, feel the way he wanted to snap my neck and make my eyes glaze over. *Flames so hot they were black. They scorched the earth, scorched everything except him. Indescribable rage.* The only reason I was spared was because he needed me, and that made his fingers loosen on my neck.

He grabbed the end of the rope and rose—and then dragged me along the ground until he secured his end of the rope around the tree trunk. My pack and belongings were left near the horse and I couldn't move, but even if I could, I had nothing to use to defend myself.

"Look, I promise I won't try to kill you for the day if you untie me."

He secured his weapons to the horse then moved to the bedroll he laid out on the ground. The snake remained in the tree branch above him, already dead asleep. It seemed like neither of them heard me.

"This is barbaric."

His hands moved behind his head, and he closed his eyes.

"What if something attacks me?"

With his eyes closed, he answered, "Nothing will attack you while I'm here."

I sank against the tree trunk, tired from my midnight escape, but too nervous to close my eyes. Some of the trees were covered in full leaves, but they were crimson red and orange, stuck in perpetual fall. Others were withered and dead, but not because of the cold winter. The mountains farther in the distance were covered with snow, and I feared our passage through the treacherous terrain. I could barely survive the night on the mountainside. I wasn't sure how I would fare under harsher conditions.

At some point, I drifted off...and slept in the shade of the mighty tree.

———

"Up."

I jerked awake when I felt his boot kick me.

My eyes opened to dusk. The sun was low in the sky, the light filtering through the trees and causing dramatic shadows. It was much colder in the evening than in the daytime, and I saw my breath escape my nostrils.

He untied me, and the snake slid down the tree beside me, its scales iridescent. He hissed quietly as he passed, his enormous body taking a full minute to pass me, his proximity an intentional threat.

I really hated snakes.

I grabbed my pack and searched for something to eat. I'd only grabbed a few things in my haste, dried nuts and apricots.

"Let's go."

I remained on the ground, my hand deep in the bag of snacks. "Can I eat first?"

"No."

"Well, I'm not going to taste very good if I'm starving, right?"

His dark eyes regarded me, the slit in the pupil identical to his pet's, and the amount of disdain he showed me in that single look was profound. His handsomeness was tarnished by his anger, the shadow masking his perfection. He finally stepped away, his cloak giving an elaborate woosh because he turned so quickly.

I tried to enjoy my lunch—or dinner, whatever it was—when I noticed movement in the distance. It happened so quickly I wasn't sure if it was real. Then my eyes narrowed, and I saw it again, something dark, something bulky. It shifted into the darkness, and another slid behind a tree. My eyes scanned all the trees, and if I looked closely enough, I could see the shapes everywhere.

Kingsnake prepared his horse, his back turned to me.

"There are things out there..."

"I'm aware."

"They're all around us." Now my food was forgotten as I felt surrounded by foes I couldn't possibly survive.

"Guardians of the Dead Woods."

"Guardians? That's what you call them? Because we call them monsters."

"The name is dependent on your status as friend or foe—and we know what you are."

I got to my feet and came closer to his side. His snake didn't seem concerned either. "We're just going to ride through their territory?"

He secured the saddle then looked down at me. I was considered tall for a woman, but Kingsnake still towered over me by at least an additional foot—and probably more. "As long as you're with me, you're untouchable."

"Why?"

"Because I'm not only the King of Vampires—I'm the Lord of Darkness."

———

We rode through the night, and Kingsnake was able to navigate the dense woods like he had memorized the trail, memorized every upturned root and low-hanging branch. When we reached the base of the mountain, I knew we'd arrived at the second part of our journey—through the blizzards and snow.

I'd probably die of hypothermia.

He reached the base of a rocky outcropping then dismounted the horse.

"Is it almost sunrise?"

He ignored me and walked up to the wall.

It was so dark that it was hard to make out his actions, but I realized he was pressing his palm against various points, like they were hidden triggers to start an unseen mechanism. Once he hit four points, the solid rock moved—and a passage was revealed.

"We're going under the mountain..." No storm. No blizzards.

"We proceed on foot."

I left the horse's back and snuck a look behind me. It was too dark to make out details, but I could feel their presence. Feel their stare. Feel their hungry eyes on my pale skin.

Kingsnake took the reins of the horse and proceeded into the cave.

I followed, and once we were in the passage, the door shut behind us.

The way was lit by a hallway of torches, torches that illuminated an endless path.

"Who lit the torches?"

"The others have already passed this way." He held on to the reins of his horse and proceeded into the tunnel. It was twelve feet high and at least ten feet wide, big enough to usher an army through the mountain, but the ground was rocky and uneven, dangerous for a horse bearing riders.

I walked behind them, the snake far in the lead as he slithered across the uneven floor. We passed torch after torch, every footstep heightened by the amplifying sounds of the rocks. It was slow progress, and I started to count the number of torches we passed until I lost count. "How long is this gonna take?"

"Three days."

"We're going to be in here for *three days*?" In the darkness. Disconnected from the sky. Trapped in a tunnel that could collapse on us at any moment.

"Trust me, it's better than going over the mountain."

"Are you sure about that?"

"I'd suggest we try—except you would certainly die."

I lowered my voice and spoke to myself. "I'm dead anyway..."

After a beat, he spoke. "I have no intention of killing you."

"Trust me, I know what your intent is toward me."

"And you think being as obnoxious as possible will change that?"

"Worth a shot."

We fell into silence, moving through the endless cave, passing torch after torch, no sign of our progress. I had no way to know how much time had passed either because there wasn't a hint of sunlight on the rocks.

I was driven mad with boredom. "How'd you get that pet snake?"

"Fang is *not* a pet."

"He obeys you like one."

"He's a companion, standing at my side of his own choosing and, therefore, does not obey."

"Well, how did he become your companion?"

"It was a very long time ago."

I waited for more, staring at his muscular back as he led the horse. "That didn't answer the question."

"How does anyone become bonded? There's a connection."

"And what is your connection?"

He halted his stride then looked at me over his shoulder. "You're awfully interested for someone who doesn't care for Fang."

"I've just never seen such a pairing."

He continued forward, silent.

"So you're never going to answer me?"

"You aren't entitled to my answer."

———

It must have been a full day of travel, because by the time we stopped, I was exhausted. We entered a larger part of the cave, a chasm with a ceiling so high that it was impossible to gauge the distance. The space was big enough for an army to rest, and I noticed several passages in different directions.

I wonder where they go...

He fed the horse, and the snake slithered elsewhere, probably to find a rat to eat.

Just when I pulled out my own food, I wondered what Kingsnake would eat.

I hadn't seen him eat since we'd started this journey together.

Shit.

He drank from his canteen then set his things against the wall.

I stared at the other passages, wondering where they went, how far I could get before he noticed I was gone. He might know the tunnels, but if I had a head start, I might be able to evade him and hide out until he gave up.

He leaned against the wall, keeping a far distance from me, like he found me repulsive. His mind seemed quiet because the waves of emotions under his exterior were flat. He drank from the canteen again, his forearms on his knees, his eyes straight ahead. "Yes?"

I flinched at his tone.

"You're staring." He turned his head and regarded me.

I quickly looked away, not realizing I'd been watching him for so long.

"I know what you're thinking."

It was hard not to keep my head straight.

"But if you run into those tunnels—you'll die."

The snake was gone, and that was my biggest adversary. With his smooth scales, he could slither at immense speed, and then he could wrap his body around me and paralyze me. Plus, he was fucking terrifying. "If I stay with you, I'll die."

"As I already said, I have no intention of killing you."

"But I'd prefer death over being prey to a vampire."

"Really?"

Now I turned to look at him.

"Then take that dagger and pierce yourself in the heart." His hard eyes stared into mine, heartless. "Do it."

The thought had never crossed my mind.

"That's what I thought." He looked straight ahead again. "There are worse things than feeding a vampire. Most of your kind even enjoy it."

"That's a bunch of bullshit." I got to my feet and secured my pack to my shoulder.

Kingsnake remained on the ground, unprovoked by my attention. "I warned you."

I walked toward the first tunnel door, ready for whatever was on the other side. "You aren't going to stop me?"

He remained on the ground. "At my side is the safest place you'll ever be. I'll let you figure that out the hard way."

Perhaps I should take that warning to heart, but I was so desperate for freedom that I was willing to take my chances. I moved into the tunnel and found a long, cold corridor. I took off at a jog, wanting to put as much distance between us before he decided to come after me. Unfortunately, the path sloped downward, slowly at first, but then steeper. Different corridors led in different directions, so I took whatever paths I could find, getting lost in the process.

But if I was lost, that probably meant Kingsnake wouldn't find me. I had enough food and water to last a few days, so I'd have to find the exit sooner rather than later.

I halted once I noticed the smell.

It smelled...like a dirty animal. Like a dog that had been out in the rain all night. Its matted fur coated with sweat and dirt. I sniffed it for a while, wondering exactly where I was going.

Should I go back?

Did I even know the way back at this point?

I stared into the darkness ahead, pondering my next step. The light from the torches was growing fainter, and soon I wouldn't be able to see. But then I saw a sliver of light far ahead, so far I couldn't gauge the distance.

If I went for it, the smell of wet dog would probably become more intense, and that could only mean one thing...

But behind me was a hungry vampire prepared to make me a slave until he fed too long or too hard and then I was dead—an empty vessel.

Straight ahead, it was.

I continued forward, moving faster than I did before, desperate to put distance between me and the king of the vampires—and his pet snake. As far as I could tell, he was nowhere behind me, but I wasn't stupid enough to believe he would really just let me go.

I descended deeper down the slight incline, and then the smell became more potent. My stomach had been gnawing consistently since we'd left because I hadn't had a proper meal once I'd been chased off into the night.

The light grew brighter. The sliver became wider.

And the smell danker.

Twenty minutes later, I realized the light was a torch around the bend in the path. Once I reached it, I saw more torches, a large cavern—and creatures.

Tall, muscular, with skin so black it was like it was covered with paint. Bent at the waist, they shuffled across the floor like hungry dogs, and the sounds they made were peculiar.

Now I knew where the smell came from.

In the corner, they roasted a pig over an open fire.

And that meant there was a way out of this place.

My heart raced, my palms grew sweaty, and the fear was enough to make me consider returning the way I came.

But I had to keep going.

I crept into the other pathway and made my way silently, pressing my back against the wall in case one of the creatures passed into another doorway. The way was dark, and they were unsuspecting of my presence, so it was easy to sneak by.

I darted into another hallway, and it appeared to be a storage room. It was easy to hide behind their barrels of wheat and fresh apples, and I stole a couple of things for myself because I wasn't above stealing from ugly-ass beings.

I made it into another hallway, and once I found a path that rose at an incline, that was the direction I took. That meant it would go to the surface and, hopefully, a doorway.

"*Rooooaaaaaarrrrrrr.*"

"Oh shit..."

"*Roooaaaarrrr.*" More of them came, rising from other directions. "*Roooaaaaarrr.*" I didn't know how they knew I was there, but they definitely knew. Maybe I smelled just as bad to them as they smelled to me.

I ran for it, not knowing if it was the right way, not knowing if I would run into a horde I could never combat.

Footsteps sounded behind me in the tunnel, and that was when I booked it. I pushed my body as hard as it would go. With a surge of adrenaline, I ran faster than I ever could have imagined. I reached another chasm lit up with torches, and then there was only one passage from this room—and it had light. Not torchlight. But sunlight.

I sprinted across the room, ignoring all the terrifying roars as they echoed off the ceiling and hard rocks, and dashed into the tunnel.

But then the sunlight disappeared.

A door had been shut.

"No..."

"*Roooaaaarrrrr.*"

I turned around to see the chasm flooded with the disgusting creatures, growling and bearing their sharp teeth, seven feet tall when they stood upright, wearing armor and blunt swords.

Shit. Kingsnake was right.

The first one came at me and raised his sword.

I was so scared I could have shit myself, but instinct kicked in and I met his sword with my own. The force of his hit almost knocked me back, but I held my own. I parried his sword then stabbed my sword right between the plates of his armor and kicked him back with my foot.

There wasn't time to enjoy my victory because the next one came down on me, slicing his sword to cut my head clean from my shoulders.

I blocked the hit then sliced him across the face. He collapsed with the other, forming a small barrier of protection.

But then they all came at once—and I had no chance. If I ran into the blocked tunnel, I would barely have room to swing my sword.

"*Stop.*" The horrible creatures could speak, their voices guttural and animalistic. "Kingsnake approaches."

One of their swords was so close to my face. I was using my own as a shield that would have collapsed under their attack. My heart still raced as if it only had moments to beat. My hands were so slippery the pommel was about to slide from my desperate fingers.

Then the creatures parted, stepping uniformly, revealing an open path to where Kingsnake entered the room. He was shorter than the monsters, but he somehow looked like the tallest being in the room. At his side was Fang, sliding across the room with his irritated eyes locked on me. Kingsnake wore no expression, his thoughts a mystery, but I felt an overwhelming sense of annoyance from him.

He stopped directly before me, kingly in his tunic with the serpent, his broad shoulders filling out his armor and cloak in a muscular way. That annoyance deepened into something more sinister. Like hatred. "The moment you left your kingdom, you stepped into mine. My power reaches far beyond the borders of Grayson, into places that only darkness can touch, and it is the only reason you still draw breath. If you wish to continue living, you will submit to me."

I should feel grateful that Kingsnake could chase away creatures that could snap my neck between their fingers, but I hated him far too much to feel any kind of appreciation.

"Do you understand me?"

I met his gaze with the same hostility.

"*Answer me.*" Now his tone deepened, and the rage in his slitted eyes matched the emotions coursing through his body.

"You said you won't kill me, so I don't have to do anything."

A tidal wave sixty feet high formed—and crashed down hard enough to wipe the earth of every rock and tree. Fire consumed whatever remained, turning the world into a pile of ashes. He stepped forward, his cloak sliding behind him, and then stopped when he was directly in front of me.

I held my ground.

His hand suddenly flew forward and grabbed me by the neck before I could stop him. His fingers squeezed me hard through his glove, cutting off my air supply. My hands tried to pry his fingers from my neck, but it was like yanking on steel. His face was directly in front of me, and then he lifted me from the ground without any sign of exertion. "That promise is conditional—conditional on you being useful to me."

He let me struggle, let me suffocate with my feet hanging above the ground. I felt myself slip, my lungs protesting without air to circulate within them. Then he lowered his voice to a whisper. "Disrespect me like this again—and I will kill you."

Everything went black.

4

KINGSNAKE

Her limp body was secured to the back of Midnight, secured by ropes and a blanket. Hours passed as I continued the journey, moving at a much quicker pace now that the human wasn't holding me back.

Peeeace and quiet. Fang slithered ahead, carefully navigating between the upturned stones so he wouldn't tarnish his shiny scales. Once upon a time, he used to perch on my shoulders, but now he was the size of a monster, far too big for me to carry.

Yes.

She's annoying—even for a human.

I know.

And unremarkable for blood so powerful.

I agree.

We continued in silence, moving past the torches that lit the dark hallway, the stench of orc fading into the background.

Fang suddenly stopped. **They're close. I ssssmell horse.** Fang continued again, sliding at a quicker pace.

After another hour of brisk walking, we made it to the next cavern. This pathway had once belonged to the orcs, but after I demanded passage under the mountain, they gifted it to me—their true sovereign. Underneath the ground was our safest route, as there was no concern of sun exposure.

Soldiers guarded the prisoners, who were all bound by their wrists and cornered against the stone. "I have another." I handed the reins to one of the soldiers and parted with my obnoxious captive. The soldiers stared at me as I passed, watching me approach the next passage, where I found Viper.

"You finally caught up to us." He turned to regard me, his cloak fastened to his armor, his eyes slits.

"I was delayed."

The general glanced past me, watching the men maneuver the woman off the horse to join the others. Our prisoners weren't only comprised of women, but men as well. So few were healthy that we'd had to take whatever was available. "That woman was enough to delay you?" His judgmental eyes turned back to me.

"Once you make her acquaintance, you'll understand."

Fang slithered over Viper's feet, sliding between his ankles as he curled around his body.

Viper glanced down. "Fang."

Fang raised his yellow eyes and slipped out his tongue.

"He says hello."

"Get off me!" Shouts emerged from the prisoners' pen against the wall, and I didn't have to look to know who was responsible.

I watched Viper glance in that direction, seeing the woman fight the soldiers by launching her body at them like a catapult.

He looked at me, his eyebrows slightly raised.

"I told you she was lovely."

"Perhaps a beating will subdue her."

"No." A single drop of blood would turn us all into a frenzy. "Let's continue. We have a lot of ground to cover."

5

LARISA

I was stuck with the other prisoners, our wrists bound, moving like livestock. The soldiers shoved us forward when we didn't keep pace with everyone else, and I got so frustrated I kicked one of them right in the knee.

Kingsnake was up ahead with his pet snake, leaving me behind.

Good fucking riddance.

We continued our trek through a dark passageway, and the only good thing about it was we were properly fed. We were given more than nuts and dried fruit, including meat jerky and stale bread. They wanted to keep us nourished for the same reason a farmer fattened a pig—so it would be a satisfying dinner.

As we made our progress, Angela started to cry. "I wish I were sick..."

"So do I," Ethia said. "Sickness and death are preferable to this."

"Let's not despair, alright?" I said. "We know how to kill them."

"We can't decapitate all these soldiers." Angela stumbled behind me, too depressed to keep pace with everyone else.

I had to give her several nudges to keep up. "We don't need to. We just need to get that asshole in the front."

"Kingsnake?" she whispered. "Impossible."

"It's not impossible."

"It is when he has that snake with him."

"Then I'll kill the snake."

Angela gave me a wild look like I was crazy.

I was crazy.

"You're going to get yourself killed," she whispered.

"He needs us to survive. Without us, his people will starve. We're untouchable."

"Maybe you're untouchable...but not the rest of us."

I turned to meet her look.

"He knows you're immune." She said it as a whisper again, as if there was a chance it could be kept a secret.

My heart dropped like a stone into a pit. *Fuck.*

"You're irreplaceable, Larisa. Use that to get yourself out of here."

"Like I would leave you guys behind..."

Her eyes softened. "You may not have a choice."

———

It was the second night in the cave, which meant the journey had almost been completed. The vampires camped for the night, laying out their small cots to get some sleep. A few of the soldiers were put on guard to watch us. My sword and dagger were still on Kingsnake's horse, so I didn't have my weapons.

Kingsnake was somewhere at the front, far out of reach, leading his pack of vampires.

I waited until everyone had gone to sleep, waited to ensure Kingsnake wouldn't make an unexpected appearance, before I made my move. There were little rocks everywhere, so I put one in my lap underneath my blanket and dragged the taut rope around my wrists against it, shredding the fibers one by one until it came free.

My hands came apart underneath the blanket, and my heart gave a jolt in excitement.

I turned to Angela and passed her the stone.

She hesitated, refusing to accept the rock, even shaking her head.

I shoved it at her. "I can't do this by myself."

She finally took the rock and sawed until her binding came free. She passed it to the next person who was awake, and eventually, four of us were free while the others slept. The guards clearly didn't see us as a real threat, probably because they were powerful vampires and we were just humans, but that worked to our advantage. When their backs were to us, I rose to my feet and crept forward to the closest soldier. A sword hung at his hip, and I gently grabbed the pommel and slowly pulled it out, inch by inch, trying to disguise the loss of weight by taking my time. It eventually came free, and I possessed a blade with black steel.

Angela's eyes had never been bigger.

I pulled the sword back, and with all my strength, I swung at his neckline.

It only went halfway through, but was deep enough that he didn't scream. But his body toppled forward, and the thud was loud enough to alert the other soldier. His reaction was so fast, pulling his sword out of the scabbard quicker than I could see.

I didn't know how to stop him, so I slammed the blade directly into his open mouth.

He stilled, his lips sliced by the blade.

I shoved my weight into it, pushing the sword out of the back of his head.

Then it was pandemonium.

Soldiers who were once asleep were on their feet, swords in hand, coming right at me. Just as I had with the monsters in the cave, I parried their blows and kicked them right in the chest, but soon, there were too many. They tried to subdue me without killing me, so I got a fist to the face before I was tackled to the ground.

I fought with all my strength and then got another fist to the face. "You fucking monsters!"

My wrists were bound once again, but this time with a different kind of rope. It was much thicker, with strands of metal through the fibers. I was shoved on my ass, and then the soldiers parted as their king approached.

Kingsnake emerged, taller than the vampires who served him, looking at me with those restrained eyes. His look stayed for a long time, so long it was like he couldn't see me. Then he examined his dead soldiers on the ground, their black blood seeping across the bottom of the cave. He looked at me again, and I felt it.

Searing heat, the kind that forged metal into steel, the kind that molded steel into a battle sword.

"Rise."

I felt the throbbing in my face, felt the discoloration immediately after the hit. He was the last person I wanted to be with, and I preferred the punches to the face to the proximity of this fiend. If I was in his captivity again, I would never escape.

"You'll pay for what you've done."

"It was worth any price."

His eyes narrowed, and just when it seemed impossible for him to be any angrier, he was. The sensations were indescribable, and instead of feeling rage, I saw the color red. It blocked my vision, just a single, bold color.

He snatched me and dragged me to my feet, lifting me with a single arm like I was weightless. When I refused to walk, he dragged me across the stone, in front of everyone like I was a toddler throwing a tantrum.

"Let me go!" I tried to fight his hold, but my hands were bound and my feet kept slipping on the stone floor.

He dragged me into the other room, into the cavern where his horse remained.

Another vampire was there, and I could tell by his armor and cloak that he was different from the others. Kingsnake dragged me to where his snake was curled into an enormous pile of scales and dropped me. "Fang will supervise—since you can't be left unattended."

Hissssssss.

I shuffled backward until my back hit the wall of the cave.

"Bite her if she moves."

The snake lowered his head on his own body, his yellow eyes trained on me without the need to blink.

I pulled my feet closer to my body, feeling the sweat start on my forehead.

Kingsnake went back to the other vampire, and then they spoke in voices that were so quiet I couldn't overhear them. While the others slept, they continued their conversation. I couldn't make out their words, but their tones made it seem like they were equals.

I didn't sleep that night.

I stared at Fang as hard as he stared at me.

———

We continued our journey, my wrists bound to the reins of the horse so I couldn't run off, and when we emerged from the cave, we were under a blanket of stars. The cold was immediate, and I missed the warmth of the cave.

Kingsnake mounted his horse then pulled me into the saddle behind him.

The other vampire mounted his horse as well.

"How much farther?" I asked.

Kingsnake didn't answer me.

Because the prisoners were on foot, we continued at a walking pace, moving in the darkness underneath tree limbs. I had no idea where we were going and couldn't see past Kingsnake in front of me.

But I did feel the cold.

It became deeper, more chilling.

And then I started to shiver.

Desperate for warmth, I clung to Kingsnake's hard body, shielding myself from the elements with his tall stature as much as possible.

Hours later, the distant light of dawn came from the sky, but it was diminished in the thick cloud bank, keeping the surface dark. Torches appeared in the distance, and they grew brighter as we approached.

A large gate was open, and we passed through, following the line of torches in the valley between the mountains. It was midday, and the terrain came alive. Mist hung in the air, and small sage plants were along the sides of the pathway. Succulents protruded from the earth, their leaves rough and thick.

We approached another gate, and once the watchmen on the tower identified Kingsnake, the metal gates swung inward—and revealed Grayson—the Kingdom of Vampires.

The city sloped downward toward the shore, and beyond that was a gray sea with white waves beating the cliffs. Sea gulls flew across the sky, perching on the rocks that breached the surface of the water. A combination of the cloud bank and the fog provided a thick veil of protection between these monsters and the sunlight.

Now I knew why they'd chosen the seaside as their home.

We entered the city, torches lining every cobblestone road and alleyway. The other vampire led the soldiers and prisoners in a different direction, while the three of us took another path.

When I glanced up the hillside, I saw a palace that had an unobstructed view of the sea—and I assumed that was where Kingsnake carried out his reign. It was a long walk up the hill, taking different paths that didn't have stairs, and we eventually reached the front, where at least one hundred stairs led up to the entryway of the palace.

Vampires in uniform took the horse from Kingsnake the moment he dismounted, and then they lowered me to the ground beside him, my wrists still bound. Despite the fact that I was a prisoner to the vampire king, several days of traveling had made me desperate for a hot shower, a bowl of soup to fight off the chill that seeped into my bones, and a real bed where I could sleep comfortably.

But then I remembered what would come afterward.

He ascended the stairs, his snake navigating the steps like they were no obstacle. When I didn't follow, he turned back to look at me. "I grow tired of this game."

"Sorry that my desperation to live is such an inconvenience to you."

He pulled his black sword from his scabbard, the threat unmistakable. And his snake stared at me the whole time, his look just as hostile.

"Fine." I moved up the stairs. "I'm coming..."

We made it up the one hundred steps and approached the blue double doors that were twenty feet in height. At his approach, both doors swung open, and vampires bearing the serpent crest on their tunics appeared.

We stepped across the enormous rug into a palace far more luxurious than the castle I used to clean. Paintings of landscapes were on the walls, some of ships coming into harbor, some of succulents on the mountainsides, but there were others...monsters ten times bigger than the humans they feasted on. Red was the color of choice in these disturbing images.

Kingsnake moved across the floor, his snake at his side like they were equals, and didn't say a word to anyone.

A man stood at the end of the hallway, not a vampire, his hands behind his back, wearing a long-sleeved shirt and trousers that had a serpent embroidered entirely through his outfit, starting at his right shoulder and moving all the way down his left pant leg.

When Kingsnake approached, he gave a slight bow.

Disgusting.

"What are your orders?"

"The human will—"

"My name is Larisa."

I stood behind him, so all I could see was the way his back stiffened. The room went quiet, and all the soldiers who guarded the hallway looked at me as if I'd just made a dire mistake.

After a long stretch of silence, Kingsnake turned to regard me. "Have you already forgotten what we discussed?" The threatening tone was unmistakable, like he'd grab me by the throat again and bring me under the veil of darkness.

"I have a name—use it." Perhaps if he saw me as a person rather than a meal, he wouldn't torture me.

Kingsnake looked forward again. "Bring her to the prisoner's quarters. Four guards will be posted, and let them be warned that she will try to escape. When she does, they have my permission to use all force necessary. If there's a second offense, then she'll share her quarters with Fang."

He must have figured out I hated snakes, because he continued to use Fang against me to ensure my compliance.

"Bring her a meal as well." He stepped away, his cloak swooshing behind him dramatically, and as he left the room, he took all the energy with him.

The human servant bowed after him. "Your bidding will be done, My King."

The soldiers grabbed me and escorted me into another series of hallways. Since Kingsnake had other matters that required his attention, I didn't expect a visit, so I didn't fight their hold as they escorted me into my bedchamber.

They opened the door, and I stepped into a room that felt nothing like a prisoner's cell. It had a king-sized four-poster bed with a deep walnut vanity and dresser, as well as a small sitting room with a couch and two armchairs, along with a circular table where I could eat.

It was an upgrade from my house in Raventower.

They shut the door behind me and locked it.

That was when I noticed the small slot under the door, big enough for a tray to pass through.

The bedspread was red and brown mixed together, with poppies blended into the pattern. A thick rug extended around the bed. When I opened the closet, I found women's clothing hanging there.

Were they for me? Or whoever was his prisoner at the time?

The one downside—there were no windows.

But that made sense since I would shatter them with a chair then make my escape.

After I examined my new home, I stepped into the bathroom to find a shower with hot water, a tub, and a vanity with hairbrushes and makeup. I undressed and left the disgusting pile of clothes on the floor then hopped into the shower.

The second that hot water touched my skin...it was divine.

I felt so good after my shower I went straight to bed and didn't wait for the dinner tray to be delivered under the door.

6

KINGSNAKE

Viper entered my study, his hands behind his back, his sword and dagger at his hip while his bow and quiver of arrows hung across his back. There'd been no attack on Grayson for thousands of years, but as the general of our armed forces, he insisted on always being prepared.

I sat at the desk, fingers reaching over the ends of the armrests, and stared at the vampire before me.

"Our people are fed and satisfied."

"How many prey did we lose?"

"Just two—but that was expected."

I'd grown tired, not just from the journey from Raven-tower, but from my abstinence. I'd fed on the animal blood I'd packed with me, but it tasted like rotten fish...or at least, how I imagined rotten fish tasted. Even when Rose was still alive, she'd failed to sustain me, to strengthen my vitalities. There was nothing wrong with her blood, but it'd grown stale like old bread.

Viper examined me with intelligent eyes. "You haven't fed."

The knowledge was known, so I didn't confirm it.

"We have prey that's immune to the plague—and you haven't had a taste?"

"I've never hated prey so much in my life." From the moment I'd laid eyes on that woman, she'd been the biggest pain in the ass. Every time she opened her mouth, her words flowed like a river of bullshit.

"Would you do anything different if you were her?"

I propped up my elbow and brought my fingertips to my jawline. The stubble was coarse against my fingertips, like tiny knives that tried to cut me. "No." But that didn't make her less annoying.

"She's decent with the sword."

"Yes, I've noticed. She killed a few orcs entirely on her own."

"Impressive."

I hated her too much to be impressed.

"You need to feed, Kingsnake. A king can't lead his people with sallow skin and empty eyes."

"Every prey I've ever had has wanted my bite. Not this one." Bloodletting was intimate, passionate, more than just a feed. A woman gave herself to me completely, clawed my back as I drained her life-force and tasted her on my tongue. "And if she doesn't want it, then I have to force it, and if I force it—I'll kill her."

Viper stared at me for a while before he sat in one of the armchairs in front of my desk. "Then tell her that."

I watched him.

"If she doesn't cooperate, your fangs could nick her and she'll bleed out. As rambunctious as she is, she doesn't want to die."

"She knows how valuable she is, so she knows I can't risk losing her." She had the upper hand in every scenario—and we both knew it.

Viper stared at me, his disappointment coming through. "You give that lowly human too much power."

"She knew she had that power the moment she realized she was immune. Thousands perish and she thrives. Perhaps if I have a taste of her blood, I can figure out why."

His eyes narrowed. "There's your answer."

I met his gaze.

"If she lets you feed, you might discover a cure for her people."

7

LARISA

When I woke up, I devoured the dinner tray that had been left under the door. An hour later, another tray was delivered for breakfast, and I ate that too. Like an animal that had nothing to live for except food, I waited for the next delivery and napped in between. There were books on the bookshelf, books that were written by humans, and that made me realize a line of women had occupied this room long before I did—and had all died since.

Days passed, and Kingsnake didn't come for me.

He went through so much trouble to capture me, but now, he acted like I didn't exist.

I knew that wouldn't last long. He captured me for a reason—and he wanted a return on his investment.

What would I do when he came for me?

My sword and dagger had been taken. All I had were the items in the room with me. I could break down one of the bedposts and slam it into his head. Pick up the armchair and throw it at him. Slam a book on top of his head. But none of those things would kill him—just piss him off.

My thoughts were shattered when I heard the noticeable click of the lock.

Shit.

The door opened, and he emerged—but he didn't look the same.

His black armor engraved with serpents no longer covered his body. He wore no tunic either. No cloak. In fact, he didn't wear a shirt at all...

All he wore were trousers that seemed to be made of cotton, the kind of attire he would wear in the privacy of his bedchambers when his presence wasn't required else-where. That made me think it was evening, or rather his evening, which was morning.

He was covered in lean muscles underneath tight skin and corded veins, and his fair skin was marked with subtle scars. Some on his arms, some on his torso, a couple on his chest. He was ripped, the strong muscles shifting with the slight movements he made. Those slitted eyes were on me, dark like the bark of a tree after a morning rain. The intensity of his stare was a little terrifying because he didn't need to blink—just like his snake.

I stepped back, putting as much distance between us as the bedroom would allow. All I had within reach was the book I'd been reading, so I held it at my side, ready to smash it on his head once he came close enough.

His eyes never left mine. "You must be as tired as I am."

"I'll never be too tired to fight."

He stared at me a moment longer before he shut the door behind him.

The lock clicked, like someone waited on the other side.

A tense silence fell between us. I stared at him. He stared at me.

White-hot fire leaped from his eyes and burned every piece of furniture. It swallowed the room whole.

I gripped the book tighter. "The feeling is mutual."

His eyes shifted slightly, narrowing just a little more. "Sit."

"No."

He came at me, still looking like a king even though he wore no clothing.

I gripped my book and prepared to strike him in the temple.

But he walked right past me, even turned his back on me, and took a seat at the dining table.

I watched him move, my fingers loosening on the edges of the spine.

He relaxed against the wooden back of the chair, one ankle crossed and resting on the opposite knee. He crossed his arms over his wide chest before he nodded to the chair across from him. "*Sit.*" His tone deepened and his jawline sharpened, like a parent that had officially run out of patience with a child.

"Why?"

"*Because I said so.*"

"You know, if you just treated me with some respect—"

"Respect is earned here in Grayson—not given."

"You haven't earned my respect either, asshole."

The flames rose, burning the entire palace that he called home. He was willing to burn it to the ground as long as I burned too. "I have a proposition for you—if you would sit and listen."

"A deal with a vampire? No thanks."

His eyes narrowed. "With Kingsnake, King of Vampires and Lord of Darkness."

I rolled my eyes.

His movements were so fast I didn't actually see them happen. His hand seized me, and then I was in the chair, my ass hitting the wood so hard it would leave a bruise. Then he walked back to his chair with slow grace, as if the ordeal had never happened. He faced me, arms across his chest, the flames still burning around him. "I have no intention of biting you this evening."

"Oh goodie..."

His eyes narrowed even more. "You're powerless here, and you conduct yourself like you're invincible."

"I am invincible. I'm the only human who's immune to the disease that's claimed the lives of thousands and poisoned the blood of thousands more. You bite the wrong human, and you're dead. I'm the most powerful goddamn person in the world right now." I wasn't stupid, and I wanted to make that abundantly clear.

He was silent, and slowly, the flames around him started to diminish.

"You think I'm a pain in the ass? Honey, you haven't seen the half of it."

Silent he stayed, watching me across the table, the intensity in his stare remaining but the flames settling. "I can offer you the one thing you want more than anything."

"My freedom?"

"Even more than that."

There was nothing I wanted more than to be free of this monster and the other monsters that followed him. "What is that?"

"A cure."

My expression didn't change, but I felt all the muscles in my body tighten automatically. Against my will, my lungs pulled in a deep breath.

"Do I have your attention?" Those angry eyes now shone with arrogance.

Stubborn to my core, I kept my mouth shut.

"We have the same self-interest. The plague has devastated our food source, and your population has been decimated by the sickness. We can find a cure together—if you cooperate."

"Cooperate?"

"Yes."

"And what does *cooperate* mean?"

He tilted his head the other way, his slitted eyes never leaving my face. "I need to taste your blood."

My stomach tightened with disgust.

"It's the only way."

"Right..."

"If I've fed on someone before, I can identify them based on the taste of their blood alone. It's the same way you can identify someone based on the sound of their voice...their scent. I can taste the properties of your blood, and perhaps I can determine what sets you apart from everyone else."

It felt like a trap. "And in the event you succeed, what then?"

"We invent a cure—and give it to your people."

"Just like that?"

"As I've already said, the eradication of this disease is paramount to our survival. It's decimating our population as much as yours."

"That's not true... You have other options."

"Animal blood is a poor substitute. Yes, it keeps us alive, but it also keeps us weak."

I stared, annoyed with his calmness, with the way his deep voice set the tone of this conversation.

"You're the savior your people need."

I broke contact and looked away.

"You can save them all...and you're unwilling to make this sacrifice?"

"I'm not stupid. I know what you're doing."

"Which is?"

I looked at him again. "You're trying to manipulate me."

"Even if that's true, what does it matter?"

"It is true."

He didn't refute it. "An opportunity has been given to us, but you would throw it away because you're afraid?"

"I'm not afraid. Just don't want a leech on my neck. Don't want to strengthen my greatest mortal enemy. I'd rather watch you wither and weaken until you're dust on the wind..."

The corner of his mouth lifted, and he grinned.

"Did you not understand what I said?"

"There are worse things than my kind in this world."

"Such as?"

"You'll see—someday."

Trepidation filled my heart, an unease that seeped straight into my bones. I wanted to press him for answers, but I would receive none, especially since I'd refused to comply with every single one of his demands.

"When I said your kind enjoy bloodletting, I meant it. Every prey I've ever had has enjoyed my bite. The only pain you feel is the moment my fangs pierce your skin. But then indescribable pleasure sweeps through you, the kind that will make you beg me to keep going, until I've had every single drop."

"I don't believe you."

His stare was motionless, eyes locked on to mine, like I wasn't even there. "I've never had to force a woman to be my prey."

"Then why don't you get someone else?"

"Humans normally travel to our gates and offer themselves as prey. We've never had to travel to the kingdoms and capture prisoners. The plague has changed everything."

"Why would they do that? Why would anyone in their right mind want to subject themselves to that?"

He gave a subtle shrug. "Several reasons."

"Such as?"

"One, physical desire."

"Desire? Desire to be bitten?"

"Desire to be with a vampire in other ways..."

I couldn't sit across from Kingsnake and pretend he wasn't a treat for the eyes, especially when he was shirtless and muscular. The other vampire I usually saw him with was the same way, though even more muscular. A lot of vampires were good-looking, but Kingsnake was exceptional. "Is that why you're half naked right now? Because that's not going to work on me."

That knowing grin returned. "I find it more comfortable."

"What are the other reasons?"

"Obsession. Some humans worship our kind. Think we're gods. To serve us is a great honor."

I'd heard about those people before. I'd always dismissed them as crazy enthusiasts.

"And the final, more important reason is the chance to become a vampire themselves."

Death would be preferable. "None of those sound remotely appealing."

"The chance to live forever isn't remotely appealing to you?"

"No—because it's not living. You don't have a beating heart. Your lungs don't draw air. You have no soul. When your time comes, you'll just be...nothing."

His expression didn't change, as hard as ever, still as stone.

"That doesn't bother you?"

"Why would it bother me when my time will never come?"

"You're that arrogant?"

"Confident. That's the word I would use."

I stared at this creature across from me, a monster that had a beautiful face, a beautiful body, but an enormous void inside his chest. "If I were to cooperate and we did discover a cure for my people...would you let me go?"

Silence. An eternity of it.

I waited, unsure what he was thinking or if he was thinking at all. His face was hard, and his emotions were subdued.

"Every prey I've ever had has fulfilled their use. Their taste grows stale, and soon, I crave something different. Once I've grown bored of your taste, I will release you. What you choose to do at that time is your concern."

"You don't kill your prey when you're finished with them?"

"No. They usually become prey to someone else. Or they leave." He studied my gaze, watched me work out the information he'd just given me. "Contrary to what you've been told, we're not monsters. We don't kill humans unless by accident. We're no different from some fishermen. After we've made our catch, we toss it back into the water."

The comparison was a stretch, but I kept my opinion to myself. "You give me your word? You'll let me go?"

He held my gaze for a long time before he gave a subtle nod. "Yes."

I didn't know him well enough to trust his word, but honorable kings kept their promises—and he seemed honorable.

"I can't force you to do this."

My arms crossed over my chest.

"Because if I do, there's a good chance I'll kill you."

When I pictured myself submitting to his bite, I was filled with self-loathing. But if there really was a possibility this could lead to the salvation of my people, it would be selfish to refuse.

"I need you to submit to me completely."

That was an impossible task.

"Can you do that?"

My hands automatically rubbed up and down my arms, fighting the chill that suddenly crept into the room. My entire life, I'd been warned about the horrors of these creatures, and to allow yourself to be bitten...was unspeakable.

"You can trust me, Larisa."

"Trust you, how?"

"Trust that I won't kill you." He hadn't moved in the last ten minutes, hadn't even blinked. His snake-like qualities became more apparent the longer I was in his presence. "Trust that you'll enjoy it."

I was horrified that I was actually considering this.

"Will you let me, Larisa?"

My heart had picked up in speed, and the fast rate made me a little sick. My palms were clammy even though this place was eternally chilly. I suddenly felt hot, like the sun could pierce through the clouds and the solid walls. "Yes… I'll let you."

8

LARISA

I didn't sleep a wink last night.

I was scared, and being scared was making this moment more daunting. He wouldn't kill me. He said it wouldn't hurt. I even had a chance to save my people from damnation. If we didn't stop this sickness, at some point, there would be so few of us that the kingdoms would fall into ruin. It had to be done, and all I had to do was lie there until he finished.

But the unease didn't stop.

The clock clicked.

The door opened.

And then he appeared, the same as he had last night, shirtless in his trousers, even barefoot. He shut the door behind him, and it locked from the other side.

I sat on the bed, looking at the vampire who was indistinguishable from a human. His fangs weren't visible. His only tell was the difference in his pupils. The second he was in the room, my heart rate turned sporadic.

"Lie down."

My instinct was to talk back, to resist every order he gave me, but this wasn't an order. It was a suggestion.

I was fully dressed, with the exception of my shoes. I hadn't worn them since I'd been barricaded inside this prison because there'd been no need to.

He approached the bed, coming as close as he had when he'd choked me by the neck. Now I could smell him, smell the hint of sandalwood and salt and ocean air...even mist. He'd always been adorned in his armor and clothing, but now his skin was exposed to my senses.

He didn't touch me. "You'll be more comfortable if you lie back."

"How long will it take?"

His eyes shifted back and forth between mine. "Not long."

I finally lay back on top of the bedspread, my head hitting the pillow.

He stood at the bedside. "Move your hair."

I grabbed the strands and shifted them away, exposing my flesh to the vampire who wanted to feast on my blood. My eyes were locked on the ceiling because I didn't want to see the look of victory on his face. I didn't want to acknowledge my fate.

He continued to stand there.

"Just get it over with."

He moved onto the bed, his knees immediately making the mattress shift from his weight. He was several inches over six feet, and even with his lean body, he had to weigh two hundred pounds.

He moved directly on top of me like he was about to do more than bite me.

Now his scent was more intense, right at my nose, smelling like a cold ocean. His body didn't touch mine, and his slitted eyes studied my face. His strong shoulders and chest were at my eye level, and that made this moment feel far more intimate.

His hand slid into my hair like he was about to kiss me.

Bumps formed all over my arms instantaneously. My nerves became tight and bundled up. I swallowed even though my throat was dry. Every time I took a breath, I held it before I let it release.

He turned my head in his hand, making me look to the right, and then he dipped his head down—and I felt them.

His fangs.

They pierced my flesh, and the sting was sharp like a paper cut. It made me wince, made me kick my legs in protest.

But then the pain dwindled, replaced by a euphoria that was indescribable. It was pain medication to numb the bite, but it was intoxicating enough to make it addictive. My body went limp with relaxation, and then the pleasure I received was so potent that I didn't want it to stop...just like he said.

My hands moved of their own accord, and they snaked up his muscular back. When they reached the backs of his shoulders, my nails dug into his skin like I wanted to draw his blood the way he drew mine.

My eyes closed, and I tilted my head back, giving him greater exposure to my neck. I was so subdued I could barely feel the rush of emotions.

An earthquake that toppled mountains. A force strong enough to destroy the world and everything in it. Trees snapped in half. Winds destroyed stone. Floods broke dams and covered the world in water.

Less than ten seconds after his fangs pierced my flesh, it was over.

He left my body and rose to his feet. His face never turned toward mine, his expression a mystery.

"What happened?" It was my first time, but I knew it was supposed to last a lot longer than ten seconds.

He stormed out of my bedchambers—and left the door wide open.

9

KINGSNAKE

The door to my study opened and closed, and Viper joined my presence.

He took one look at me and identified the change. "You fed."

It'd been hours—and I still felt the same.

"But your eyes...they're a different color."

"It used to be worse." They'd turned to green, but slowly, they were returning to their previous color.

Viper understood the severity of the situation and lowered himself into one of the armchairs.

"Her blood...is unlike anything I've ever tasted." Those ten seconds were chaos. The second I tasted her, I wanted to suck her dry, extinguish her life so I could have all of her in a single bite. "I wanted to kill her."

Viper stared.

"I've never felt that way before." Blood only tasted good because it was new. But once the flavor felt dull on my tongue, it was forgettable. But this...it would never get old. "I could taste the power. It's beyond immunity. There's more to this woman than meets the eye..."

"Are you saying she's not who she says she is?"

"No. I'm sure she has no idea who she is...or *what* she is."

Viper relaxed further in the chair, and his eyes shifted away, like he was deep in thought.

My hands tightened under the desk, my tendons stretching over stronger muscle than before. "It was brief, but it was enough to make me feel whole. Weeks of hunger washed away with just a few drops. The taste of animal blood...is like it never happened. My ability to focus is tenfold. I feel a thousand years younger."

His eyes shifted back to mine. "Did you recognize the elements in her blood?"

"The frenzy was too deep." I couldn't identify anything—not in the blizzard of bliss. "Once the shock has worn off, I'll try again."

"I can check myself."

My eyes halted on his face, and I felt the tightness maneuver through my body. It was the same tension I felt before drawing my sword, before carving an enemy to pieces. My rage was misplaced and misdirected, but it was real nonetheless. "She's mine."

Viper held my gaze, stonelike. "If you can't feed—"

"I can feed."

"If you kill her—"

"I won't. If I were unable to control myself, she would already be dead."

A heavy silence passed between us, a cloud of tension releasing raindrops upon us both. Thousands of years of trust existed between us, but that quickly came into doubt when something as desirable as Larisa entered the fold.

"I suppose you don't hate her anymore."

I'd forgotten about my prejudice the moment I tasted her.

"Did you desire her?"

"No." She was an attractive woman, but not particularly attractive to me. Maybe that would have been different if she hadn't been so disobedient. I was used to women following orders, getting on their knees, and begging for my bite.

"Do you desire her now?"

I knew the reason why he asked—because he wanted me to share her. "I'm starting to."

———

"There's been unusual activity at the Evanguard border." The scout entered the war room where General Viper and I conferred with the commanders about our military stance. We shared our lands with monsters and orcs, and while our invasion had been peaceful, there was always deep-rooted resentment from the people we subjugated. Someday, there could be an uprising—and we had to be prepared for it.

I regarded the scout with furrowed eyebrows. "What kind of unusual activity?"

"Shipments of some kind. Their cargo is well hidden in their carts, but there're so many..."

I looked at General Viper.

He stared back at me.

I turned back to the scout. "Continue to watch their borders. I want to know where these shipments came from."

He gave a swift bow then departed.

I stood at the table with the map of our lands on the surface, our neighboring kingdoms farther away. The commanders stood with their hands at their backs, waiting for orders. "We don't need proof to know exactly where this plague is coming from." I stared at Evanguard, the stronghold of the elves, the mythical creatures that believed they were gods. "With their magic, they created this devastation—and unleashed it on the world."

"By decimating the human population, they've decimated ours." General Viper crossed his arms over his chest, his thick armor covering his massive body. "A smart plan. If they have the poison, they probably have the antidote."

"Which they'll never give to us."

"There may be something we could trade."

"No." I straightened, my eyes lifting from the map. "They want our annihilation, and if we don't stop the disease, they'll succeed. Most of us will die from starvation, and the others will subsist on animal blood, making them too weak to fight. They'll march on our borders and defeat us once and for all." I could see their plan clearly in my mind, and the fact that it was a good plan only made me angrier. "Soon, this world will belong to them—and only them."

Viper looked at me, his thoughts written clearly on his face.

If we couldn't get the cure from Larisa, we would all be doomed.

10

LARISA

The only way I could measure the passage of time was by the trays placed through the flap in my door. It was easy to distinguish breakfast, lunch, and dinner, so I realized two days had come and gone since Kingsnake had rushed away from my bedroom.

I continued to examine my neck in the mirror, seeing the two small punctures from his fangs. They'd healed quickly, but the scar still remained days later. Sometimes I would touch it, and if I pressed hard enough, I could feel the sting of the cut.

When I grew frustrated waiting for Kingsnake to return and explain what had happened, I banged my closed fists on the door and screamed, "Let me out!" I hadn't seen sunlight in nearly a week. Hadn't seen a cloud or a bird. Trapped as I was in these four walls, every second that passed felt like it belonged to a single day.

There was no response.

"I want to talk to Kingsnake!" No one would open the door for me, and I suspected they needed his permission first. And the door was probably prohibited from being opened without his presence because I was such a flight risk. "I mean it!" I grabbed the armchair from the living room, and with all my strength, I threw it at the door.

Didn't make a dent—not even a scratch.

I picked up the chair again then swung it a couple times before I threw it.

Right when the door flew open.

With his quick reflexes, he caught the chair without effort. But his hard face showed just how annoyed he found my erratic behavior. He set the chair to the side and entered the room. In his full uniform with his sword at his hip, he stepped inside and towered over me. "Yes?"

"*Yes?*" My eyebrows practically jumped off my head. "I've been trapped in here for a week, and that's all I get from you?"

"Would you like to take a walk?"

"You can't just treat me like— Wait—*what?*"

He left the room and stepped into the hallway, the ceilings thirty feet high, the stonework carved with elegant serpents.

I watched him go, looking through the open doorway, unable to believe I could just...walk on out. I followed him into the hallway, his cloak shimmering across his large back as he moved, not waiting for me to catch up.

Even from the rear, I could see his power, see it in the way he carried himself. My people didn't know much about the vampires because they'd always been secretive, always been the enemy, but I knew Kingsnake had been around for many generations, according to the texts on my bookshelves.

I came to his side. "Where are we going?"

"Wherever you want." After a couple turns, we exited the stone palace and emerged at the top of the one hundred stairs, looking over the city as it curved and descended down the mountain. To the left was a breathtaking sight of the ocean, gray clouds above the water, the sun hidden behind the blanket that covered the sky.

I'd never seen the ocean.

It was cold and gray, large whitecaps rising to the surface before they broke on the shore. The smell of salt was in the air, the cold humidity against my skin. It was chilly.

My eyes shifted to his when I felt his stare.

"You've never seen the ocean."

I was the one who could read emotions, but it seemed like he could read minds. "Is it always this cold?"

"Most of the time."

"That's why you live here...because there's no sun." The cloud bank constantly blocked out the sun, dimmed the rays so this nightwalker could be a daywalker. The rays were so dim and refracted that they didn't pierce their flesh.

"There is, occasionally."

"What do you do when that happens?"

The question didn't seem worth his time because he didn't answer. He walked forward and began to descend the long path down the stairs, never stepping on his cloak as it trailed behind him.

I looked at the ocean again before I followed him, reaching the bottom that led to the route deeper into the city. The other buildings appeared to be made out of the same material—impenetrable gray stone. They were all carved with various images of serpents, some wrapping around pillars, others engraved above windows and doorways. "Where's your snake?"

"He's not my snake...and his name is Fang."

"Alright. Where is Fang?"

"We don't spend every waking moment together."

"What does a snake do in its spare time?"

He halted before we reached the beginning of the city, turning to regard me, a subtle rage simmering beneath the surface of his expression. "*He*. Not it."

I could feel the anger bubbling, feel the heat rise. It was my first time outside underneath the sky, and the last thing I wanted to do was jeopardize this moment of freedom. "Sorry..."

"You need not fear him."

"He's a snake. An enormous snake with big-ass fangs. You obviously keep him around for the very reasons I fear him."

"But he would never hurt you."

"You can't control him. He's a wild animal—"

"He would never hurt you—unless I asked." He continued on his walk, dismissing the conversation.

I waited a moment before I followed, catching up to his pace. As we entered the city, we saw vampires pass, impossible to differentiate from humans. They seemed to know exactly who he was because anytime they crossed his path, they either went in the opposite direction or crossed to the opposite side of the road to stay out of his way.

"They're afraid of you."

"You mistake fear for respect." He kept going, escorting me past the homes and shops. There seemed to be different districts, a separation between residences and shops, and I saw trees in pots, succulents in planters underneath windows. For creatures that were dead, they still seemed to appreciate life.

Everywhere we went, Kingsnake had the same effect—making everyone disperse. No one greeted him. No one said a word. In Raventower, if the king ever made a public appearance, the townspeople were expected to greet him with bows and curtsies, to throw flowers at his feet as he passed.

But in Grayson, they diverted in different directions and didn't make eye contact.

"Is the crown your birthright?" The crown was usually passed from father to son, staying in the royal family, saying it was their birthright as granted by the gods. But vampires didn't sire children, so how did that work?

"Yes."

"So your father was king before you?"

"You could say that." He took another path and we descended farther, and that was when I realized we were approaching the shore, the white-sand beach before the powerful waves.

The stone path reached the cliffs, and then it turned into a dirt path that hugged the cliffside. He moved to a large cypress tree, and underneath it was a stone bench. He adjusted his cloak before he took a seat, his strong back perfectly upright, and his dark eyes took in the breath-taking view.

I sat beside him and stared out at the endless sea of never-ending gray, staring until sky met ocean. The breeze stung from the cold, pierced my eyes like small knives and made tiny tears roll down my cheeks because I couldn't with-draw my stare. I'd heard stories of the ocean, of large wooden ships exploring uncharted territory, of how big the world truly was.

He stared as well, saying nothing.

The taste of freedom was indescribable, to feel the fresh air directly on my skin, to see more than solid walls. "I can't go back in there..."

No reaction. No emotion.

"Give me a window, at least."

"I'll give you whatever you want—if you don't run away." He turned to look at me, his dark eyes packed with both cruelty and intelligence, his hard jawline sharp as any dagger. "I'm a king, not a babysitter."

"I let you bite me so we could find a cure to save my people. You think I'm going anywhere?"

He looked forward again. "Do I have your word?"

"My word what?"

"That you won't run."

"Does my word mean anything to you?"

"You've trusted me to let you go. I'd like to reciprocate that trust."

For just a moment, a flicker, I stopped hating him.

"But I must warn you. My trust is like glass. Once it's shattered, it can never be repaired. Not only will you lose my trust, but also my respect and my protection. I've already told you the safest place for you in this world is by my side."

"I don't need your protection..."

He slowly turned my way. "I'm not talking about orcs and goblins."

"Then what are you talking about?"

"Soon, everyone will know your value. That your blood is immune to the sickness that's claimed the lives of our kind. Every single one of them will want a taste—and won't be able to resist a bite. My protection is the only thing standing in their way."

When I'd walked through the streets with Kingsnake, I'd never once felt vulnerable. But if I were alone...surrounded by hungry vampires...I'd be utterly terrified.

"While my people respect my rulership, they're hungry. My previous prey didn't heed my warning—and you can guess how she ended up."

I swallowed, imagining her lifeless body left behind a building. "Did you care for her?"

"No."

"She offered herself to you...and she still meant nothing?"

"So did every woman before her. So will every woman after her."

"That's a bit cold."

He cracked a smile, a sad one. "And I'm cold-blooded —literally."

I looked forward, trying to get that cruel smile out of my head. "I give you my word." If I returned to Raventower, I would only be able to comfort the dying, not cure the sickness. It was a pointless endeavor. But if Kingsnake could give me the antidote, I could return to my people as a savior.

"Don't leave the palace without General Viper or me as your escort."

I'd fought him the whole way here, and now I was a willing prisoner—to none other than Kingsnake. "What happened when you bit me?"

He turned silent, but his mood intensified. *Black clouds swirled around him in an angry storm. Hurricanes crashed against the shores of his mind.*

"I don't know much about this, but I'm sure it was supposed to last longer than that."

His mood deepened, the storm now in a frenzy, rage and annoyance racing for first place.

"Why does my question anger you?"

The storm instantly disappeared. The waves went calm. His head had turned in my direction, his eyes narrowed.

There was no way he would discover my secret, but I should tread carefully nonetheless.

"I'm not angry."

"Yes, you are," I snapped. "And annoyed."

His eyes shifted back and forth between mine. "The taste of your blood was far more potent than I anticipated. I couldn't handle it—so I had to withdraw."

"Potent?" I asked. "Potent how?"

"Strong. Powerful. Irresistible." His anger had disappeared, but a deeper feeling surrounded him, a darkness that couldn't be described. The clouds turned gray, and then everything went dark.

"Could you...discern anything?"

"No."

"Are you going to try again?"

"Eventually."

I studied his gaze, trying to read his emotions on his face. The feelings within him became murkier, like a puddle of mud, intense but indescribable. As I stared, I realized his eyes were a slightly different color, more green than brown, practically hazel. I noticed the subtle brightness in his skin. It took me a moment to understand the implications of our situation. "You wanted to kill me..."

His slitted pupils were fascinating because they had more depth than any other eyes I'd ever held. Whenever he went still, he was like Fang, focused on his target like a predator focused on its prey. "I didn't want to stop—that's a better description."

Now my heart started to race. My palms were clammy again. I was supposed to be safe at his side, but now I felt like I was in battle without a sword or armor.

"I would never claim your life."

"But you wanted to—"

"And I stopped." His tone deepened, sharpening like the edge of a blade. "I will always stop."

"How do you know—"

"Because I already did." His eyes were hard like the gates to their city, impenetrable, made of solid stone. "And I will again."

———

My new quarters were much better than the previous.

For one, I had windows.

Windows through which I could see the pines in the forest, see the ocean in the distance, that could be opened to let the salty sea air chase away the staleness. I even had a balcony with a table and two chairs.

It was too cold to be outside for too long, but it was still nice to have the option, to mark the passage of time by the sunlight rather than the meals slipped underneath my door. Now when my meals arrived, the servant carried them to the table in my bedroom, treating me like a person rather than a dog that got his food in a bowl on the floor.

I was also given better clothes, long-sleeved dresses that I could wear throughout the palace. They were tight on my chest and waist, and they flared out slightly around my hips. They were all in dark colors, black, dark green, and even a snake pattern.

I still didn't understand the relationship between vampires and snakes, but clearly, there was one.

Days had passed, and I hadn't seen or spoken to Kingsnake. I rarely left the room, because all I really wanted were windows. If I couldn't go into the town safely, there was nothing for me beyond these four walls anyway.

It was early in the morning when a knock sounded on the door.

My heart jumped into my throat because I suspected Kingsnake had come for a visit. When the servant knocked on the door, he always added, "I have your breakfast." Or whatever meal it was.

When I didn't say anything, he knocked harder, announcing his annoyance.

"Come in."

The door swung open, and he entered, shirtless and bare-foot, his intentions heavy in his eyes. He shut the door behind him then approached me where I sat on the bed. It was so early that I hadn't even had breakfast yet, let alone a chance to get ready for the day.

But he looked at me like he didn't notice those things.

His body looked slightly different, the muscles more prominent under the skin, like he'd been on a long journey that made him stronger. The cords were more noticeable over his biceps and up both sides of his neck. His slitted pupils regarded me with hunger.

The energy emitting from him was overwhelming. Unrequited yearning. Desperation. Need. It came from him in waves, leaving his shores and coming to mine.

I pulled my legs closer to my body under the sheets, withdrawing as much as I could. I was in just a silk tunic to sleep in, but I wore nothing below but my underwear.

He came closer around the bed, undeterred by my terror. "Remember how it felt last time?"

Once his fangs had pierced my flesh, all the toxins dumped into my blood, and all I wanted to do was let him feed. My arms hugged his large body, and I pulled him deeper into me, squeezing his hips with my thighs. Bliss overcame me, and I reveled in the inexplicable pleasure that bite ignited. "That's not what I'm worried about."

He stared at me, his features hard and etched in stone, his desperation still vibrating.

I knew I had no say in the matter. His excitement was too deep.

He grabbed the sheets and tugged them down.

My knees came closer to my chest to hide whatever I could.

His eyes remained locked on mine as he grabbed me by the ankle and dragged me toward him.

I felt like a flimsy piece of rope in his hand, gliding across the sheets as if I weighed nothing. I let out a whimper as my heart raced in desperation.

He inserted himself between my ankles and then my knees, moving on top of me on the bed, his weight making the mattress dip like last time. "I'm not going to kill you." His face was directly above mine, his naked skin pressed against the areas of my body that were exposed. "If I do, I can't feed again, and that's the last thing I want."

I panted underneath him, nervous to let those fangs pierce me again. They put me under a spell that I couldn't shake, and if he was under that same spell, I had no hope of making it out alive.

"I can't help you if I can't taste you."

I was trapped there, pinned underneath his massive body, but I still had power because he gave it to me. Without my permission, he wouldn't start, and that calmed me slightly.

"Tap my shoulder if you want me to stop."

Like I would ever ask.

His eyes continued to bore into mine.

"Promise me..." I relied on the word of a man I hardly knew, as if that would make any kind of difference once he was high off the power in my blood.

With his eyes locked on mine, he slid his hand into my hair and fisted it. "I promise." He didn't even wait for me to blink he was so anxious, and he dipped his head to my neck and pricked me with the points of his fangs.

I gasped before I sucked in a deep breath at the sharpness of his bite, but then it passed immediately, replaced by the exquisite pleasure that I remembered. I quickly felt warm, and my hands found their way to his muscular back, gripping his muscles like rocks as I climbed up a cliff.

My knees pulled to my chest, and I squeezed his torso with the insides of my calves. My eyes closed, and I dragged my fingers down his back, marking him with my nails the way he marked me with his fangs.

An explosion erupted from his mind. *The storm that snapped trees in half. The hurricane that moved mountains.*

The fire that burned water. It rushed through him with the force of the gods. His hand tightened on my hair, and he sank his body into mine.

I felt it between my legs, the definition of a man. Thick. Pulsing. Hot. It was so hard it felt like the stone that made these halls. Between his pants and my panties, I could feel his size...and none of my previous lovers could ever compare.

He continued to feed, his arm snaking underneath my back to pull me closer into him, all the while his emotions slowly built higher and higher, a crescendo nowhere in sight. He squeezed me. Dug his fangs deeper. Fed like a new vampire that had never tasted blood.

The euphoria began to wash away...and I felt weak.

Weaker with every passing second.

He'd taken too much...and I wasn't sure if he would stop.

My hand made it to his shoulder, and I tapped him.

Reluctantly, he pulled away. His fangs were still exposed when he looked down at me, drops of red blood on the white teeth. He quickly withdrew them at the sight of my face. His hand cupped my cheek, and all the desperation was replaced by concern. "Larisa?"

"I feel tired..."

"That's normal. Let me get you something to eat." He left the bed and poked his head out the door to give someone an order. He came back a moment later, a tray in hand, and set it beside me. "Take a few bites."

It took all my strength to eat whatever he gave me. I wasn't sure what it was, so weak from the blood loss and delirious from the high that lingered. My eyes were only half open most of the time.

He took the tray away, and then he tucked me into bed. "Get some rest."

"Don't leave me..." I had no control over the things that came out of my mouth. It sounded horrible on my ears, but I still couldn't get myself to stop. The high in my veins continued to make me a different person.

He came back to the bed, and this time, he slid into the sheets beside me. "I'm here."

I immediately moved into his body, used his shoulder as a pillow and his body as a teddy bear. My eyes carried the weight of boulders, and once they closed, I was dead asleep.

11

LARISA

When I woke up, I was alone.

There was no sign that Kingsnake had been there, other than the couple of drops of blood on the sheets. My tray was at the end of the table, the plates empty even though I didn't recall eating it.

I felt a lot better.

The weakness felt like a haze at this point, a distant dream. The euphoria had washed away like silt in the bottom of a riverbed, and then the creek ran dry. Kingsnake fed on me as much as he could, and I wondered how much longer he would have gone if I hadn't asked him to stop.

I was surprised he stopped at all, not when I remembered the rush of pleasure that thudded through his body...and the hardness too.

That came back to me, distinct and hard, like I could feel it against my body all over again.

Guess he wasn't totally dead...

When I got out of bed, my legs were initially shaky, but I walked it off and felt fine. I showered, put on a change of clothes, and then looked outside to realize that it was almost nighttime.

Now I had the sleep schedule of a vampire.

A knock sounded on my door. "His Majesty requests your presence."

"You can come in."

The servant entered my quarters, no tray in hand.

"What does he want?"

"For you to join him for dinner."

Dinner? Did vampires eat food? Or was I the dinner? No way he believed he could get another meal out of me so soon. "Will I be eating or...?"

"You both will. Join him in the dining hall when you're ready." He shut the door.

I stood there for a solid minute as I tried to figure out what to do.

I put on one of the black dresses in my closet, slipped on the heeled boots that came with it, and then made my way through the hallways of the palace until I reached the dining hall. It was a private room with floor-to-ceiling windows showing the ocean at the bottom of the cliff. It wasn't visible now because it was dark, but I knew it was there.

Kingsnake was already seated, his back to the window, wearing his king's uniform without the armor. His eyes were on me the second I entered the room, and their heaviness told me he wouldn't look away.

His look made me swallow.

I approached the table and took a seat under the enormous chandelier, which was aglow with candles even though the palace had electricity. Now there were only a few feet between us, and the scent of sandalwood hit my nose once again.

I wanted to fire off questions, but his hard stare steadied me. He'd never looked at me that way before. It was the stare a commander gave his enemy across the battlefield. It was the look an eagle gave to a rat before he broke its neck with his beak. His stare had that intensity, but not the threat.

And I felt nothing from him. Nothing at all.

The servant interrupted the stare down when he brought two plates and two goblets to the table. The wine was poured, and then he silently excused himself so we could enjoy our meal. It was a rare steak with roasted potatoes and asparagus.

I looked at his plate and saw the same thing. "I thought vampires didn't eat."

"What you thought was wrong." He laid the napkin across his lap, picked up his utensils, and then sliced into the meat.

I watched him put a bite into his mouth, watched his hard jawline shift and move as he chewed the meat. Then his throat gave a twitch when he swallowed. There was a subtle hint of facial hair, a little shadow, and it made me wonder if he shaved.

He reached for his glass of wine and took a drink. "Eat."

I was shaken from my position, realizing I'd just been sitting there and staring. "So...why don't you just eat instead of feeding on blood?"

"Because food is for pleasure, blood is for sustenance." He took another bite, elbows off the table, his back straight.

I didn't expect someone like him to have manners. "I'm relieved I'm not on the menu tonight."

"I won't need to feed for a while. That's how powerful your blood is."

Ever since the moment I looked at him, I'd noticed a change in his appearance. It was subtle, a brightness in his eyes and his skin. His shoulders seemed slightly bigger too, rising higher than they did before. "Then why did you ask me to join you?"

"Because I wanted to." His tone was sharp as an ax, like he didn't appreciate all the questions.

I didn't know how to have a conversation with him without asking questions. I decided to turn quiet, focusing on my dinner, waiting to see if he would explain the reason for this candlelit meal.

When five minutes of silence passed, I knew that wouldn't happen.

"How are you feeling?" He finally asked his first question.

"Better." I'd felt so weak, weak enough that I wouldn't be able to fight off any kind of attack. Food and sleep helped me recuperate, but I didn't enjoy the way his bite made me feel. "Good thing I asked you to stop. Otherwise, you may not have."

"I would have."

"When I was dead, maybe."

His eyes flashed with a look of annoyance. "You can trust me."

"Like I'd ever trust a vampire..."

That look of annoyance increased tenfold. "I stopped on my own when I questioned my strength. And I stopped the instant you asked me to. I've earned more respect than you've given."

"*Respect*?" I asked incredulously. "I should respect you for eating some of me but not all of me?"

Now his eyes narrowed. "You don't want to know what the others would do to you—"

"You only keep me alive so you can keep feeding. Don't act like this isn't self-serving."

Silence. Heavy silence. And then fire. "It is self-serving. Completely and utterly. But this is also self-serving for you."

"Self-serving for me?" I asked in disbelief. "I'm sacrificing myself to help my people. That's pretty damn selfless."

"I disagree."

We glared at each other, our dinner now forgotten.

"Answer me this." I stared him down across the table, wanting to bash my plate over his head. "What elements have you identified in my blood?"

His stare was hard, like the stone underneath our feet.

"I'm sorry, I didn't catch that?"

Flames erupted again, rising up the walls and consuming the building. "It's complicated—"

"You aren't even trying. You're just enjoying it."

He sucked in a hard breath through his clenched teeth. "You don't understand—"

"I understand you're an asshole. That's what I understand."

His gaze was lethal. Silence passed as the flames slowly withdrew from the room. Gradually, they were pulled back, bringing the room back to its previous condition. "I need to acclimate to the taste before I can be objective about its properties."

"You act like you're a teenage boy who needs to fuck a couple of times before he stops blowing his load so soon."

His stare was cold. "It's exactly like that."

"Well, I don't want to be here longer than I have to be."

His elbows moved to the table, and he folded his hands together.

"And I'm sure you want me gone too."

He said nothing.

Trepidation moved through me, making my fingers twitch underneath the table. "You promised you would let me go..."

"I know what I promised."

"You can't go back on your word—"

"When did I give you any indication that I had?"

"I said you must want me gone...and you didn't say anything."

Again, he didn't say anything for a long time. A very long time. "Just because I don't want you gone doesn't mean I won't release you when the time comes."

"My blood tastes so good that you would rather put up with me than find someone else to eat?" I knew I was a pain in the ass. The more I inconvenienced him, the more he'd want to finish this project.

His eyes stared at me, still and cold. "There's no comparison."

Ice moved through my veins, a horror I couldn't shake. "Why did you ask me here tonight? If it's not to discuss an antidote to this horrible disease and it's not to feed on me, then why?" What did this monster want from me?

His fingers rested against his bottom lip as he stared at me. Ten seconds passed. Thirty seconds. Then a full minute.

His eyes were so green they looked like the moss on trees. Normally brown and the color of soil, the new color of his eyes changed his appearance entirely. Then he lowered his hands and sat back in the chair. "I want more."

I knew he had an agenda. "You said you wouldn't need to feed for a while."

"I'm not talking about your blood."

I took a breath, and that was the moment I realized I'd read his intensity incorrectly. Emotions were specific to each person. They felt them on different levels, in different ways. He expressed a horde of emotions in the same way— as blinding rage. Now I realized what he wanted—and that made my stomach tighten into a fist.

His eyes didn't leave my face. That intensity slowly rose like smoke in a room, surging to the ceiling.

My mouth was suddenly dry. "You despise me."

"I do."

I remembered the way his hard dick felt against me, so hard it was like a pillar of stone. "Then why would you want...?"

"Because your blood makes me crazy."

I shifted my gaze away when his stare became too much. I'd never felt more like prey in my life.

"I want you. All of you. In every way imaginable."

I kept my eyes on the dark window.

"Look at me."

I didn't.

"Look at me."

The command in his voice forced me to obey.

"I know the feeling is mutual."

"It's not."

He was as still as everything else in the room, but his eyes possessed so much energy. Every little shift. Every little movement. He absorbed my reactions, absorbed my emotions the way I absorbed his. "Your ankles were locked around my waist. Your nails clawed at my back like I was buried inside you, and you didn't want me to stop. I'm sorry to be the bearer of bad news, but the feeling is mutual."

"It's the toxins in your venom. You said yourself it makes your prey feel good."

"Makes them relax. Makes them feel pleasure. Doesn't make them wet—and I could feel how wet you were against my pants."

I tried so hard to keep a straight face and not look mortified, but it was like trying to tip over a mountain.

The asshole had that arrogant look in his eyes—like he'd won.

As if I'd ever let him win. "I hate to be the bearer of bad news, but you misinterpreted my actions."

There was a little smirk on his lips and playfulness in his eyes that I fucking despised. "My mistake."

I moved to my feet and shoved the chair back. In my haste, it toppled backward and struck the floor. I stormed away from the table and into the hallway, trying to get away from this disgusting nightwalker.

I'd reached my bedroom door when I felt a large hand grab me by the arm.

I twisted around and shoved him, but he was so heavy I only pushed myself back into the wall. He was on me, pinning me to the wall with his hand on my throat. He was so powerful I couldn't move at all. "Please don't do this..." My choice had been stripped from me, and my strength was no match for his, not after the power I'd let him take from me.

His eyes had been hard a moment ago, but now they were a little softer. "I don't get off on that shit. I like to fuck women who beg me not to stop, who leave claw marks on my back that last for days. I fuck women who let me bite and fuck as hard as I want."

I tried to look away, but his hand forced my chin up so I would meet his gaze.

"Don't fight it."

"Let me go." My hands grabbed on to his arm, and I tried to pry myself free. It was pointless.

"I said, don't fight it."

"Fuck you." I slammed my hands down as hard as I could.

It didn't affect him at all, but he decided to let me go anyway.

I darted into my bedroom and tried to shut the door on him.

He shoved it aside and came at me again. The flames burst from his body and consumed the entire bedroom. A new level of rage exploded from his body when he didn't get what he wanted. "Why are you being this way?"

"Because you're a fucking monster." I wanted to pick up the chair and throw it at his head. "You think I want to screw someone who's been feeding on my people for centuries? You think I'd fuck the man who dragged my friends from their homes in the night and forced them back here to feed your kind? I *despise* you. You're a damn curse on this earth, and if I could kill all of you without killing my own, I would."

His angry eyes watched me, standing there in silence, the flames consuming the curtains on the windows, the comforter on the bed. Silence passed, like he might say something if he found the right words. But then he marched out of the bedroom, and as he went, he pulled the flames with him, taking the soot and smoke.

12

KINGSNAKE

"There's some unusual activity going on with the goblins in the north. Our scouts claim there's been a sudden increase in production in their forges, measuring by the smoke in the sky. The same is true for the orcs under the mountain."

I spun the scotch in my glass before I took a drink. A fire burned in the fireplace, and my eyes stared into the flames as I pictured a face that had been seared into my mind for every waking moment.

"Are you listening, Kingsnake?" Viper's irritated voice caught my attention.

I slowly turned to him before I took a drink.

His dark eyes started to smolder in his quiet rage.

"Do you ever wonder what the point of it all is?"

His rage slowly faded, and confusion replaced it. "The point of what?"

"*This.*" I gestured to the room around me, at nothing in particular. "Eternal night. Neither living nor dead. Immortality. Instead of days and months blurring together, decades blur into a single instant."

Viper watched me in silence, his eyebrows furrowed. "Where is this coming from?"

"Just a thought..."

"Humans would do anything to have what we have."

"Some. Not all."

"*Most.*"

I took a drink before I looked at him.

"It's a gift."

"Is it?" I asked. "Or is it a curse?"

His eyes shifted back and forth between mine. "What did she say to you?"

"Who's she?"

"You know of whom I speak."

I took another drink.

"You've been different ever since she arrived."

"Stronger than I've ever been...that's how I've been different." I could feel it in my veins, feel the unbridled power I took from someone else. She couldn't harness the benefits, but it still felt like theft.

He studied me like a map on the desk. "Tell me what's on your mind."

"You want a heart-to-heart?" I set the empty glass on the table.

"Yes," he said, sitting in the other armchair, dressed the same way—pants without a shirt. It was sometime in the morning, the beginning of our night. The windows were blocked out with wool drapes. "Who else will you have it with?"

"Her blood has changed me."

"I can see that."

"It's changed me in ways you can't see. I have the strength to march to Evanguard and strike them down without an army. My mind moves at a speed greater than a hawk on the descent. My body has the energy of a hundred men put together."

"If this is true, then you should share her."

Just the suggestion made me angry, but I swallowed it back. "I can't do that..."

"You would strengthen your kind—"

"The answer is no, Viper."

"Are you fucking her?"

"No."

"Then I don't see the problem—"

"But not because I don't want to."

He leaned back in the chair and watched me.

"I've never been in this position before." Every prey I'd ever had had wanted more than just my bite. They'd wanted my body. They'd wanted my immortality. And on some occasions, they'd wanted my heart. "Ever since I tasted her...I've wanted her. And with every bite, it gets worse."

"She'll come around."

I shook my head. "Her stubbornness knows no bounds."

"Offer her something in return."

"I already agreed to release her once I've identified the immunity in her blood."

"Offer her something else."

"Such as?" I looked at him, wondering if I'd missed something.

"Immortality." He said it like it was the most obvious thing in the world.

"That won't interest her." I hardly knew her, but I understood her wants and desires as if I'd known her for years. "She's made her opinions for our kind very clear."

"But once she's offered the chance to live forever, she'll feel very differently. No one can resist the temptation. Never once in my long life has anyone ever turned down the opportunity—even those who've called me their enemy."

"She's different."

"Just because her blood is different doesn't mean she is."

I sat back in the chair and stared at the fire.

"I've given you the solution, but you remain unhappy."

"Because I know it won't work."

———

I approached her door and tapped my knuckles against the wood.

No answer.

I knocked again, this time louder.

Nothing.

I invited myself inside, panic flooding my body when I thought she'd broken her promise to me. But my eyes quickly found her sitting on the balcony, trying to absorb whatever sunlight she could under the blanket of fog that blocked the sun. She sat cross-legged at the small table, a book in her hands, her brown hair down her back. She wore a long-sleeved dress, and the way her legs were crossed made the slit open so one of her long, slender legs was on display.

Just a glimpse of her flesh made everything in my body tighten. Images flashed across my mind at a speed no one would be able to catch, her naked body underneath mine, blood on the pillow from where I'd bitten her, tears down her cheeks because I'd just made her come so hard.

Fuck.

She suddenly sat upright in the chair to look at me, like she'd heard my footsteps when I hadn't moved. Her eyes were wide and guarded, not the least bit pleased to see me in her personal space.

She hated me—and that feeling was mutual.

But the command in her blood was so powerful that I couldn't deny its magnetism. I'd never wanted someone more in my life, felt a raw attraction I couldn't dismiss. It was hard to believe it was for the same woman I'd shepherded across the land, the one who was so aggravating I considered snapping her neck just to make her stop talking.

I stepped onto her balcony and took the seat across the table from her. The sunshine was hot on my clothing and immediately irritating. It was a mild annoyance, a tolerable one, but impossible to ignore entirely.

She righted herself and adjusted her legs so they would be covered.

The damage was already done, sweetheart.

She shut the book, slipping a flower between the pages to mark her spot.

"I have a proposition for you."

"The answer is no."

She was like a fan to my flames. "Never turn down an opportunity without knowing the details."

"Unless it's with a vampire."

Every time she pissed me off, it just made me want to bite her more. "You're unfairly prejudiced against my kind."

"I'm very prejudiced—but not unfairly so."

My patience had always been limited, even when I was a human, so my words came out as a threat, naturally. "You're going to listen to every damn word I have to say, or

I will make you listen to every damn word I have to say. Which do you prefer?"

Her only response was a miffed look—so she folded.

"I'm going to tell you something personal about me, something that's not freely given, only earned."

Her features slowly relaxed, making her eyes critical but gentle, her lips soft and not pursed. A subtle breeze was in the air, and it moved her hair slightly, sometimes blowing it into her right eye and sometimes away.

"I was born fifteen hundred years ago."

Both of her eyebrows jumped up her face.

"I've had the luxury of watching regimes rise and fall. I've witnessed the greatest storms that have swept across this world. I've watched the long lines of kings wither and fail, to be replaced by a new line. I've watched cities be renamed, cities be reclaimed, seen snow in places where it no longer falls. I've had more lovers than I can count, have experienced all the luxuries of youth because my appearance is frozen in place."

"Okay...why are you telling me this?"

There was no jealousy. Not a hint of it. "We rarely offer this gift to others—but I'm willing to offer it to you."

"*Gift?*" A snort escaped her lips. "You think everything you described sounds remotely appealing? You've watched entire families come and go...disappearing to dust. That's the most depressing thing I've ever heard. Why would I want to watch that? Why would I want to watch every person I've ever cared for die...while I live centuries with those horrible memories? Why would I trade sunshine for darkness? Why would I want to fuck a bunch of men I won't remember for decades? I want to love one man for as long as I can and make that love grow with children. Why the fuck would anybody want to live in a permanent state of monotony? I don't want your gift, Kingsnake. I pity you."

It was the first time I'd listened to someone denounce immortality, and after lifetimes of humans offering them-selves to us for the opportunity to live forever, it was shocking to hear someone reject it without a second thought.

I'd suspected that might be her answer, but I hadn't expected her to have so much conviction. There was no hesitation. I looked at her in a whole new way. It was the first time I had nothing to offer someone.

I was powerless.

She stared at me across the table. "Are you happy?"

I said nothing, not understanding the question.

"Are you happy?" she repeated, like she knew I was confused. "Because if you aren't happy, living forever truly is a curse. Have you ever been in love?"

I stayed quiet.

"If you're fifteen hundred, it must have happened at some point, right? What happened to her?"

She somehow flipped the conversation and interrogated me instead.

She stared at me, waiting for an answer.

"Your parents? Are they vampires too? Siblings? Are you alone?"

"Yes."

"Yes to which part?"

"My father and brothers still live. And no to your previous question."

"Which question?"

"You asked if I'm happy," I said. "No, I'm not."

———

Once my armor was fitted and cloak fastened, I stepped into the hallway and approached her bedroom. I knocked several times, and then her quiet voice came from inside. "It's open."

I stepped inside and found her on the couch in the sitting room. Darkness had spread across the land, so it was far too cold for her to go outside. A book was on the table, the dead flower sticking out from between the pages.

She looked me up and down, her eyes appreciating my black armor with red accents.

"I'll be gone for three days. Guards will be posted outside your chambers in my absence. I ask that you don't leave this bedroom until I return."

"Why?"

"For your own safety." My people had been given food, so there was no dire need to take my prey, but knowing her blood had the power of immunity would be tempting to anyone. Could invite betrayal from the most faithful subject.

"Where are you going?"

"North."

"But why? You're dressed for battle."

"The first battle always begins in a time of peace."

"Why don't you send your general?"

My eyebrows furrowed. "Because I'm not the kind of king to send others to do my bidding. And it sounds like you wish I would stay."

"If you're worried for my safety in your absence, then yes, I'd prefer it if you stayed." She rose to her feet so our eyes were level with one another. She was in one of the dresses the servants provided, and it was tight on her chest and her slender stomach. Her face wasn't painted with darkness around her eyes and a bright shade of red on her lips. She was natural, with fair skin and a couple freckles that were so small no one could see them but me. Her cheeks were rosy, the blush of blood just underneath the skin. Her appearance was so tantalizing I struggled to move my feet.

I turned away. "I'll see you in three days."

"You still haven't told me where you're going."

I looked at her again. "That's my business. Not yours."

"What if you don't come back?" she asked, the panic rising in her voice. "What will become of me?"

I stared her down, my imagination twisting her concern into something that was self-serving. "I've lived fifteen hundred years because I can't be killed—so your concern is misplaced."

"At least give me back my sword before you go."

I stared her down.

"If you aren't here to protect me, I need to protect myself."

I continued to stare.

"I promised I wouldn't run. I just want my sword if I need it."

I realized that was what she truly wanted—not immortality. "Then I'll give it to you."

13

LARISA

My sword was at my bedside, easy for me to grab if something came in the middle of the night. Just as Kingsnake had requested, I stayed in my bedchambers and never entertained the thought of leaving. I was in a land of sharp-toothed vampires. The only reason I would even think of leaving this room would be to escape.

But since we needed a cure to save humanity—I stayed put.

A day came and went, and all I did was sit on my ass and eat from the trays the servant brought. I finished my book then started another. Being idle for so long made me crave a physical demand, like the journey we took to get here.

I wondered what Kingsnake was doing—and truly hoped he would return.

If he didn't...someone else would take me.

I'd just gotten ready for bed when I heard a sound that made my blood go cold.

Thud.

The sound of a body hitting the floor.

Thud. And then another.

My two guards. I hopped out of bed and grabbed the blade. I unsheathed it from the scabbard then positioned myself around the corner, giving myself the advantage of surprise once they stormed into the room.

The doorknob turned quietly, like I would be dead asleep and unaware of the dropping bodies on the other side of the threshold. There were no footsteps. They didn't make a sound as they approached the bed, thinking my body was underneath the bunched-up sheets.

When the first one had turned his back to me to look at the bed, I swung my sword with all the strength I could muster. I had only one shot to take one down, and if I didn't, it would be two on one, and there would be no chance I could succeed.

The sword swiped through the air—and embedded halfway through his neck.

He stilled, shocked by the blade carved deep into his flesh.

I tried to tug my blade out, but it was too deep. Since he was lifeless, I grabbed his sword and finished the job.

The other one jumped straight over the bed and came at me.

"Ah!" I backed up into the sitting room and swung my blade, striking his as steel met steel. It turned into a spar between our blades, the reflection off the steel the only way for me to keep track of the weapons as they sliced through the air. On instinct alone, I blocked his strikes and held my own.

Hiiiiisssssssssss.

Fang's black body was difficult to see in the dark, but I saw the reflection on his scales as he slithered between the vampire's legs then squeezed, making him tip over and drop his sword. Fang lifted his body and extended his fangs.

I stumbled back onto the couch, disturbed by the horrific sight in front of me.

"No—"

Fang bit him on the face. Bit him again. And again. His strikes were so fast there was no possible defense.

The vampire went limp.

Fang uncoiled his body and let him slide to the floor. *Hiii-issssssss*. He turned his yellow eyes on me.

It took several seconds to find words because I was shocked by the events that had transpired. "Thank you...."

Fang gave a very subtle nod—as if he understood exactly what I said. Then he slithered back into the other room and coiled up into a circle of scales on the rug in front of my four-poster bed.

By the time I had finally gotten to my feet, other guards came into the room, asked if I was okay, and removed the dead bodies from my presence. Once they were gone, Fang remained behind, still in a pile on the floor.

There was no way I could sleep now, but I got back into bed because I didn't know what else to do in the middle of the night. I crawled to the edge and looked down at the enormous snake that watched the door. "You can come up here if you want..."

He slowly lifted his head and turned his neck 180 degrees.

"You don't have to lie on the floor... There's room."

He studied me with intelligent eyes before he rose up onto the bed and climbed up the bedposts to the canopy. He was so long that he covered every single corner of the bedposts, his undulating body hanging like curtains from every side. His head rested on the corner that faced the door.

I got under the covers and made myself comfortable, admiring the way his scales reflected the moonlight outside the window. His body was black, but there was a subtle design in his scales, a swirl of dark clouds. I'd never noticed it before. "I meant on the bed...but that works too."

14

KINGSNAKE

We stepped through the open gates and passed through the desiccated trees and gray earth. The moon was unnaturally bright that evening, its potency enough to rival the sun in daylight. On nights like these when the moon was big and full, I felt the slight burn across my cheeks.

Grazkan, the goblin chieftain, came forward in armor made of sharp bones from the animals they'd killed. Unlike orcs that towered over us by a foot, goblins were nearly a foot shorter—but they were quick.

I dismounted my horse and came forward to approach him.

"Your Majesty, to what do we owe the unexpected but appreciated visit?" Grazkan said all the right words, but the murderous tint to his gaze showed his hand. I'd been an unwelcome dictator to their lands, and their resentment had blossomed like a rose garden.

"Your forges burn day and night, Grazkan. Some might assume you were preparing for war." I faced him with my chin slightly down, my sword sitting at my hip and ready to be pulled. A midnight breeze rushed through the land and lifted above the ground.

Grazkan said nothing, caught on the spot without an explanation.

"Your enemies are my enemies. If someone has provoked you, it's my job to resolve it."

He stared at me with gray eyes, jagged teeth pointing in all directions spilling out of his mouth.

I gestured to my men.

They moved forward, carrying buckets of Varnish, a mud-like substance that hardened to stone once it combined with water.

Grazkan stared at me.

I stared back.

The buckets splashed as they were dumped into the forges, extinguishing the flames the goblins coaxed with the driest wood in their forest. It would take months to rebuild the forges, and once they did, I would return and do the same.

There was a tremor in his face, a rage he couldn't suppress.

Good.

My men returned, leaving the empty buckets behind.

My eyes remained on the goblins. "I see everything, Grazkan." I turned my back to him and walked back to my horse, exposing my back just to taunt him.

General Viper was beside me, his bow slung across his back, watching my enemy when I couldn't.

I clicked to my horse, and then we turned back, making our departure from their unremarkable lands. We passed through the open gate, and the second the last horse had passed, the gates shut.

General Viper rode beside me. "It's exactly as we feared."

"They arrogantly thought they could fool us—but now they've been warned."

Kingsssssnake.

What is it, Fang?

They came for your prey.

I brought the horse to a halt—and every vampire behind me did the same.

Viper stared at me, waiting for an explanation.

They killed the guardssssss. She killed one and I the other.

Is she hurt?

No.

Are you?

My ssscales are impenetrable. I will guard her until you return.

Gives me their names. I had a list of culprits in my head. Their spouses would be decapitated as punishment for their treachery.

I can't—because they aren't our kind.

15

LARISA

I sat on the couch and read my book while Fang hung in his canopy above the bed. He hadn't moved since he'd taken up the spot, his eyes always on the door. When he suddenly uncoiled and moved to the bedspread, I knew something had happened.

The door opened, and Kingsnake entered. He was in the same armor as when he left, so I knew he had rushed straight here the moment he had returned. His bare hand reached for Fang's scales and rested there, almost as if he was trying to find a heartbeat on the serpent. Fang gently wrapped his tail around his wrist and part of his arm. They stared at each other. Seconds passed. And then they both withdrew from each other.

It took me a moment to understand what I'd just witnessed.

Love.

Kingsnake turned his attention to me next and entered the sitting room. "You're alright."

I left the book on the table and got to my feet. "I wouldn't have been without my sword...and Fang. He hasn't left my side since the attack."

"I know," he said without explanation. "I hope your fear of snakes has ended."

"I mean...I'll always be afraid of snakes. But not this one."

When he stood in his black armor, he was just as intimidating as when he was shirtless. His power came from somewhere deeper than the sword on his hip and the plates that protected him from harm. He could be stark naked and still have the energy of a king. I'd never felt that sort of presence before.

"Pack your things."

I blinked twice, replaying his words in my head. "What?"

"I said, pack your things."

"And where am I going?"

"My bedchambers."

Now I didn't blink at all. "*What?*"

He snapped, his fury overflowing. "Stop sounding like an idiot and get your shit together."

"I'm not going into your bedchambers—"

"Would you rather I leave you here and vulnerable to another attack?"

"We killed those assholes, and Fang can stay here."

His eyes narrowed. "Fang is *mine*, not yours." The possession in his voice was unmistakable, and I quickly realized the snake meant more to him than anything else in this world. "And those assholes you killed were not my subjects. Our security has been breached—and you aren't leaving my sight."

"What do you mean? They weren't vampires?"

"They were—but not from Grayson."

"There are *other* vampires?"

He gave me a hard look, looking at me the way a father would when scolding a child. "You know nothing of this world."

———

What few things I had were moved to Kingsnake's quarters. My wardrobe, my essentials, and my books. His bedchambers were far more massive than mine. His four-poster bed faced a grand fireplace, and his sitting room had a formal dining table, a study, and the wall that faced the ocean was nothing but a solid window. The door to the balcony was open, and the sound of the waves was so loud it felt like the ocean was just a few feet away.

A tree was planted directly into the floor, the floorboards closed around the trunk, and the branches reached out along the ceiling. Because it was by the window, it was exposed to sunlight, so there were green leaves on the branches. I stared at it, finding it odd inside someone's bedchambers.

Then Fang slithered past me, up the trunk, and made his large body comfortable along the branches.

"Stay here until I return."

I turned around to face him. "Where are you going?"

Annoyance billowed out around him like waves crashing against a shore. "I'm a king. My job is to protect my people every moment of every day. So anytime I leave, just assume that's what I'm doing."

———

It was late, so I'd gone to sleep sometime after he left. With Fang and his poisonous venom in the room, it was easy to fall asleep without concern. My sword was also at my bedside, so it was within arm's reach if something unexpected came through the door.

At some point, I knew he'd returned because I heard the door open and close. He wasn't in the room for long before he entered the bathroom.

I fell back asleep.

He came out again sometime later, and I felt the bed shift and move when he joined me under the covers.

Half asleep, I mumbled, "What are you doing?"

He was quiet.

I sat up, squinting. "I said, what are you doing?"

His hand was propped underneath his head as he lay there with the sheets at his waist. "What does it look like I'm doing?" His gaze was directed to the ceiling.

"Sleep on the couch."

"Sleep on the couch." He said every word slowly, like it was amusing. "Kings don't sleep on the couch."

"Well, I'm not sleeping with you."

"You didn't have a problem with it the other night..."

"You mean when I was so weak I couldn't keep my eyes open? Wasn't exactly in the right state of mind..."

"Listen." He suddenly sat up, bringing his body close to mine, the smell of his shower fresh on my nose. "I'm not moving, so if you have a problem, then get your ass on the couch." He stared me down, and the longer he did, the more the pocket of intensity grew. Bigger and bigger, becoming a storm cloud over our heads.

My heart started to race, and my palms grew sweaty as if they were held up to a fire. The longer I felt his intensity and the deeper it became, the more unnerved I grew. Now that I could read his emotions better, I understood exactly what he wanted from me...exactly what he was feeling in that moment.

I continued to lie there, thinking about the cold couch in the other room with Fang. I didn't see any spare blankets, so it would just be me in my clothes. And if I were cold, I wouldn't sleep at all.

But if I stayed...I would have to feel this. "Don't touch me..."

He didn't blink. Didn't hesitate at my coldness.

"You stay on your side...and I stay on mine."

Somehow, my words made everything worse, made the intensity start to hum like distant drums. The more I denied him, the more he wanted me. His eyes narrowed slightly, looking like a hawk that had found his prey from the skies.

"Stop it."

"Stop what?" he asked calmly.

"Stop..." How could I describe it? "Stop looking at me like that."

His stare remained, and so did the crippling desperation.

It was almost too much to bear.

"Until I'm buried deep inside you with your come all over my dick, I'll never stop looking at you like this."

The heat flushed to my cheeks and forced me to swallow.

He gave me another hard look before he lay down.

The stare finally stopped—but I still felt it.

16

KINGSNAKE

"It's the Barbarians." Viper sat in the armchair by the fire, his bow and quiver of arrows hung on the hook by the door because he wouldn't use them in close quarters such as this. "It has to be."

"How would they know?" I stared at the fire.

"Spies."

Bile bubbled up my throat. "I refuse to believe our people would betray us."

"I don't think it's our people. I think they've managed to live among us. Probably just a handful—so no one would notice."

"If that's true, some will remain."

"Which means Larisa is always in peril."

We hadn't spoken to each other in two days. After my last outburst, she put up her walls and kept me out. "We need to speak to Cobra."

"That's a long journey."

"You know he's behind this. If our situations were reversed, I would probably do the same."

Viper gave a slight nod. "What of Larisa?"

I didn't want to leave her without my protection, but I also didn't want to take her with me—right into my enemy's hands.

"I could speak to Cobra and you stay here—"

"No." I fought my own battles. "You'll stay with her. You're the only person I trust to protect her."

"What about Fang?"

"He's coming with me."

———

She was on the couch in the sitting room when I walked inside. She didn't acknowledge me even though she must have heard me. I removed every piece of armor before I took a shower in the bathroom, and when I came out, I continued to wipe myself down with the towel.

She turned to look at me, and when she caught a glimpse of my naked body, her eyes doubled in size before she quickly looked away and pretended she hadn't noticed.

Too late.

I put on my boxers and lounge pants before I joined her in the sitting room. The balcony door was cracked open so she could hear the ocean, and there was a fire going in the fireplace, which Fang seemed to enjoy as he rested in his tree.

I sat in the armchair and watched her pretend to read.

She'd been on the same page for several minutes now.

"Your thoughts?"

"I'm reading," she said coldly.

"If you read at that pace, you'll never finish a book."

She lifted her gaze from the page and gave me a furious look. Her eyes were so vicious and her lips were pushed tightly together, and the look was far more sensual than she realized. Every time she burned hot, I burned hotter too. "You can finish up in the bathroom. No need to march in here like that."

"It's my home. I can do whatever I want."

"Well, you have a guest. And I don't like it."

"Yes, you do."

She looked angry again. "I don't—"

"Whatever you say."

She got so mad, she chucked the book at me.

I caught it with a single hand then tossed it onto the cushion beside her.

That pissed her off more, so she threw it again.

With a small smile, I caught it again and tossed it back.

This time, she crossed her arms over her chest and focused on the view. It was dusk, so only a few more minutes of daylight remained. Soon, the sight of the gray waters would be gone until sunrise.

I watched her, watched the way she tried to make her body as small as possible, like she might disappear on the spot.

"I didn't ask you to marry me."

The statement made her turn.

"Letting me make you come isn't a betrayal."

"Wow...that's an impressive ego."

"Then prove me wrong." I could slake my need with another woman, but it would be a grand disappointment, especially when there was one woman I thought about day and night. All the shit she used to do that annoyed me seemed comical now.

"You really think that'll work on me?"

"You're right."

She stared.

"Why would you take a bet you know you'll lose."

She gave a slight shake of her head.

"How long's it been?"

Her eyes shifted back and forth in confusion.

"Since the last time someone made you come."

"I'm not having this conversation—"

"So it's been a while. And who knows how long you're going to be here..."

"My hand works just fine. Thanks."

My train of thought died on the spot. Now I pictured her naked in my bed, rubbing her clit aggressively, writhing on the sheets, touching herself exactly as she liked to in order to make herself explode.

Like she knew what she'd evoked, she looked away. "The answer is no."

"I don't accept that answer." Passion and rage fueled that response. It flew out—out of my control.

Her head snapped back. "Excuse me?"

"You heard me." I said the words, so I had to stick with it now.

"Just because you're an entitled asshole who gets what he wants all the time doesn't mean you're going to get what you want from me—"

"You want me too."

"Fuck you, I don't," she said savagely.

I stared at her, remembering the stain she'd left on the front of my pants, the stain I didn't hesitate to smell when I was back in my room. My pants had been dropped and my dick was in my hand a couple seconds later. Her blood had rejuvenated me, made me whole, but it also made me want her more, to the exclusion of all else.

She looked away again.

"What are you afraid of?"

She ignored me.

"Larisa."

"I'm not afraid of anything. I'm just not going to fuck the asshole who terrorizes my people."

"Your people *come* to me."

"Not the ones you took from Raventower."

"That was an extraordinary exception."

"Call it what you want—it's still barbaric." The only person more stubborn than me was this woman. Any other woman would have caved the second she saw me. "What if I agree to release half of them?"

She slowly turned to look at me, her eyes guarded.

"That's a fair exchange."

"That's extortion."

"Call it whatever you want. You have the opportunity to free half of the people you came here with."

"*If I fuck you.*"

"Which you want to do anyway, so now you have a good reason to justify it."

"You're a monster..."

I gave a small smile. "A monster you want inside you."

She grabbed the book again and chucked it at my head.

"How many times are we going to do this?" I caught the book, and this time, I set it beside me.

She launched herself to me, arms swinging, ready to give me a black eye.

I deflected both of her hands from my face when she landed on me then pinned them behind her back. Without her arms to balance her, she fell against me, and then her knees slipped across my pants, making herself sit right on top of my dick.

My rock-hard dick.

Her face was right next to mine, cheek to cheek. She stilled for a few seconds, her breaths deep and uneven, but then she tried to wiggle free again, to get her hands away from my hold.

My fingers moved across her ass, and I pulled her into me, dragging her clit right over my dick between our clothes. She sat straight up, her wrists still gripped in one of my hands.

Face-to-face, just inches apart, we stared at each other.

We hadn't been this close since I'd last bitten her, and while the flush of her cheeks was appealing to me, that was the last thing on my mind. I wanted her flesh, her body, her smell. I wanted those plump lips on mine, on my dick, caressing my balls with soft kisses.

I tugged her close and angled her right into my lips.

Our mouths came together like rose petals, soft and delicate. It was a gentle landing, a subtle introduction between our mouths. Her lips were everything I thought they would be, absolutely delicious.

My mouth opened farther and took hers.

She tilted her head and mimicked my movements.

I won.

My fingers slid into her thick hair the way they did when I fed, grasping her with ownership, clenching her so she couldn't escape my kiss. A sudden burst of air left my lungs because her taste was so damn good. I could feel the pulse in her neck. I could feel her desire as she kissed me back, as both of her arms circled my neck and brought her body closer.

My tongue dove into her mouth, and hers met mine in return. In a slow dance, they moved together, mixed with our heavy breaths. Every time my fingers pressed into her body, she gripped me harder, let a sexy moan escape into my mouth.

Fuck.

I'd never felt this in my life...whatever the fuck it was.

And I knew she felt it too.

I guided her hips over my lap, getting her clit to drag over my hardness so her panties would soak with her arousal. My hands gathered the dress higher so the material wouldn't be between us. I wanted her to feel my hardness even more, to experience a taste of the pleasure I could give her when the clothes were gone.

The heat level changed, a forest fire erupting from a single match. Her palms flattened against my chest as she took my mouth with that sexy tongue. Her hips dragged over my dick in my pants, turning her heavy breaths audible with quiet moans.

Then I felt it.

The stain on the front of my trousers.

Fuck.

I got to my feet as I supported her in my arms, my hands gripping her tight ass underneath the long dress. I moved forward, pinning her against the first wall I could reach.

She continued our kiss like she didn't even notice she was suspended in midair. Her fingers were deep in the back of my hair, kissing me like I was the love of her life, not the man she despised.

I tugged down the front of my pants and felt my spine shiver as I prepared for the moment I would slip inside her. Tight. Wet. Fucking paradise. It was too difficult to pull her panties to the side and keep them there, so I chose to rip them off instead.

That was when she stopped.

Her passionate kisses evaporated, and she stared at me like they had never happened in the first place. She looked at me with loathing, or perhaps it was self-loathing, and then withdrew her touch altogether. "Put me down."

I couldn't do it.

For the first time, her eyes flashed with a look of fear.

I could do it anyway, bring her back into the moment once she felt my dick stretch her in a way no other man had before. It would be so easy to turn that no into a yes.

But the fear in her eyes pulled at something inside me, something I thought I didn't have anymore.

I put her down.

She stormed off, moving to one corner of the room and then the other, trying to escape with nowhere to go.

"Stay." I pulled up my trousers and headed to the door. "I'll go."

17

LARISA

I slept alone that night.

Well, Fang was there, hanging in his tree in the other room.

I realized we'd had the erotic exchange right in front of an enormous snake.

Kinda awkward.

I was hot and bothered after he left, even the following morning, but the overwhelming self-loathing stopped me from finishing the job. He was the king of the vampires, the leader of the nightwalkers, our mortal enemy, and I *kissed* him.

And worse—I liked it.

It wasn't just his touch that made me melt. It was the way he wanted me. I could feel it in my mind, feel his desperation like a hand around my neck. It was a need I'd never known before, never having felt it myself or been with a man who felt it toward me. It was probably the biggest turn-on—even though he was a damn good kisser.

I showered and got ready for the day, even though I had nowhere to go. He would return eventually, and I wondered where he'd spent the night. Did he spend it alone in his study with a glass of scotch? Or did he spend it with someone...?

The door opened unexpectedly, and he entered the room in his king's uniform, the fabric proudly showcasing the serpents that seemed to be embedded in every part of their culture, for reasons I didn't understand. He was back to his usual coldness, his eyes regarding me like the enemy that I was.

I wondered if he'd returned in the middle of the night to change or if he had clothes stashed elsewhere.

He didn't say a word to me, just stepped into his closet to gather his armor.

I could feel it—his anger.

"So you're going to be an asshole because I didn't sleep with you?" The words were out of my mouth before I could stop them. His ice-cold greeting got under my skin and pressed every single one of my buttons.

There was a pause, and then he stepped out of the closet. That sinister stare was back, like he didn't know whether he wanted to strangle me or bash my head against the headboard.

"You're the one who kissed me—"

"And you're the one who jumped into my fucking lap. If you don't want a man, then don't jump on his dick. Word of advice."

"I wanted to punch you in the face—"

"Then you missed." His anger intensified, like a fire with fresh fuel.

"You're such an asshole."

"Get used to it, sweetheart." He moved to the door, fully dressed in his armor like he had somewhere important to be.

"Don't you dare call me that—"

"I'll call you whatever I please." He walked out and slammed the door shut.

I ran into the hallway, watching his magnificent cloak shift and move behind him. "Are you leaving?" He only put on his armor if he left Grayson, so I worried he had another mission that required him to leave the city—and me.

He ignored me.

"Kingsnake."

He turned the corner and disappeared.

———

I sat at the dining table alone, eating the dinner his servant had brought me.

Fang was in the tree most of the time, always sleeping, trying to stay in the sunlight to keep his blood warm.

I wondered if and when Kingsnake would return. I pushed my food around before I looked at Fang. "Wish I could sleep all day..." Being cooped up in a bedroom all day had made me restless. It was hard to sleep at night because I wasn't remotely tired.

Fang opened one eye and stared at me. Then he slithered from his tree, across the floor, and wrapped himself around the chair across from me and raised his head, sitting across from me like he would join me for lunch.

"You can understand me, can't you?"

He stuck out his tongue and slipped it back in between his fangs.

"I wish I could understand you..." It seemed like Kingsnake and Fang could communicate, but since it

182

wasn't verbal, I had no idea how they exchanged information. "You're my only friend in this place."

He tilted his head slightly, regarding me with his bright-yellow eyes.

The door opened, and Kingsnake entered, kingly in his armor and uniform. His eyes immediately went to us in the other room, and they narrowed.

It seemed like something was exchanged between them because Fang slithered off and returned to the tree.

I stared at Kingsnake. "Can you talk to him?"

He went into the bathroom and shut the door—and ignored me.

The sun had finally set, and darkness entered the bedroom. I started the fire to bring some warmth to the room, because the cool climate at this oceanside paradise seeped through the window frames and brought a chill to my skin.

Kingsnake returned a while later, rubbing the towel through his short hair, buck naked.

I only caught a glimpse before I looked away—but I saw it all.

He was six-foot-something of mass and muscle, cords over his arms and neck, muscular thighs with dark hair—and a dick no woman could complain about. His stomach was as hard as his back, with the muscles defined by lines of tightness. He had rounded shoulders where the muscle bulged from the rear. He was still on the leaner side, but damn, he was strong.

He tossed the towel on the floor for someone else to pick up then pulled a pair of boxers from the dresser.

"It didn't work last night, and it won't work tonight," I said, my gaze averted.

"I disagree." He shut the drawer, and it made a thud.

My eyes fought to stay elsewhere, but I felt them shift to his face.

Tall and proud, he looked down at me where I sat in the chair. His stare was hard and piercing, with the fierceness of the tip of a blade. An old rage filled the room, the very one he'd felt for me during our travels to Grayson. Then he pulled his gaze away and got into bed, sitting up against the headboard as he stared at the fireplace.

His gaze was elsewhere, so I stared at his profile, seeing the shadow of facial hair across his hard jawline. It matched the color of his eyes, which had returned to their normal shade of coffee and earth. The rage he'd exhibited a moment ago had disappeared. Now there was nothing from him at all.

"I'll do it—if you release all of them."

He stared at the fire a second more, like it took him a moment to understand the words I'd just spoken. Then his gaze shifted to me, his stare hard. "Half."

"If you want me, it's going to cost you."

"And half is a hefty price."

"I won't budge."

"Nor will I—because I can't." His fierce stare was locked on my face. "My people will be angry when I take half their food source away, but if I take them all, there will be anarchy. Trust me, you don't want that."

"It's not my problem."

"It is your problem, because they'll either feed on you or travel to Raventower and feed on whomever they can find."

My heart dropped into my stomach because the truth was undeniable.

"Half is my only and final offer."

I couldn't believe I entertained the offer at all.

"You can choose who goes home."

That meant I could pick Angela—if she was still alive.

"I would tell them you negotiated their freedom. You wouldn't be known as a traitor, but a hero."

He was manipulating me, and it was working.

He fell into silence, his stare doing all the talking.

I was hot and cold at the same time. Excited but also scared. Motivated and deterred. I was stuck in this horrible place until a cure was found, but they didn't have to share my fate. The others could return to Raventower, to live their lives as people rather than prey.

He waited for my agreement, still and quiet, his emotions empty like a finished glass of wine.

I swallowed before I answered. "Fine...half."

The moment I spoke, the rush of adrenaline crossed the space between us in the blink of an eye. The very same desperation he'd shown the night before was back in full force—but now it was stronger. Yearning so powerful it could rip a person to pieces, his desire rivaled a hurricane that lashed the shore. He experienced all of this instantly, but he hadn't moved a muscle, hadn't released a breath. "Get over here."

If I weren't so absorbed in his desire, I would have ignored his order. But I got to my feet and entered the bedroom, the heat of the flames against the right side of my body as I walked. I stopped at the foot of the bed, facing him head on.

He was upright against the headboard, his arm resting on one propped knee, his shirtless body aglow in the light of the fire. Just like Fang, he didn't blink, his stare locked on my features. "Undress."

"I agreed to fuck you, not be bossed around—"

"You agreed to let me fuck *you*. And this is how you're going to get fucked." The small flames that burned underneath the surface suddenly became higher, became hotter. He sounded pissed off by my disobedience, but his emotions showed that he actually enjoyed it. "Undress."

I tolerated his hot stare before I unfastened the back of my dress. It immediately released its hold around my body, and I was able to slip out of it without pulling it over my head. That left my bra and panties.

But he boiled like I was buck naked. Even if his emotions didn't melt me, his look sure did. His jawline was so hard it seemed like he ground his teeth together. The cords in his neck thickened to the size of ropes. His fingers automatically tightened into a fist, and the exposed knuckles turned slightly white.

Now it was easy to forget who he was. Easy to forget that we were enemies turned allies. Easy to forget that we were frenemies. Never in my life had I felt so desirable, been less concerned with the imperfections of my body. My skin was so fair it looked like rice, but he didn't seem to notice or care. My tits were small, but he acted like they were perfect. When Elias had told me he loved me, I didn't feel even a fraction of Kingsnake's emotion.

I unclasped my bra and let it fall to the floor.

His eyes dropped to my tits and stayed there. His emotion didn't waver whatsoever.

My thumbs hooked into my panties, and I pulled them over my hips.

That was when the flames turned into a bonfire.

I pushed them down my legs then stepped out of them, stark naked at the foot of the bed, his eyes eating my flesh.

He released the fist he held, then made another, like he wanted to slam his hand down on the nightstand because the desire was too much to contain. "Come here."

I moved around the bed and approached.

His eyes followed me, and when I came close, he lifted his hips so he could pull down his boxers.

It was even bigger than I imagined.

His arm circled my waist, and he guided me onto my back in the middle of the bed.

"This is for only one night..."

His arm locked behind my knee, and he adjusted me into the position he wanted. One hand gripped my tit, and then he pressed his face right between my thighs—and kissed me so good.

The breath I inhaled came out as a gasp because his touch was such a shock. I expected him to enter me and get his dick wet as soon as possible, but he circled my clit with purposeful swipes of his tongue, giving me so much pressure that my hips automatically bucked against his mouth. "Fuck..."

Sometimes he kissed me. Sometimes he sucked me into his mouth. And sometimes his tongue did all the work.

It felt so good, I was delirious.

He pulled away and shifted up my body. "You spoke too soon, sweetheart." With my taste on his lips, he dipped his head and kissed me, igniting an unquenchable fire in my belly. His hand slipped into my hair, and he fisted it like last time, his desire so intense he suffocated me with it. He tugged on my hair and commanded my mouth, giving me his tongue, giving me his soul, or lack thereof.

My hand started on his chest, his body so solid it felt like a wall. My fingers pressed into his skin, feeling the strong muscle underneath. My other hand cupped the side of his face then moved around his neck, pulling me to him.

He ended the kiss, and as he pulled his head back, I lifted mine, chasing the mouth that made me so weak. An arrogant sheen came to his eyes, but it was quickly replaced by his intensity as he directed himself to my entrance. "I can't wait to watch you come." His head was fat and swollen, like fitting a square into a circle, and he had to push several times to get past my tight opening, to feel the slickness that my body made just for him.

It hurt like it was the first time, but it felt so good I started to claw his skin.

His eyes were locked on mine as he made his slow entrance, watched me struggle to take his big dick. The fire in his blood was rising, burning forests and fields, turning wood into soot, turning the blue sky black with smoke. He burned so hot, his flames turned white. He tugged on my knee and folded me deeper, changing the angle so he could slide in easier. Once he was past my tightness, he sank the rest of the way, moving until he made me wince when he reached my end.

He paused, his eyes so intense they looked angry, his big dick taking up every available space I had. The world suddenly went still as we stared at each other, both breathing irregularly, connected in a way both of us least expected.

Then he started to move inside me, slow at first, letting his dick become slick from my wetness so he could glide into me harder. He picked up the pace and found his rhythm, fucking me hard and fast, getting right to the point.

It felt so damn good.

I'd never been pounded like this. Elias and I always had to be quiet, and on the off chance we didn't need to be, he couldn't keep himself together long enough for either of us to enjoy it.

But Kingsnake fucked me like he didn't share the same struggles. Fucked me ruthlessly. Fucked me like he hated me.

I could feel his enjoyment soak into my skin, feel how rock hard he was, see a desire so deep in his eyes that it had no bottom. My hands planted on his chest because I was folded underneath him, my body shaking as he did all the work. He screwed me like he was turned on just by my lying there, like he was so thrilled to be inside me that he didn't care if I just lay there and took his fat dick.

It came so quickly, I didn't see it before it arrived. A searing heat that rivaled Kingsnake's formed in my stomach and my extremities. That heat traveled everywhere, making me white-hot like a ball of fire. Then it dissipated, replaced by the most sensual pleasure right between my legs, right where he fucked me so hard.

"Come on, sweetheart," he said amid his deep breaths. "Show me those tears..."

My fingers curled, and my nails dug into his skin. My body suddenly felt weightless, like I could bend and move at any angle I wanted. I felt myself squirm, unable to contain all the pleasure inside my little body. My head turned, and my hips bucked automatically as the quiet scream tried to escape my clenched jaw.

"You can't hide from me." He grabbed me by the neck and forced my gaze on him. He pinned me to the bed, and our eyes locked.

The restraint on my jaw broke, and my lips parted, a throaty scream erupting as a feminine roar. When my vision blurred, I knew my eyes had watered from the ecstasy, and if I hadn't noticed, I would have figured it out based on the look on his face.

He'd never looked so intense. A vein popped out of his temple. The cords in his neck were so tight they might snap. The fire that burned his fingertips had deepened into something more—possession. "I'm going to come inside you." He didn't ask the question, but he gave a moment for me to say no.

I didn't.

"You want me to." He kept up his pace, grinding me into the bed with his weight, rubbing his pelvis right against my clit.

I reached for his lower back and pulled him into me, wanting more of his dick even though it wouldn't fit. I was coated in sweat and still high from the pleasure that electrified me, delirious in euphoria.

"Say it."

"Fuck you."

"*Say it.*" He ground into me harder, rubbing my clit so good it felt like my own hand.

I didn't think it could happen again so soon, but I felt it. Hot. Throbbing. Blissful. "Yes..."

The victory was so bright in his eyes it looked like starlight. Like he'd sailed to my shores and conquered them in his name, his possession grew. It was hostile and angry. Even terrifying. Every emotion he felt in that moment increased tenfold. "Beg."

I was right on the verge, but his command still shattered my focus. "You fucking asshole—"

"*Beg.*" He decreased the pressure, making my clit ache for his touch.

"I hate you."

His hand fisted my hair, and he moved farther over me, bringing his pelvis back to where I needed it the most. He ruled over me as a king and unleashed his command. "Say please." With his dick rock hard inside me, he ground his body over and over, pushing into my tenderness, bringing me to the edge of a knife.

I wanted it so bad I didn't care about the price. "Please..."

He started up again, pounding into me like we'd just started from the beginning. "Louder."

"Please."

"Again."

The heat kicked in, and my entire body tightened. The match had been lit, and the fire spread. My head rolled back, and I fell into the throes of bliss. "Please...please... fucking please."

He gave a moan that sounded like a growl then finished with his final pumps, filling me with seeds that couldn't grow. His eyes grew heavy, but the intensity remained at its peak. He looked at me as he filled me, victorious in his conquest. He remained, and as the seconds passed and turned into a minute, he stayed just as hard as when we started. Then his hips started to rock once more. "Again."

18

KINGSNAKE

"Change in plans." I stood at the grand table holding the map in the war room. Fang was draped over my shoulders, his tail wrapped around one of my arms, the rest of his body hooked around my torso. He weighed at least two hundred pounds, but the extra weight didn't bother me when it was dispersed across my body. His head was raised next to mine, looking at the map like he could read it. "Larisa will accompany us."

Viper stared at me from across the table, his stare hard and stoic. "Why?"

"Leaving her here would be a bad idea. They came once—and they'll come again."

"It doesn't matter if they do when I'm the one protecting her."

I stared at the map between us. "I've made my decision." I lifted my gaze to meet his.

"And it's a stupid one."

My eyes narrowed.

As did his.

"What's this really about, Kingsnake?"

My hands gripped the edge of the table.

"Taking a hot dinner straight into a den of wolves is a bad idea."

"We won't take her with us. She'll wait in the forest."

"Unprotected?"

"We'll leave men with her. We'll sneak her out of the city so everyone will think she's still here."

Viper continued to give me that cold look. "I'm the general of the Grayson army, but you doubt my abilities."

"I don't doubt your—"

"Then what is it?" He would never speak to me this way in the company of others, but now that we were alone, he spoke his mind in the most candid way.

You can trusssssst him.

I can't trust anyone.

Viper waited for my answer.

I didn't have one.

Viper's eyes narrowed slightly more, showing a hint of his offense. "You can't trust your men, not when the temptation is too great, but you can trust me. Not because I'm the general who fights alongside my soldiers—but because I'm your brother. Others may stab you in the back to take what's yours, but I never would." He was a man of few words, but he managed to pierce me through my armor and straight into my heart.

"I don't doubt your intentions—"

"But my resistance."

My hands stayed on the edge of the table, looking for the right way to conduct this conversation. It would be easy to scream and shout, but that wasn't kingly. "Can you fault me after what happened with Ellasara?" I said her name, a name I hadn't spoken in who knew how long.

Viper's reaction didn't change, hard as ever, but underneath that stoicism was a fire. "That was a long time ago—"

"Not for our kind."

The stoicism remained, but his eyes hinted at his anger. "Different circumstances."

"You hated me. Yes, I remember."

Now he gave an annoyed sigh as he scratched his neck.

"I'm pretty easy to hate, so that could happen again."

"Kingsnake." His words were short, his temper shorter.

"Viper."

"You intend to punish me forever?"

"I haven't brought it up until now."

"So you've resented me all this time."

"I don't resent you," I said. "But I wouldn't be a very good king if I didn't learn from the past."

"She's at far greater risk if she accompanies us."

"And she's at even greater risk if she's parted from me."

He came closer to the table, standing in his armor and red cloak. "You had no issue with this days ago. What has changed?"

I didn't speak a word, but flashbacks came through my mind, so searing hot they made my dick hard underneath the table. Tears. Kisses. Screams. It surpassed the endless fantasies that had gripped me from the moment I tasted her blood.

His eyes shifted in understanding. "I see."

I didn't confirm nor deny, and not because I was a gentleman, just a territorial and possessive asshole.

"Then you have even more to lose."

"The answer is no, Viper."

His eyes showed his anger, but he didn't argue further.

"Prepare the men for our departure. We leave at nightfall."

————

When I returned to the bedroom, she was asleep, naked in bed—exactly as I'd left her. Our rendezvous had stretched deep into the night, so she hadn't gotten much sleep. Now it was midday, and she was still knocked out.

I wanted to let her sleep—but preparations needed to be made. "Larisa." I stood at her bedside, looking down at her as she hogged all the covers and wrapped them around her body like she didn't share the bed with another person.

Her eyebrows shifted slightly, but she kept her eyes shut tight.

"Larisa." I hardened my voice.

She moaned like a child and turned over. "Leave me alone..."

I grabbed the sheets and yanked them off.

Buck naked on the bed with firm tits and hard nipples, she immediately tightened her body to fight the cold. "Why are you such an asshole?" She sat up and snatched the covers out of my hand and covered herself once more.

"Because you need to get ready."

"Ready for what?" she snapped. "Staying inside all day and never leaving?" She closed her eyes.

"I have to travel east—and you're coming with me."

Her eyes opened, and she finally looked at me. "Why?"

"Why what?"

"Why are you traveling east?"

I dismissed the obnoxious questions and walked away. "The seamstress will bring your clothes. In the meantime, bathe. You may not get another chance for some time." I headed to the door.

"Wait."

I stared at the door for seconds before I grudgingly turned back to face her.

"You said you would release my kin."

"I know what I said." Didn't need to be reminded. "Give me the names, and I'll have them escorted back to Raventower. Only six remain—so three names."

"Two of them died?"

"Unfortunately."

"Fuck...do you know who?"

I turned to the door and opened it. "Make a list with alternates." When I stepped into the hallway, she spoke again.

"You're just going to act like last night didn't happen?"

I steadied before I turned back around. "What do you want from me, Larisa?"

My cold look must have stifled her words.

"A kiss good morning? A flower on your nightstand?"

Her eyes kindled with renewed anger.

"Just because I want to fuck you doesn't mean I care for you—"

"Trust me, the feeling is mutual."

"Good." I moved into the hallway.

"But I would hope for some respect...for a change."

I entered the bedchamber hours later and found her in the sitting room. The table was covered with playing cards, and across from her sat Fang, most of his body in a ball on the floor with his head upright. His tongue slipped in and out through his closed mouth before he picked up a card and placed it in the center of the table.

"Dammit." Larisa threw her cards down. "You've got to be cheating."

Fang released a low growl.

Larisa should be terrified, but she pooled all the cards in the middle of the table and started to return them to the deck. "Sorry...I've always been a sore loser."

My brain struggled to believe what my eyes witnessed. "What are you doing?"

Larisa looked up when she realized I was there. "Playing cards. What does it look like?"

Fang turned his head toward me, luminous eyes on me. ***She'sss good. But not good enough.***

Larisa returned the cards to the box then stood up, dressed in the traveling clothes my seamstress had provided. Black leather leggings with wool sewn on the inside, and a long-sleeved black shirt that fit the natural curves of her body perfectly. On top was the serpent armor, black and red, with her sword at her hip. Her dark hair was in layers around her face, and every time she moved, the strands shifted like there was a breeze in the room.

I noticed all of those details within a second or two. "Are you ready?"

"Yes." She put the deck of cards in the pocket of her leggings then looked at Fang. "We'll play later."

He gave a nod.

You don't have to entertain her.

I know.

Then ignore her.

I enjoy her company.

My eyes shifted back to her face to see her staring at me.

"Are you talking to each other?"

I looked at Fang again. *She's obnoxious.*

As are you.

My eyes narrowed.

"You *are* talking to each other..." She studied the inaudible exchange. "How does that work?"

"It's time to go." I picked up her pack and held it out to her.

The fiery look was in her eyes, but she took the pack without asking another question. We exited the bedchambers and moved down the hallway. Instead of heading to the front door, we went to the rear of the palace and entered a private room.

Fang crawled up my body, securing himself around my shoulders.

Larisa looked around, clearly confused by the route we'd just taken.

I locked the door then moved the enormous bookshelf out of the way before I pulled up the loose stone. "Take this passage. We'll be waiting for you at the end."

She looked into the dark hole then at me again. "Uh, why?"

"I don't want anyone to know you've come with me."

"Because?"

Her incessant questions never stopped. "Just do as I say."

"Sure, I'll get right on that," she snapped.

"The more questions you ask, the more time it costs."

"You had all day to tell me this plan and chose not to—"

"Because I'm not obligated to explain a damn thing to you. Now, go."

You're making it worse. Her eyes look like fire.

I don't care.

They're beautiful—like my own.

I don't care about that either.

"I can't believe I let you fuck me." She moved past me to the top stair of the trapdoor.

"I can."

She gave me her most furious look yet.

And she looked so irresistible that I nearly shoved her up against the wall and kissed her.

"That's never going to happen again."

"Yes, it is." The angrier she became, the more I enjoyed it, like a psychopath. "It'll happen after we make camp."

"Then you're going to have to force me because there's no way in hell I'll let you touch me willingly."

Why do you antagonize her?

Because I like it. "I won't have to force anything, not when you beg me the way you did last night."

Her anger was subdued by the humiliation that spread across her face.

You just kicked the hornets nesssst.

Her embarrassment was short-lived. Her palm struck me across the face.

I'd known it was coming. Could have easily stopped it. But I didn't.

She took the stairs into the darkness. "Fuck off, asshole."

19

LARISA

Kingsnake and General Viper met me with their soldiers when I emerged from the tunnel. A brown mare was saddled and ready for me, and I was relieved I didn't have to share a horse with that pompous prick.

It was pitch dark, but we headed out anyway, maybe because they could see in the dark. There was a straight path we took, and the soldiers carried torches, probably for the benefit of the horses and not me.

Because we were in their lands, they must have felt safe from harm.

I would never feel safe, surrounded by vampires with a dickhead as a king.

I grew tired quickly, used to spending my nights asleep rather than awake and guiding a horse, but I pushed because I didn't want to complain—not to avoid being a nuisance, but to avoid appearing weak.

After a long night, sunlight crested the horizon, making the sky a gentle blue rather than a stark black. It was winter, so the temperature was freezing, and while my well-made clothing and heavy armor gave me a substantial amount of warmth, it wasn't enough to fight the bite of the cold. It seeped through my gloves and made my knuckles ache.

The sunlight grew brighter, and we eventually made camp under a heavy canopy of trees, the foliage so thick that sunlight couldn't penetrate through the brush. The soldiers got to work building the camp, and I noticed Kingsnake and General Viper conferring away from the others, Fang wrapped around Kingsnake's body like a bird perched on a man's shoulder.

I chose to stay on my own, sticking with my horse at the very edge of camp. I had a bedroll and food, so I didn't need anything else. It would be uncomfortable to sleep in the armor, but it was better to be warm than freezing cold.

The camp was set up with black tents everywhere. Only a few soldiers stayed awake to keep an eye on the terrain.

Kingsnake left his tent then came straight to me.

Shit.

His uniform and armor were gone—and he was shirtless.

It was freezing cold, and he chose to walk around half naked?

He reached me then looked down at me with his signature look of displeasure. He didn't say a word, just stared at me like that was enough to convey his wants and desires. To be fair, it was, because I knew exactly what he wanted.

"I'm staying here."

He didn't move. Didn't feel anything. "You'll freeze."

"You're half naked, and you're just fine."

"It's different for me."

"Because you aren't alive?" I couldn't believe I'd slept with him last night. And worse...I liked it.

"For many reasons."

I stayed in my bedroll.

"Larisa."

"Kingsnake." I stayed tucked under the blanket, unafraid to make a scene in front of his men.

"We can do this the hard way, if you want."

"Whatever is more inconvenient for you is convenient for me."

Now his anger started to rise to a dull heat. "Alright." He grabbed the bottom of the bedroll and dragged me across the earth.

"What the hell are you doing?"

He dragged me with a single arm through the lines of tents, heading to his tent near one of the bonfires.

"Stop it."

He pulled back the flap and dragged me inside before he let go.

"I'm not sleeping with you."

"You said that last night."

"But that was to save my people. Now you have nothing to offer me."

"Nothing?" He faced me and dropped his bottoms right in front of me, revealing that dick he was all too proud of.

I looked away, fighting the searing memories that popped into my mind.

He didn't have a bedroll like I did. He had a foldable mattress and real sheets, all the stuff carried in the carts in the rear. Everyone else probably slept on their bare backs, but he had luxury wherever he went.

It was only the first night, and I missed my bed back at Grayson.

"Where I go, you go. Do you understand me?" He stood in front of me, his enormous dick right in front of my face.

I got to my feet, so I could look at his eyes and not his junk. But once I was face-to-face with those dark eyes that had endless depth, I wasn't so sure which was better. He had hard eyes in a hard face, chiseled with masculinity, with power that radiated all around him. "Don't boss me around. Do you understand *me*?"

The fire continued to burn, low like a candle. "It's for your protection. I trust my men, but when it comes to a food source more powerful than any other, it's hard to resist. If I were in their position, I'm not sure if I'd be able to. And then to stop...is another matter entirely."

I kept my eyes on him and ignored the strength of his body, the way his arms and shoulders were separated by prominent lines that segmented the muscles. There was no amount of hate that could diminish the attraction, to deny that he made me feel more alive than anyone else...even though he was dead.

"I know you hate me, but not enough to put your life at risk, not when the survival of your people depends on it."

"Stop manipulating me."

His hard eyes narrowed. "I'm reminding you what's at stake—"

"You think I could forget? I'm surrounded by vampires every moment of every day...except when I'm with Fang." I looked around the tent because I realized he wasn't there. "Where is he?"

"Sleeping."

"Sleeping where?"

His eyes glanced to the corner of the room.

I turned to see him inside a cotton bucket, a lid on top. His scales were visible in the small crack.

"As the temperature drops, he needs to stay warm."

"But you don't?"

He obviously grew frustrated by my questions because he got into bed. "Sleep on the ground if you want, but don't leave the tent." He was under the covers, still naked even though the thin flaps of the tent couldn't keep out the cold. He lay on his back, his hand on his stomach, and then closed his eyes.

I stared at him for a while before I looked at the bedroll.

It was just a blanket on the cold earth. Next to the mattress, it really looked pitiful.

Kingsnake already appeared to be asleep.

I decided to take off the armor, because it did weigh twenty pounds, and then take the other side of the bed. The second my back hit the mattress, I realized just how hard and cold the ground had been. I pulled the sheets over my body and immediately felt my mind slip away because I was just so tired.

It took a moment for my mind to wake up, to register the warm kisses right between my tits. I lay there, still in the land of dreams, but I woke up when I felt my bottoms come off. My eyes opened to Kingsnake's handsome face on top of me, my shirt yanked up to expose my tits, his naked body already wedged between my soft thighs. "What are you doing?" I mumbled, squinting.

He yanked on my body and folded me underneath him, ready to fuck me the way he did last night.

Now my mind became sharper. "Stop."

He dipped his head so his face was just above mine, dark eyes looking into mine.

"I told you I didn't want to sleep with you." I should be yelling right now, but I spoke quietly, whispering to him like a lover.

"Then why did you get into my bed?"

"Because the ground is frozen and hard..."

His dark eyes regarded me with coldness, but the rest of his body hummed to life. The desperation had returned, the intensity that rivaled the fierceness of a raging snowstorm. His dick pulsed at my entrance, but the rest of his body pulsed too, with a need so potent it made the earth shake.

It cast a spell over me, made me forget our mutual hatred, because being so desperately wanted by this beautiful man was intoxicating. Everything he said earlier in the day didn't matter, was immediately forgotten when his body screamed for mine like his life depended on it.

How could a man make me feel so beautiful without ever saying it?

"Tell me you want me." His face was close to mine now, so close he could kiss me. He moved his hips slightly, grinding his fat dick right against my aching clit. He pressed into it over and over, bending it to his will.

Game over.

I lost. He won.

He dipped his lips to my ear and continued to rock into me, pressing a little harder each time. "Sweetheart."

My hands snaked up his back, and my nails sliced into his flesh. My thighs hugged his hips entirely on their own. I was swept away by the tide, pulled deep into the abyss, at the mercy of the man who gave me these highs.

He whispered into my ear, "Ask me to fuck you."

With every thrust, I was a little closer to the edge. My hips rocked back, my wetness kissing him every time we came together. "Fuck me..." My fingers sliced into his back, nearly deep enough to draw blood.

"Say please."

I wanted his dick so much I didn't care if I had to sell my soul. "Please, Kingsnake."

The second I said his name, an explosion of pleasure swept through him, amplifying all the desire he already had. The candle had been consumed by a wildfire, and when he slipped inside me, a bottle of liquor was thrown on top.

I gasped when I felt him.

He moaned like it was the first time.

His hand fisted my hair like before, using the strands like reins on a horse, and he fucked me just as hard as last time. One of his arms bent my knee back, opening my body to him and his big dick, folding me to take me at the perfect angle.

My hand planted against his chest as he leaned over me, my body shaking because he gave it to me so hard. The cold was nonexistent when we moved our bodies together like this, when we were making our own heat.

It took almost no time at all to reach the threshold. I had been dragged into that tent by a man I hated, and now our eyes were locked together as we made each other writhe in the most exquisite pleasure.

My head rolled back when I felt it arrive, slowly invading all my senses, taking over my entire being. It made me burning hot, made my pussy so tight, made his dick feel enormous.

He moved his face over mine and kissed me, pressed his lips against mine to stifle the screams I wanted to unleash. He wouldn't let me go, muffling our sounds as we came together, his dick dumping all his seed inside me.

He pulled his mouth away once the high began to decline. We both breathed hard, both a little sweaty even though he'd been the one doing all the work. Slowly, we came down, our eyes still locked on each other.

I'd thought last night was an anomaly, a clash of sexual tension and loneliness, something that couldn't be repeated. But it was repeated—and it was even better. He'd finished, but his emotions still vibrated with the strength of an army, like it was just as good for him as it was for me.

He rolled off me then lay on his side of the bed.

I felt cold once he was gone and immediately grabbed the sheets to cover myself.

Kingsnake was the best sex of my life—and he was a goddamn vampire.

He lay on his back, looking at the canopy above the tent. "I don't want any more bullshit."

The comfortable haze was wiped away. "What?"

"You resist out of spite—not because you want to. Stop the charade."

"Trust me, it's not a charade."

He turned to look at me, still breathing slightly hard, looking at me in bewilderment after the fucking that had just ensued.

"If you treated me with respect, I wouldn't hate you so much."

"I've protected you since the moment you came into my possession—"

"That's not the same thing. Just treat me like a person, and maybe we'll get along. All your insults...they get old."

He continued to stare at me.

"Just be nice."

"Be nice..." He said the words like he didn't understand.

"Yes."

He looked at the ceiling again.

"You know, like frenemies."

"Frenemies?" He propped himself up and looked at me. "What the hell is that?"

"It's when two people who hate each other are nice to each other because of their circumstances."

He looked away and rubbed the back of his head, like he had no idea what to make of that.

"If you have nothing nice to say, don't say anything at all. I'll do the same."

He lay back down again. "Alright."

"Alright..."

We both got comfortable in bed, the gentle light coming in through the fabric of the tent. It took some time to get tired again after his touch had brought me to life, but eventually, my eyes became heavy...and I fell asleep.

20

LARISA

The tents were packed, and the fires were extinguished.

Now it was nightfall, but the vampires acted like it was a brand-new day.

Kingsnake mounted his horse then waited for me to mount mine.

I climbed up on the brown mare, wearing the heavy armor he had designed for my slim size.

He stared at me, commanding my gaze.

I looked at him.

"Stay with me at all times."

He ordered me around like one of his men, and I wanted to resist and shove him off his horse. But after our pillow talk last night, I learned that we needed to get along if we had any hope of tolerating each other.

He pulled on the reins of his horse and took the lead with his general.

I trailed behind them both, the rest of the soldiers in a line behind me. The moonlight reflected off the stalks of grass and leaves in the trees, painting a muted outline of our terrain. Details were difficult to make out, but the path forward was clear.

As we moved farther east, it became colder. I could feel it pierce through the armor and the leather underneath. My gloves weren't enough to protect my skin from the dry air. I followed behind them, catching a word here and there of their conversation.

Hours passed in silence, and we continued to move farther into the harsh terrain of barrenness. I blindly followed them, unsure if we traveled to mountains or creek beds. When I started to hear crunching underneath the hooves, I knew we'd struck snow.

In front of me, I could see Fang's outline as he covered Kingsnake, probably staying warm with his body heat.

We finally came to a stop, but it was nowhere near sunrise.

Snow was shoveled out of a clearing, and bonfires were placed in a circle around the perimeter. Tents were erected, as if we would make camp for the rest of the evening. Kingsnake and General Viper continued to confer in private, the two of them inseparable since this journey had started.

My horse was tied up with the others, so I went to Kingsnake's tent, seeing that Fang was already there, tucked under some blankets on the bed like a dog trying to fight the cold. "The snow is no place for a snake, huh?"

His head lifted slightly, making the sheet slide back on his smooth scales. He slipped his tongue in and out, his yellow eyes showing his agreement.

"I'm not a fan of the cold either." I wanted to remove my armor, but it was so damn cold I didn't want to take off a single layer. "I hope we aren't here for long."

The flap to the tent opened, and Kingsnake appeared, tall and powerful in his serpent armor. His handsome face constantly wore an angry stare, making his sharp jawline even sharper. He looked perpetually angry, but no amount of rage could dampen his looks. "General Viper and I will be gone for a few hours. I'll leave Fang here with you."

"Whoa, what?" I got to my feet. "Where are you going?"

He gave me a hard stare.

"I think I have the right to know, considering you're leaving me here alone in the freezing cold."

His eyes switched back and forth between mine. "I know who sent those men after you. We will have words."

"What else lives in these woods?"

"Nothing you need to worry about."

"Well, it's pitch dark, and I can't see...that's a little worrying. Can't I just come with you?" I'd rather take my chances with the king and his general than a snake in the dark.

"Trust me, you don't want to be anywhere near their kind."

"Their kind? Aren't they vampires?"

"But a different kind of vampire."

How different could they be?

"My men understand the consequences of betrayal. Just stay in this tent until I return." He turned to depart.

I'd hated this man since the moment we'd met, but now I was scared shitless of him leaving, out in the middle of nowhere...in the dark...and the snow. "How long will you be gone?"

"Just a few hours." He opened the flap to leave.

"And what if you don't return?"

"I will."

"But how do you know—"

The flap closed. "Trust me, I'll return."

———

Instead of going to sleep, I sat on the edge of the bed, my ears straining to hear everything around me. I'd slept throughout the day yesterday, so I was too awake to go to bed. Besides, that would require me to remove all my gear —and there was no way I was doing that.

Fang continued to sleep underneath the blankets, the top part of his head poking out so he could breathe.

I stayed quiet and let him sleep.

Then Fang suddenly jerked up, throwing the blankets off himself and hissed so loudly it sounded like a scream.

"Fuck." I jumped to my feet and stepped back. "Nightmare?"

Fang released a loud growl then faced the entrance to the tent, as if he expected unwanted visitors. His tail was up like he intended to use it as a weapon, and his fangs continued to drip venom.

"What's happening?" I whispered, unsheathing my sword.

The flap opened, and a man's face was revealed. It was one of Kingsnake's men, judging by the serpent crest on his armor.

Fang growled louder, issuing his warning.

The flap closed.

"The snake is in there." Voices from outside suddenly became audible.

"We'll have to kill it first," another man said.

Fang hissed.

"Oh shit..." Now my heart raced as I gripped my sword. It was the two of us versus all the soldiers in the camp. Even with Fang's large body and deadly venom, those weren't good odds.

The stakes in the ground were suddenly knocked over, and the top of the tent collapsed. My vision was obstructed as the material completely covered me. Then a hand grabbed me and shoved me to the ground. Someone grasped my ankle and dragged me across the cold earth. The tarp disappeared from over my eyes, and I saw the night sky in the opening between the trees. Vampires with the serpent crest seized me and started to bind my hands and wrists with rope.

"Let me go!" I tried to thrash out of their hold, but it was like fighting an iron grip.

"Hiiiisssssss." Fang launched his heavy body at the guys on top of me and knocked them over.

I twisted out of the binding and grabbed my sword from where it'd fallen on the ground.

Fang took on two men by himself, fangs protruding, venom dripping.

More men were about to descend on me, their own fangs exposed, something I'd never seen before. I rolled out of the way then got to my feet before I swiped my sword at the first. They were armored, so my blade did little damage. They unsheathed their blades, and it turned into a battle, two of them versus one of me.

One tripped, Fang's long body grabbing him around the ankle and tugging hard, all the while dodging the blades of his own foes.

When the other vampire was distracted, I swung my blade at his neck—and chopped his head off. The other one was still on the ground, so I took the opportunity to plunge the tip of my blade right into his neck. He made a strange gurgling sound then went still.

I looked up to see Fang's body wrapped around one of the vampires, squeezing him to death while he took on another soldier. I rushed to his aid and swung my sword, making him retreat to evade my attack.

Crunch. Fang collapsed all his bones with his body.

It was disturbing, but also impressive. "Good one."

"Hiiisssssss."

The others came, all the soldiers in the camp turning against their king the second the temptation became too much.

"We have to run. We can't kill them all."

Fang looked up to the sky, seeing the hint of sunrise, and then looked at me.

We shared the same thought.

"Run." I sprinted into the tree line, having no idea where I was going or where I'd end up. Fang was fast, slithering across the snow like he was flying, his long body able to move at speeds that didn't even seem possible.

We ran into the dark forest and through the trees.

Fang suddenly stopped and buried himself in the snow.

I kept running, knowing he had a plan.

He jerked his body up, taut between two trees, and tripped all the men who came for us.

I continued to run but then stopped when I realized Fang hadn't caught up to me. I turned back around, seeing him flail about in the snow, stuck underneath a net weighed down with rocks. He squirmed to break free, but even his heavy weight wasn't enough to burst through.

Then I saw the sword. The vampire raised it, ready to stab Fang to death because he had nowhere else to go.

"No..."

I ran back, stumbling through the piles of snow, tripping more than once. "Stop!"

Fang hissed, trying to gnaw at the net with his sharp fangs.

The vampire looked up, ready to stab Fang right beneath the head.

"Let him go!" I stopped fifteen feet away, not willing to come any closer.

He continued to hold the blade, and a disgusting sneer spread across his face. "Why should I?" Behind him, the other vampires stood, all eyes on me, looking at me like a roast pig over the fire.

"Let him go...and I'll do what you want." I swallowed, knowing it would be nothing like it was with Kingsnake. He was gentle and always gave me a choice. But these assholes wouldn't show me the same respect.

"You know we can't let him go." He withdrew the sword and returned it to his scabbard.

"Then leave him until Kingsnake returns." I hoped saying the king's name would remind them of the retribution they faced when he returned, but they didn't seem to care whatsoever.

"Hiiissssssss." Fang stared at me through the holes in the net, furious.

"We have a deal." He raised his hand, gesturing for me to come to him.

Fang continued to hiss, trying to undulate his body until he came free.

I stayed rooted to the spot, terrified of what I'd just signed up for. Was my life more important than a snake's? Probably not. But I couldn't run off and leave him behind. I wouldn't have been able to live with myself, knowing he suffered a fate so cruel...to be trapped like that.

I swallowed before I came forward, approaching the hungry vampires that didn't take their eyes off me. Now I was more aware of the pulse in my neck. More aware of the warm blood right underneath my skin. Maybe one vampire would feed and spare me, but if I had to feed them all...there wouldn't be enough to go around.

21

KINGSNAKE

Viper and I were permitted passage beyond the gate to the mountain, and then we were escorted to the throne room, made of stone with high ceilings and no sunlight. Braziers burned with fire at all corners of the room, giving light and warmth in this lifeless place.

Viper and I stood side by side and stared at the empty throne, waiting for our company to join us.

He turned his head slightly to look at me. "Has Fang reported?"

"The camp is quiet." I kept my eyes on the throne made of stone, a throne that looked too painful to sit on. I personally didn't have one, because I was too busy leading my people to sit on my ass all day.

The door finally opened, and he appeared.

Cobra.

He entered the chamber in armor that flashed gold and black, with a cloak that dragged across the floor. Guarded by two soldiers just as heavily armed, he moved past them as they took their positions on either side of the throne on the lower step.

Cobra flashed us a smile before he took a seat. "The three of us together again. To what do I owe the pleasure?" He had the same dark hair, the same dark eyes—just without the slitted pupil.

I took a step forward.

Both of his men aimed their arrows right at my heart.

I ignored the threat and moved forward.

"It's alright." He sat with his knees wide apart, one elbow propped on the side of the chair, his fingers curled into a fist underneath his jaw. "My brother loves to make an entrance..."

We approached his chair, the three of us just feet apart now.

Cobra rose to his feet, meeting us at eye level. "You've traveled far for a moment of my time." That obnoxious smile returned to his face. "I'm flattered."

"Let's cut the shit," Viper said.

My eyes were locked on Cobra's. "I second that motion."

"Right down to business...I see." He walked off toward the door from which he'd entered. "I think we'll need a drink for this."

We followed him into another antechamber, a room with a large fireplace and leather furniture. A rug was on the floor, and there was a wet bar full of preserved booze. He took a seat in the armchair closest to the fire, and Viper and I made ourselves comfortable on opposite ends of the couch.

A woman in gold lingerie that barely covered her ass and tits served us, pouring us liquor into glasses with balls made of ice. She set the decanters on the table between us so we could grab our own refills then walked out.

Now we were alone.

I stared at Cobra, a man who shared my blood but not my likeness. We had little in common, from our ideologies to our morals.

Cobra took a drink, downing the entire glass as if it was some kind of competition. He set the empty glass on the table then wiped his mouth with the back of his forearm. "What can I do for you?"

"Stay the fuck out of Grayson, for starters." I set the glass down, the alcohol no match for my rage.

Cobra grinned, like this was all a game.

"You think this is funny?"

"I think it's funny you thought we wouldn't discover your secret."

"So you admit it?" I stared at my older brother, the favorite in the family.

He gave a slight shrug. "Maybe I did. Maybe I didn't."

I wanted to smash this glass over his head. "Well, in case you *did*, just know there will be consequences next time you enter my lands uninvited."

"Like a smack on the wrist—"

"Like war."

He continued to grin, as if my threats bounced right off him. "Remember what mother told us when we were younger? That we should always share—"

"You have an entire city of people to feed on." Cobra had his own village of humans that lived behind the mountain, people trapped with no chance of escape. They lived normal lives—except when they were called to feed Cobra and his men. That was the difference between us. Cobra thought humans were akin to livestock, to be taken and used for his own benefit, whereas I took those who offered their blood to us freely. "You're free from this plague, isolated from the rest of the world."

His fist was propped against the side of his face, and then he swiped his finger across one of his fangs, catching a drop of liquor before he closed his mouth again. "But to taste blood so powerful...that would be a real treat."

"That'll never happen, Cobra."

He turned his gaze and looked at Viper. "Has he shared with you?"

My brother said nothing.

Cobra looked at me again. "A dick move, don't you think?"

"My people are fed."

"People are different from family." Now Cobra's smile dropped.

I knew exactly what he was doing. "You can't turn Viper against me."

"You sure about that?" he asked. "No one likes a dictator..."

"No wonder I don't like you."

The grin was back, and he let out a quiet chuckle as he looked away. "Father will laugh once I tell him that..."

I didn't ask about him. Hadn't spoken to him in a very, very long time. "I believe our enemies to the west are the origin of this disease."

"A disease that doesn't concern us."

"It will concern you if we don't find a cure. If we lose our food source, where do you think we'll turn?"

Cobra turned his gaze back on me. "Is that a threat?"

"It's a promise."

He stared at me with his brown eyes with flecks of gold. His smile was long gone. "Your proof?"

"I have none," I said. "Just suspicions."

"And you think it's wise to declare war on the elves based on suspicions?"

"I said nothing of war."

"You didn't say it, but I heard it, nonetheless."

I stared at my brother, a man I'd butted heads with since we were boys. We were like two rams getting our horns stuck together. "I suspect they've poisoned the humans to make us malnourished and weak, and once they succeed, they'll move to annihilate us."

Cobra stared, his eyes shielded and unreadable.

I waited for him to say something.

"If they take us down, they'll come for you next. We'll need to stand together and fight."

"Again, suspicions..."

"You suggest we outright ask them?" I asked incredulously.

He ignored the question. "How close are you to a cure?"

In truth, I hadn't even started. "It's hard to say." Every time I tasted her, I was so high I couldn't think straight. To have the objectivity to identify elements in her blood was beyond my restraint right now.

Cobra stared at me.

"We need to put aside our differences and work together."

"We have no differences," he said. "We're exactly the same —despite what you seem to think."

Kingsnake.

My attention was immediately withdrawn from the conversation.

They're coming for us—and I can't hold them off.

Cobra must have said something and I missed it, because both he and Viper stared at me.

Hurry.

I'm leaving now. I rose to my feet. "I must depart."

"What's happened?" Viper asked when he should have kept his mouth shut.

I ignored the question and stared at Cobra. "Encroach on my lands again, and you ask for war." I turned away.

"What an interesting conversation," Cobra said. "First, you threaten me, and then you ask for my help not one minute later. Kingsnake, you need to work on your negotiation skills, for they are lacking."

We left the antechamber and the throne room and returned to the snowy landscape where our horses and men waited.

"What's happened?" Viper repeated.

I mounted my horse and dug my heels into its sides. "Larisa will die if we don't hurry."

22

LARISA

I was scared.

I was bound by the fire, wrists secured above my head, my ankles tied together. Fang had been left in the snow, and I knew if Kingsnake didn't return soon, he would freeze to death. The vampires made sure I was warm before the first one dropped his knees on either side of my hips.

I'd done this before, but I was still scared.

He wasn't gentle like Kingsnake had been. He fisted a handful of hair and tugged too hard on my scalp before he forced my head the other way. Then his fangs were in me without preamble, and the bite hurt far more than I remembered it.

The chemicals that numbed me entered my bloodstream to make it more bearable, but there was no pleasure with it.

My thighs didn't grip his hips. I didn't feel lost in an oasis of joy.

It just hurt.

"Enough." Another tugged on his arm. "Remember the rest of us."

He wouldn't stop. He probably couldn't.

They finally yanked him off, and there was a wildness in his eyes that hadn't been there before. He tried to rush back to me, but the others kept him at bay.

"Fuck, that's like nothing I've ever tasted..."

As if the men standing there weren't already hungry enough.

The next one dropped to his knees and did the same.

It hurt even more, having a second bite mark in my flesh.

It went on that way for a while...and I started to grow weak. "Stop. You're going to kill me..." My warning fell on deaf ears. Maybe they would have stopped if they were sane enough to, but now all of them were wild like a pack of hungry wolves. "Stop..." My eyes grew heavy, so heavy I couldn't hold them open any longer.

I woke when I felt the fangs slice across my skin as they were torn out of my flesh. Screams erupted in the early morning. I could see sunlight in the canopy above. The vampire who had just been on me was flung away as if he weighed nothing.

That was when I saw Kingsnake, his dark cloak billowing around him as he swung his blade and struck down the vampire who had taken what was his. He stabbed him in the heart then dragged him into the fire pit, where the flames immediately engulfed his flesh.

I looked away, the sight far too disturbing to handle.

It was chaos, vampire fighting vampire, Viper and Kingsnake slaying their own men and tossing them into the fire so the smell of flesh penetrated the night. I tried to wiggle free, but I was too weak to do more than just shift my weight.

Kingsnake eventually returned, his face appearing above mine. He cut my bindings then pressed a cloth to my neck to stop the bleeding. "Where's Fang?"

I could hardly focus my gaze.

"Larisa, I need your help right now."

"Fang..."

"Yes. Where is he?"

"The woods..."

"Where in the woods?"

"I... Over there."

His eyes lit up in fury, but he didn't scream at me. "If you don't help me, he's going to die. Do you understand?"

I nodded.

"Come on." He pulled me up then scooped me into his arms. "Show me."

I looked around, my face resting against his chest. "That way..." I pointed, raising my arm as best as I could.

He walked and turned to Viper in the process. "She needs something to eat."

"Alright."

He jogged to where I'd pointed, his boot crunching on snow.

"Keep going..."

He carried me into the woods, holding me steady despite the uneven terrain. He must have spotted him on his own because he started to run. He stopped where Fang's body lay underneath the trap. Without asking, he put me down against the tree then yanked the net free from its hold. "What the fuck did they do to you?"

Fang's lifeless body lay there, his eyes open.

"No..." I breathed hard but couldn't shed tears, not when I had nothing left to give.

Kingsnake scooped him up in his arms, picking up his long body and hoisting it over his shoulders, elevating him from the snow. "Come on, Fang." Without looking at me, he said, "I'll come back for you." He left, running as he carried a two-hundred-and-fifty-pound snake over his shoulders.

I sat there, freezing in the cold, too weak to rise.

Someone appeared in front of me. I didn't notice their approach because I was so delirious. He scooped me into his arms then carried me back to camp. It took me a while to realize it was General Viper.

He set me in front of the bonfire and handed me a plate of food. "Eat this."

I took the plate with shaky hands then looked over to where Kingsnake was. He'd placed Fang on the mattress we slept on in front of the fire, his body rigid and misshapen, and turned him over every few seconds, trying to warm his body.

I couldn't eat. All I could do was watch.

Viper kneeled at my side. "I told you to eat."

"Fang...is he going to be okay?"

"I'm not sure." He pushed the plate at me. "But you won't be if you don't eat."

I forced myself to eat whatever he'd made me, some dry jerked meat and fruit with a piece of stale bread.

Kingsnake seemed oblivious to everyone else in the camp, solely focused on the snake he clearly cared deeply for. The remaining vampires who hadn't been killed were tied to trees at the outskirts, while the soldiers who had been loyal to him remained on patrol. He continued to rotate Fang, getting the warmth on all sides of his body.

Finally, Fang started to move, his body tightening into a ball.

The searing hatred that had been in Kingsnake's eyes a moment ago disappeared. His hand rested on the back of Fang's head, like an owner touching their dog with affection. Sunshine in a garden. Flowers in bloom. Weightlessness like clouds. So many things ran through him, emotions that couldn't truly be described. His anger and his intensity had been replaced by something I'd never witnessed. Then his head snapped up instantly, his eyes locked on me.

Those emotions instantly changed, the intensity back in full force but stronger than ever before. He didn't blink as he regarded me, just pierced me with eyes so powerful they could cut right through me.

He got to his feet—and walked toward me.

I flinched at his movement. It was instinct, seeing a predator striding toward me with rage in his eyes.

He kneeled down beside me, and now my urge to run was thwarted by my weakness. Even with the food in my stomach, all my life-force had been drained. I was at the mercy of whomever I crossed.

My eyes held his, and I struggled to breathe.

"Fang told me what you did."

I dropped my chin and turned away, relieved that was all he wanted to say.

His fingers reached for my chin and slowly turned me back to him. "Thank you..."

I held his gaze, understanding the intensity in his veins was gratitude. Unlike others, his spectrum of emotion was limited, so several feelings could be expressed in the same way...like anger and gratitude...intensity and arousal. "He's my friend." That was all I could bring myself to say. If Kingsnake hadn't arrived when he did, I would have been dead, my life forfeited to save a serpent. But he was more than a snake. "I'm so glad he's alright."

His fingers stayed on my chin. "Are you okay?"

"Not really...but I will be."

He regarded my neck, which had been bandaged to stop the bleeding. "They'll pay for what they've done." He pulled his hand away altogether. "It was foolish to leave your side—and it won't happen again." He rose to his feet and walked away, joining his general where the prisoners were tied up.

I looked over at Fang, who had his stare locked on me. He remained flat on the mattress, as if he were too weak to raise his head and regard me. His tongue didn't slip in and out like it normally did, and his scales reflected the dancing flames.

A scream caught my attention, and I turned back to Kingsnake.

He dragged one of the prisoners across the ground and dropped him in the dirt. "Death is too good for any of you." He turned to Viper and raised his open palm.

Viper placed a metal rod in his gloved hand, and the end glowed red after sitting in the fire.

I swallowed.

Kingsnake returned to the vampire on the ground and kneed on top of him. "I won't take your life—but I'll take your sight." He slammed the metal rod into one eye, bursting the pupil then cauterizing it with the heat.

The screams...I would never forget them.

I looked away, horrified by the barbarianism.

Kingsnake destroyed his other eye then left him lying there. "Who's next?"

I cupped the side of my face to hide my vision, and I wished I could run into the woods so I wouldn't bear witness to this horror.

It'll be over ssssoon.

I heard the words directly in my mind, an echo that came from all directions. My eyes immediately lifted, focusing on Fang next to the fire. His yellow eyes were still on me.

Do not pity them. I don't.

23

LARISA

I couldn't recall going to sleep, but I woke up warm and bundled up, the world silent around me. The tent had been resurrected, and I could tell by the light coming through the fabric that it was late in the day.

I sat up and looked around, discovering Fang inside his bed made of cotton, a little crack in the lid that showed a glimpse of his scales. Yesterday had been forgotten, until a moment later, when it all came flooding back to me.

The flap opened, and Kingsnake entered, his eyes blood-shot and tired like he hadn't slept in three days. His eyes settled on me, and then instantly, I sensed a cloud of energy that emitted from him, like a high frequency my ears could barely detect. It wasn't anger or joy. I wasn't sure what it was. Perhaps another version of intensity.

He released the flood then approached me. "You're awake."

"Yes." I was in the same clothes, but my armor had been removed before I was tucked into bed.

"You've been asleep for two days." He didn't approach the bed, but instead pulled up a stool to take a seat across from me. He leaned forward, forearms on his knees, his cloak behind him.

"Wow..." That explained the headache—and the emptiness in my stomach. My hand immediately went to my neck, feeling that the bandage had been removed. Their bites were probably still visible, but faded.

"Can you travel?" He normally ordered me to do things. I didn't have much say in the matter. But now I had options...which was nice.

"After I eat something."

He left the tent.

I looked at the bed on the floor. **How are you?** I asked the question in my mind, and while I talked to myself all the time, it was strange to address someone else in that way.

He lifted the lid with his head then looked at me with those intelligent eyes. His tongue slipped in and out. ***Much better. I feasted on a family of rats.***

That's nice...

He left the bucket and slithered to me, his body impressive every time I saw it, and he slowly occupied my bed, taking up most of it with his gargantuan size. He curled up beside me, his head resting on my shoulder. ***People always assume I'm a monster because I'm a snake. But you saw something more.***

A lot more.

He rubbed his head against my cheek then made a humming noise. ***We can't tell Kingsnake about this.***

What?

That I've spoken to you.

Why not?

He's a very possessive man—as I'm sure you know.

Yes, I did know.

The flap opened, and Kingsnake returned, carrying a tray of food. He glanced at Fang beside me before he handed it over. "Fang doesn't show affection—not even with me. He's very fond of you."

"And I him."

He sat on the stool again, this time fully upright, his eyes on me.

His stare made me self-conscious, so I didn't touch my food. "Is there something else?"

His shoulders were even broader in his armor, and something about the fatigue in his eyes made him more handsome too. "I allowed this to happen. For that, I'm sorry."

"You didn't know—"

"It doesn't matter. As King of Grayson, I'm responsible for everything, even things that are out of my control. I won't let this happen again, and next time I go somewhere, you're to come with me. After what you've done for Fang, there's nothing I wouldn't do for you."

His stare became too much for me, so I looked down at my tray of food.

"I'll let you eat." He left the tent, leaving me to eat alone.

He really loves you.

Yes.

I've never seen that side of him before.

What side?

You know…nice. Not an asshole.

He's still an asshole. He's just less of an asshole to me. And now, to you.

How long have you...been together?

Since the beginning.

The beginning of what?

His eternal night.

As in...fifteen hundred years?

Yes.

That left me speechless for a moment. **So...how did this come about? I noticed his eyes are slitted like yours. Is there a connection?**

Now Fang didn't say anything.

I continued to wait.

I can't share his secrets. Only he can. Perhaps he'll tell you...now that he cares for you.

You think he cares for me?

I think he respects you—which is the same thing.

———

We returned to Grayson on horseback, stopping only once to avoid the high sun, and returned to the foggy coastline. The water was in the air, and I could feel it fleck against my cheeks as we rode. Despite the overcast sky and the humidity, it was still warmer than the snow in the east, so it was nice to be back.

We returned with half the men we'd set out with—and I wondered if that would be a problem. I walked between Kingsnake and General Viper through the city, Fang wrapped around Kingsnake's strong body. I felt like one of them, wearing their armor, walking through the streets like royalty.

We arrived at the palace, and I was excited to be grounded in a familiar place. I headed to the bedchambers, and Kingsnake joined me, which was unusual because he normally had something to attend to most hours of the day.

We entered, and he immediately removed every piece of armor, placing it in the closet along with his cloak. Then he removed his gloves and the rest of his uniform, stripping down until he was buck naked.

I tried not to stare.

Wordlessly, he went straight into the bathroom. The water turned on a moment later.

A shower sounded nice after our travels, but I decided to wait my turn.

Minutes later, he emerged, his hair wet and slightly over his forehead. His towel was in his hands, and he scrubbed his damp hair, the rest of his body on full display.

I kept my eyes elsewhere as I entered the bathroom. Once I was under the hot spray, my bones thawed after days in the snow, and I just stood there and enjoyed the warm water as it soothed my skin. I wished I could take a bath, but there wasn't a tub in his room. Once all the grime was out of my hair and the soap had been lathered into my skin, I stepped out and covered myself with a soft towel.

I felt like a new person.

Wrapped in my cotton towel, I returned to the main room and halted in my tracks when I felt it.

Overwhelming power. Violent intensity. My eyes flicked to where he sat against the headboard, his hungry eyes locked on mine with ferocity. To anyone else, it may have just been a look, but coupled with the tidal wave of need, I was paralyzed.

It took a moment to gather myself, to be aware of the fire in the hearth, the warmth that had entered the bedchambers since we returned. The curtains were drawn shut now that it was nightfall.

I gripped the towel and tore my look away.

As if his emotions were a person, they followed me, pressed right up against my neck like a pair of eager lips. I opened the top drawer of the dresser and found clean clothes to wear to bed, a loose shirt with matching bottoms. When I turned around, I flinched because he was right there, right behind me, like his lips really had been on the back of my neck.

I took a few deep breaths, unable to hide my surprise.

He grabbed the clothes out of my hand and tossed them aside.

My fingers opened and let it happen. I was powerless to do anything, and I succumbed to the potency of his thoughts, the stare that burned hotter than the sun. His naked body was right in front of me, his hard chest at my face, his chin tilted down to look at me. His desire surrounded me on all sides, and I felt like a treasure for the taking.

He grabbed the towel and gave a gentle tug, his eyes on me the entire time.

My hand let go.

The towel slipped down my body until it landed with a thud on the rug.

He didn't glance down to look at me, but the fires in the forge of his eyes burned that much hotter, like he was that much closer to having me.

I felt out of breath, even though I hadn't moved. I felt weak, when I'd been revitalized after those bites. For a woman so confident, I couldn't even remember my own name. Speech left me.

His hand slid into my damp hair and angled my head back, forcing my chin up so our eyes were locked together. He held me there for seconds, our eyes glued together in a seductive dance of stares. I melted in his heat, desperate for his kiss but equally terrified.

He finally dipped his head and kissed the corner of my mouth, his eyes still open, getting a taste and watching my reaction to it.

My heart instantly quickened.

He kissed the other corner, eyes remaining open, and then tilted his head as he kissed my whole mouth.

My eyes closed, and I felt my lips part to let him take me. All of me.

His inferno reached the sky, burning everything that came too close.

I was backed up against the dresser, his kiss invading my mouth, his big hand gripping one of my ass cheeks. My arms circled his neck, and I felt his tongue dive into my mouth as his fingers dug deeper into my hair. It was an out-of-body experience, being the prey of this man who wanted me so deeply.

His strong arms lifted me and carried me to the bed without disrupting our intense kiss. My back hit the bed, and he was on me, his mouth kissing my neck, his hand gripping my tit. I hugged him to me, my hand on the back of his neck, my fingernails deep in his back.

He migrated down, sucking each nipple before he went over my belly toward the apex of my thighs.

"No." I reached for his biceps to tug him back to me. "I don't want to wait…"

He was back on top of me, his hips between my thighs, his brown eyes locked on mine. One arm scooped behind my thigh, and he bent me into position as he pushed inside me, his fat head breaking through my tightness before it began to sink in.

I inhaled as I felt him invade me, felt him take up every open space within me. He went too far and hit me where it hurt, but I even enjoyed that. The fact that his dick was too big turned me on to no end.

He thrust the second we were combined, fucking me like it was the first time he had the opportunity. He smothered me with his desire and pleasure. Moans and grunts escaped his lips, but they didn't compare to the intensity beneath the flesh, the way my body drove him mad. Face-to-face, our breaths escaping together, our bodies slamming into each other with slickness, we fucked hard.

My arms hooked over his shoulders, and I tugged him into me more, wincing when he went too deep.

He pulled back slightly when he felt my body resist his size.

"No...I like it." I pulled him back.

Lightning struck the earth, and the radius of his desire increased. "You like it when I hurt you?"

"Yes..."

He brought himself back into me, hitting me hard every time.

"Yes." It hurt, but it hurt so damn good.

We writhed and moaned, shared kisses when we had the breath, made the bed slick with our sweaty bodies. I felt the ecstasy a moment later, given little warning of its approach, and it struck me so forcefully it made my toes curl. My nails clawed at his back, and the tears sprang from my eyes.

He watched my reaction, the intensity of his emotions burning everything around us. The desire was elevated to new proportions. His skin tinted red, a vein popped on his temple, and he came with a moan that made me wet all over again. "Fuck..." His face pressed into my neck, and he continued to rock until the high completely left his body.

My ankles locked around his back, and my fingers played with his hair, my eyes seeing stars because I was so satisfied. His inferno was gone, and now it was emptiness. Like music that had been cut, there was only silence, silence that made you feel alone.

———

Fang's head rested on my thigh as I read from the book in my hands. I didn't read aloud, just with my thoughts. **Huntley took up his sword, and with the power of a thousand suns, he stabbed one of the three kings. He sank to his knees and collapsed, no more. But when Huntley looked for his wife, he realized she wasn't there—**

The bedroom door opened, and Kingsnake entered the room, in his king's uniform without the armor. His eyes immediately went to me on the couch, and the second our eyes locked, that same heated intensity returned.

It was always there now, anytime he was in my presence.

I want to know what happenssss next.

Kingsnake took a seat on the other armchair, looking at us together. "Are you reading to him?"

"Yes." I closed the book and set it on the table.

"What is it?"

"The Forsaken King."

"I've never read it."

"Well...it's a romance. I found it in my old bedroom."

It's thrilling.

He sat there, his arms on the armrests, his hands gripping the curvature at the ends. His mood was always stark, and he didn't know how to be anything but intense. The only time he was relaxed was when he was asleep. "Would you like to join me for dinner?"

Now there was no hesitation. "Sure."

"Then I'll see you in the dining room this evening." He rose to his feet and prepared to depart.

"You're leaving?"

"The day may end for you, but it never ends for me." He walked out and shut the door.

"Has he always been this uptight?" I asked, still staring at the door.

Yesssss.

"You'd think he'd loosen up after getting laid so often..."

Nope.

It made me wonder about the others, if he'd ever felt the same intensity toward them. "How long does he keep a lover?"

Dependssss on the lover. But generally, not very long.

"Longer than I've been here?"

No.

The answer gave me relief, even though it shouldn't.

Except for Ellasara.

I turned to look at him. "Who's Ellasara?"

Someone from a very long time ago.

I knew he wouldn't betray Kingsnake and give me the information, so I didn't ask. But I definitely wanted to.

A knock sounded on the door, and the seamstress entered. "His Majesty asked me to outfit you for this evening. Here you are." She placed a dress on the bed, red and black, along with a pair of heels.

I walked over to take a look and found the long slit up the leg. It went all the way up, stopping right at the hip. "This is a bit...much...isn't it?" It had a low-cut front, *very low*, so I definitely couldn't wear a bra. The sleeves were supposed to hug the upper arms. "I mean, I should just wear my bra and underwear at this point."

"This is what His Majesty requested."

"He specifically asked for *this*?"

"Well, he said something sexy…and revealing."

Then she'd hit the nail right on the head. "Thank you."

She gave a gentle bow and left.

I picked up the dress and held it up to my body so I could see exactly where the slit landed on my thigh. "Isn't it ridiculous?"

Fang slithered over then propped himself up to look at me. *I like it.*

"You do?" I asked with a laugh.

He nodded. ***You look like a queen.***

"A slut queen, maybe…"

Wear a dagger right at the top of the slit. Then it'll be perfect.

"Not a bad idea. Didn't realize you knew so much about fashion."

I don't. But I know what he likes.

I stepped into the dining hall, wearing the high-cut dress with my tits nearly falling out the top, and approached the table.

His eyes combed my body from top to bottom, taking his time, and then focused on the dagger at the top of my thigh. A small line of my panties was visible too, and he seemed to notice that.

The depth of his emotion was so powerful I thought the windows would shatter into shards of glass all over the floor. It had the strength of a tornado that could rip the roof off this stone palace.

I took the seat across from him and felt like my tits would fall right onto the table.

With eyes fixed on me, he said nothing. His shoulders were broad in his uniform, and his tired eyes showed endless depth. Brown eyes had never intrigued me, but I found his beautiful. Silence passed, and he continued to stare.

"What are we having?"

His stare continued, as if he hadn't heard me.

The servant entered with a bottle of wine and poured our glasses before he departed.

I took a drink, just to have something to shake that stare. "This is good. Did you pick it out?"

"I've never cared for wine."

"Then why do you drink it?"

"Because you enjoy it."

"How do you know I enjoy it?"

"Because I've seen you."

I usually had a glass with dinner, and then another after dinner. Back at Raventower, wine was a luxury that I could only afford sparingly, so having unlimited access was a nice treat. "Do you grow your own wine?"

"No."

"Where do you get it?"

"We trade. Our trees have the strongest timber, so we trade that for wine and other luxuries."

There were other kingdoms, so he must be referring to one of those. I'd noticed the magnificent trees once I arrived, fifty feet in the air with trunks wider than five men standing shoulder to shoulder.

"You and Fang have become close." It was the first time he said something on his own, but it wasn't a question, just an observation.

"Well, we spend a lot of time together."

"He doesn't warm up to people easily."

"I did save his life..."

"He enjoyed your company prior to that."

"He did?"

"That's what he said."

"Aww...he's so cute."

"Cute?" He tilted his head slightly, almost offended. "He's a poisonous two-hundred-and-fifty-pound snake."

"So?"

"And you used to be terrified of him."

"I would still be terrified of him if he didn't like me."

A distant smile moved on to his lips, and his intensity dimmed to a dull simmer. "Why do you fear snakes?"

"I was bitten as a child."

He stared at me in silence, and then the servant brought our dinners. It was roast chicken with potatoes and vegetables. The steam rose to the ceiling as he continued to stare at me like he didn't notice the food had been served.

The pressure of his stare made me continue. "I was in the fields outside the village. Didn't realize it was there...until it bit me."

"What kind of snake was it?"

"I—I don't know."

"What did it look like?"

"I don't know that either."

"How do you not know?"

"Because I never saw it. It hissed, bit me, and then I passed out..."

Now his eyes were narrowed on my face. "Did someone find you?"

"When I woke up, it was dark, so I headed back to the village. My parents were worried sick."

"Did you show them the bite?"

"I never told them. I was afraid they wouldn't let me explore outside the village again."

"The snake must not have been poisonous, so perhaps it was a garden snake."

"No, it was bigger."

"You said you never saw it." His food was left untouched, the two of us more absorbed in the conversation.

"But the bite mark was too big for a garden snake. I was little at the time, but the bite took up a large part of my forearm." I extended my arm, pointing to the scars that were so old it was hard to tell they were even there. I pointed to one circle and then the other.

Kingsnake stared for a full minute before he grabbed my wrist and turned my arm slightly, bringing it closer to the candle flame. His eyes didn't blink as he stared at the markings, and another minute passed.

"What is it?"

He dragged his fingers across the flesh. "I didn't notice this before..."

"It's one of those things you wouldn't realize if you didn't know beforehand."

He finally released my arm, but his expression had darkened. His interior was silent, no detectable emotion. His eyes lifted to mine, but his mind seemed to be elsewhere.

"Can I ask you something?"

My question seemed to snap him out of it because he grabbed his utensils and began to eat.

He didn't invite or reject my question, so I carried on. "Why are serpents such an important part of your culture? It's on your clothing...in the stonework...everywhere."

He stared at me for so long I thought he might not answer. "Because that's the type of vampire we are."

My eyebrows rose.

"I told you there are different kinds of vampires."

"Yes, I remember."

"We're the Kingsnake Vampires."

"You just...like those types of snakes and decided to name yourselves after them?" It reminded me of a child playing with friends in the street, where they decided they were werewolves or monsters and pretended to be them.

His expression didn't change, but his mood had dropped several degrees. "Kingsnake venom is essential to sire another vampire. It's not only blood."

"That's why your pupils are slitted..."

"Yes."

"How many other vampires are there?"

"Several. Cobra Vampires. Diamondback Vampires. The Teeth. And the Originals."

"The Teeth?"

"Distant relations. Very distant."

"What are they?"

"They are creatures that feed on human blood, but instead of possessing two fangs, they dislocate their jaw and extend all their teeth."

"That's the scariest shit I've ever heard." I hadn't touched my food yet, and now I had no appetite. "I've never heard of them."

"Because they don't reside on our continent. They're far away."

"What about the others?"

"They're here."

"And the Originals...what are those?"

"The first vampires."

"And how did they come to be?" Humans knew nothing of vampires, just that they were nightwalkers, that they were monsters, that they were evil. But their history and their politics...we were ignorant.

"The Golden Serpent." He stared at me as if that was a thorough explanation.

"Then Originals are still being made."

He shook his head. "That type of snake hasn't been seen in thousands of years. They kept them in captivity, not understanding that's a death sentence for a creature independent and proud."

I immediately thought of Fang, and picturing him locked in a cage made my heart ache.

"They perished—and then there were no more."

"How are Originals different from Kingsnakes?"

"Stronger. Faster. Have powers we're not privy to."

"And the Cobra Vampires? How are they different?"

"They're stronger—but only slightly."

"Why didn't you choose the Cobra venom over the Kingsnake venom, then?"

His arms were on the table, his skin hidden underneath the sleeves. He looked down at his food, as if trying to decide if or how he should respond. "That's a story for another time."

I should be grateful he shared at all, because it was the first time he ever had, but I wanted to know more. "As far as I know, Raventower doesn't know any of this. As for the other kingdoms...I'm not sure."

"How would you know what the royal family knows or doesn't know?"

Because I'd bedded the prince for years. Thought we would get married. Have children. It was the first time I'd thought of him in a very long time, and I wondered whether he cared I'd been taken by the King of Vampires. "I guess I don't..."

He continued to stare at me, his eyes shifting back and forth between mine, as if trying to read me.

I looked down at the table and picked up my fork. We'd been talking so long that the food had gone cold. "Do you have a relationship with the Ethereal?" Our world consisted of smaller kingdoms, but King Elrohir of Ethereal ruled us all, promising those most worthy immortality. It was extended to kings and queens—but rarely.

"Relationship isn't the word I'd use to describe it."

"Then how would you—"

"Mortal enemies. That's how I would describe it."

We'd been taught that the Ethereal were godlike beings, elves that had an iron grip on immortality. When they walked across the earth, they looked like they glided. Their eyes were luminous, like the sun was always in their face, even in the rain. They were worshipped by us all. I'd never seen one in person, but I'd seen illustrations in books at the library. They were fairer than all other beings, blessed with profound handsomeness and delicacy. "Can I ask why?"

"Do you want me to explain their prejudice or ours?"

"Both, I guess."

"Neither man nor nightwalker has entered their borders and returned, so the details of their realm are unknown to us. But in our brief conversations, they have made one thing very clear—they're the true immortals."

I didn't know what that meant, so I continued to stare.

"And we're just a curse."

For my entire life, I'd thought the same. "And why do you hate them?"

"Because they're arrogant. Why do they believe they're the only ones who deserve to live forever? Why are they allowed to grant immortality, but we aren't? They were born with that privilege, but it's despicable for others to strive for the same blessing. They just want to keep the status quo. They want to thrive while others suffer. Humans assume they're angelic with their porcelain skin and beauty, but they're worse monsters than we are."

We'd been taught to revere the elves like gods. Because of their generosity, some of us lived forever. And those who didn't, passed on to the afterlife, also controlled by them. They didn't have to offer those gifts to us—but they chose to.

"They've wanted us gone since the Originals. Battles have been fought, so long ago that your history books probably don't even mention it. Their skill with the bow is unparalleled, but our skill with the blade is greater."

I'd had no idea. All I'd known was that the elves were good —and the vampires were evil. "If you eradicate the elves, what will be our fate?"

His eyes locked on mine.

"Our entrance to the afterlife will be barred."

"You don't really believe that, do you?"

I remained quiet, my tongue stuck in my mouth.

"It's a lie. An empty promise in exchange for your submission."

"Can you prove it's not true?"

"Can you prove that it is?" His voice rose slightly, his anger no longer internal.

Words left me.

"Humans may be our prey, but you're livestock to them."

"If that were true, why not just kill us?"

"Because it must be fun to be revered by an entire race," he snapped. "Why kill their admirers? You inflate their egos. You bring them the best of your crops. You raise statues and temples in their honor. You're no threat to them, just playthings."

"Better than being food..."

Even without feeling his mood pressed right up against me, I knew I'd pissed him off. The energy of the entire room changed. The threat was in the air, unmistakable. Instead of seeing me as an irresistible woman he wanted to claim every night, I was now his enemy.

"The only humans we feed on are those who offer themselves to us—"

"Did I offer myself to you?"

"But I gave you the choice—"

"It was extortion. And you haven't held up your end of the deal."

"I need more time—"

"Oh, look how that worked out—"

He slammed his hands down on the table so hard all the dishes shifted. "There are vampires who raise humans like livestock, but I'm not one of those vampires. Every woman I've ever fed on has offered herself to me freely. To compare me to the others is not only offensive, but untrue." He stared at me, daring me to interrupt him. "I've offered you a chance to find a cure to save your people, so we're allies in this endeavor, not enemies. You know who your enemy is? The one who released this sickness into the world."

"And who is that?"

His eyes narrowed in disbelief, like I should have figured it out sooner. "The Ethereal."

24

KINGSNAKE

Too furious to sit still, I left her at the dining table in search of a strong drink.

I entered my study, a large room with a grand fireplace and private bar, where I conferred with General Viper and his commanders more times than I could count. I sank into the oversized armchair with a glass in my hand, my feet up on the table, the fire warm against my clothing.

The door suddenly opened, and a part of me hoped to see Larisa in her high-slit dress and heels with her tits bursting out...ready to apologize to me.

On her knees.

With her pretty mouth apologizing to my dick once she was done.

But it was my brother.

He stepped inside, fully dressed in his uniform like his patrol had just ended. "I saw the light in your window." He helped himself to the bar and poured a glass before he took a seat across from me. He seemed tired because he sat there and didn't say anything, just enjoying his drink, his thoughts somewhere else.

I wasn't in the mood for conversation anyway.

"You're angry."

My eyes stayed on the fire. "I'm always angry...so not an impressive guess."

"You seem angrier than usual."

"I guess that's true."

"I thought all was well after she saved Fang."

The reminder of her heroism only angered me more. I was in her debt for the rest of time. "It was." Everything had changed in that moment. The taste of her blood fueled my desire, but it reached new heights after that. Even now, with this burning anger, I would fuck her on my desk. "But then she opened that goddamn mouth."

"And what came out?"

"Lies and bullshit."

He drank from his glass and waited for an explanation.

"I told her the truth about the Ethereal, but she still thinks we're the monsters."

"What does it matter what she thinks?"

"It matters because..."

My brother stared.

"It just does."

"That mythology has been ingrained in their minds since birth. One conversation with you isn't going to change a lifetime of indoctrination."

"But she's smarter than others of her kind."

"Really? I distinctly remembering you saying the opposite."

That was a lifetime ago, when I was forced to escort her to Grayson. "She and Fang wouldn't have survived without her skills with the blade. Fang can only do so much alone. He said she killed several vampires entirely on her own— which is inexplicable."

"Perhaps she had a good teacher."

"Women aren't trained for battle in their world."

Viper took another drink.

"Sometimes I consider training her myself...just to see what she can do."

"That wouldn't be wise. She's our enemy after all."

She was no enemy to me.

"The Ethereal may be cheats and liars, but we're no better, Kingsnake."

"You really think so?"

"We marched to Raventower and took eight of their healthiest. Two of them died from blood loss. Three will remain a food source until they're too old. The others were returned only so you could get laid. Tell me, when do we start to look good in this story?"

I stared at the fire.

"The difference between us and the Ethereal? We're honest about who we are—and they're liars."

I looked at him again.

"Maybe we're tame in comparison to our other kin. Maybe we only feed on volunteers—unless absolutely necessary. But we're all the same kind of monster. We all feed on human blood. I'd judge her if she thought anything less."

I grabbed the decanter from the table and poured another glass.

We sat in silence for a while.

Viper spoke. "What will we do about Cobra?"

"Hope he speaks to Father."

"I doubt that."

"He knows I'm right—even if he pretends otherwise."

"If we march on the gates of Evanguard, their scouts will see us coming, and then we'll have to fight the armies of the Kingdoms before we get there."

"What armies?" I asked. "They're all sick, remember?"

"Not all. A fraction of their combined forces is still enough to deter us. Then those who survive will have to face greater foes with depleted energy reserves. The only way we win this war is if they come to us."

"So the Ethereal and all humankind at our borders?" I asked incredulously.

"It's a fair fight if we have the Cobras, the Diamondbacks, and the Originals to fight alongside us."

Nepotism hadn't gotten Viper promoted to general of the Grayson army. His unparalleled skill with the blade and his strategic mind had earned him the right. His military advice was the best I'd ever heard—so I needed to listen to him now.

"What if we could get humankind to join us?"

"Their mortal enemies? The ones that subsist on their blood? There's no scenario where that happens."

"There is—if we convince them that the Ethereal are the ones who made them sick in the first place."

I stared at him, my glass resting on my thigh. "I'm not sure that's possible."

"If we discover a cure from Larisa, we would be the saviors —and our word would be gold."

My fingers gripped the glass a little harder.

"With their armies, we would destroy the Ethereal."

"But we would also destroy their salvation."

"That won't matter to them. Not when they realize these creatures that consider themselves gods purposely annihilated a third of their entire population. Not when people have lost their mothers, their fathers, their children..."

"I suppose."

"So this is our plan," Viper said. "You extract the cure from Larisa before the Ethereal march upon us. We'll forge the alliance between the vampires. And then we'll head to the kingdoms to incriminate the Ethereal as the monsters they really are."

25

LARISA

"He's such an asshole..." I sat on the couch, flipping my knife in the air and catching it by the hilt.

I know.

"Then why do you tolerate him?"

Who says I do? Fang hung in his tree, his large body dangling in different places.

I caught the knife by the hilt then balanced it on the back of my hand. "Why do you stay?"

Because this is home.

"You just said he's an asshole."

But he's more than just an asshole. He's also brave, loyal, and kind.

"Well, I've never seen any of those things."

Give him a chance, and you'll see what I see.

At that moment, the door opened, and Kingsnake emerged into the bedroom, his expression furious the moment he stepped inside. His emotions hit every single wall, intensity mixed with fire.

I looked away and tossed my dagger into the air again.

He pulled his tunic over his head and left it on the floor like a child then joined me in the living room. His hair was a bit messy because the strands had gotten caught in the fabric, but of course, it made him look better.

Bastard.

He sat in the armchair and looked at Fang, as if they were having a conversation.

I continued to toss the knife into the air.

He eventually looked at me again. "I understand why you'd prefer not to believe me, but the Ethereal have spread this crippling sickness intentionally. I'm sorry."

"And why would they do that?" I gripped the knife as I looked at him. "You said we're their admirers, their playthings. Why decimate us?"

"Their target is us—not you."

I stared at him.

"Without a food source, we'll grow weak. And once we do, they'll march on our lands and defeat us. We've fought many times before, both losing battles but neither winning the war. This is their path to victory."

"And they would poison innocent people? Children?"

"They couldn't care less, Larisa. If we feed on an infected person, it could kill us. So as your population dwindles, so does ours. Despite what you've been told, we're not the enemy."

I looked away, my blood boiling in ferocity.

His stare was focused on my face, piercing my cheek. "Larisa."

My head snapped back in his direction. "What do you want from me?"

He sat back in the armchair, elbows propped on the armrests.

"You want to convince me to like your kind? Not possible. I'll always detest vampires. *Always.*"

He stared, blinking once or twice, his mood detached. "It doesn't seem like you hate my kind when we're in bed together."

I rolled my eyes. "Fuck you."

"You can't have that kind of passion for someone you hate—"

"We made a deal—"

"For one night. What about all the other nights?"

I wouldn't look at him now. "You can be physically attracted to someone and still hate them."

"Then why did you save my snake?"

"I saved him for him—not you."

He paused. "Larisa, look at me."

I'd never look at him now.

Just when I expected him to say *now*, he said, "Please."

That got my head to turn.

"There's a piece of your story that you aren't sharing with me. I'd like to hear it."

"Why do you assume that?"

"Because it's obvious it's personal."

I stilled at his astute observation.

"What did we do to you?"

I looked away, the memory too painful for eye contact. My fingers gripped the hilt of the dagger in my hand as the blade rested across my thigh. "My mother told me a very different version of this story...but I figured out the truth once I was older. I never told her what I knew, not even when she was on her deathbed."

His stare was hot on my cheek.

"Vampires came to Raventower. I was so young, maybe five years old. My memory is poor, but I remember seeing one in particular. A woman more beautiful than any I'd ever seen before. Lucious dark hair, almond-shaped eyes, a petite little thing..." I remembered seeing her on the street as I spied through the window. "My father took one look at her, became infatuated, and abandoned us both to be with her. He naively assumed she wanted him, but she only wanted his blood. Once they returned to Grayson or somewhere in the woods, I'm sure she fed until he died." When I finished my story, I looked at him again. "Now you know why I wish you were all dead."

———

Kingsnake slept elsewhere to give me space, and I didn't even have to make the request. He didn't bother me for several days, and I spent that time on the balcony looking at the ocean with Fang beside me, or in the sitting room in front of the grand fireplace. Fang was my only company, and in that duration, we'd become even closer friends.

He checks on you often.

I forgot that Fang was also his surveillance system, his second pair of eyes.

Wants to know when it's the right time for him to return.

"I don't know if there's ever a right time..."

He was disturbed by that story.

"Why?"

Because that visit to Raventower was never sanctioned by him.

"Doesn't matter. All vampires are evil—whether they're led by a king or not."

That's an unfair generalization. You could say the same for snakes, but I only kill to protect those I love. I crush bones with my powerful body, but I love to cuddle in front of the fire while someone reads to me.

My smile was uncontrollable.

I'm sorry about what happened to your father.

"Thanks..."

He would like to return. Wants to know if the moment is right.

"I've never had that kind of power before."

As I said, he respects you.

"I guess." I couldn't avoid him forever.

He's coming.

My heart started to race as the nerves got to me. I didn't fear him, but my body tightened like it did.

A moment later, he entered the bedchambers, dressed in his black uniform, his eyes immediately locked on mine. It'd been a long time since I'd felt that heavy intensity surround him like a thick cloud, and now it was back. That unbridled desire was hot like a summer breeze, and it wafted right toward me. His eyes drank me in like my appearance was a feast and he'd been starving since the last time he saw me.

I realized then how much I missed that. No other man had ever made me feel so wanted. I swallowed and looked away.

He removed his tunic, showing hard muscle under fair skin, shadows in the lines that segmented the muscles. His shoulders were broad, his chest was powerful, and then his waistline was tight.

I watched all of it from the corner of my eye.

He approached the sitting room, the top part of his pants undone, a thick vein descending from his belly button and out of sight underneath his trousers. He took a seat in the armchair, his body shifted forward with his forearms on his knees, and he stared at me with that same purposeful stare.

How could I feel this intensity for someone like him? Not just a vampire—but the king of the vampires. The night-walkers that fed on my people. The beautiful creatures that stole my father away and killed my mother through devastation. But he was the man I wanted more than any other. Even if I could go back in time and change history so Elias and I could be together...I wouldn't. "Once we find that cure, I'm gone. I'll never return. But for now..."

"You're mine." His desperation intensified, flames in his eyes, desire boiling like a pot on the stove that overflowed at the sides.

His undeniable handsomeness pulled the word from my lips. "Yes."

———

My back hit the bed, his hips slipped between my soft thighs, and then he sank into me with the sexiest groan I'd ever heard. He folded me underneath him, his heavy weight pinning me to the mattress, and with possession in his eyes, he fucked me good and hard.

It was the position he always took me in, with me on my back, like he was more than happy that his job was to do all the fucking, while my job was taking that big dick. He ground his hips and pressed right against me, rubbing me in the magical place that made me writhe.

My palms flattened against his chest as I watched his ripped body tighten and flex as he moved, as he made both of us sweat. Just watching him work so hard to fuck me was a turn-on. He always gave it his all, never took a break, was so enthusiastic to be between my legs that he couldn't help himself.

He was so hot.

And the way he felt...was indescribable. So aroused, he was constantly on the verge of releasing. He wanted to explode the moment he was inside me, but his pride wouldn't allow that, so he gave his best to make me come first.

I did...and it felt so damn good. "Yes..."

He ground his hips harder, rubbing my nub until I was finished, until my hips stopped bucking on their own. His dick was harder than it'd ever been, desperate for its own release.

I didn't want him to wait, not after he'd earned it. "Come inside me..." I grabbed his ass and tugged, wanting that enormous dick deep inside me to catch every last drop.

A vibration moved the air around him, and he suddenly felt on fire. His flames burned all the furniture in the room, burned everything except the two of us. "I'd love to, sweetheart." He closed his eyes briefly, still thrusting inside me, his brow sweaty from all the hard work he'd been doing.

He made his final thrusts, eyes locked on me, and then he finished with a loud groan. He shoved his entire length inside me and ignored the way I winced when it hurt. He kept it there, watched me struggle with the pain, and gave it all to me.

It fucking hurt, but I fucking loved it.

He finally withdrew a few inches but kept most of his length inside me. He was still rock hard, like that fuck was just an appetizer. "I want to feed." He held his face above mine, his eyes demanding his desires.

Despite the sweat all over my body, my blood went cold.

"It'll feel even better."

I knew he wouldn't analyze my blood in that moment. There was too much heat and passion to be objective. This was only for pleasure.

I should have said no, but inexplicably, I nodded.

The glimpse of his fangs was brief before they were impaled in my neck. The initial bite stung, but then the pleasure was surreal. His hips continued to rock into me, much slower now, and my ankles hooked around his waist. My arms locked underneath his shoulders, and I pulled him closer.

It was nothing like the other bites he'd given me. There was no explosive pleasure racing through my veins. It didn't make me slip away in a dreamlike state. He felt even better between my legs, our bodies sliding together in perfect harmony.

He gripped the back of my hair and switched sides.

I released a moan and clawed at his back.

We stayed that way for a while, and then I felt it, an explosion that would burn the sky. My eyes closed, and I felt it pull me away, floating across a powerful tide. I moaned again and again and felt my hips buck against him. His fingers were steady in my hair so my head wouldn't move. He continued to drain me, taking my blood but giving me something better in return.

His hips increased in speed as he brought himself to another climax, his fangs hooked into my skin, feeding and writhing at the same time. When it became too much for him, he withdrew his fangs and finished with a groan, his fingers leaving my messy hair.

I felt the drops of blood slide off my neck to the sheets below.

My eyes locked on his, seeing them deep green, the color of serpent scales. I noticed subtle changes in his body everywhere, strength he didn't have before. Muscles were more prominent, his body tighter.

He moved to the bed beside me and rested with his arm behind his neck. The shine of sweat was still visible on his skin, but he breathed normally, like he was no longer winded. He stared at the ceiling.

The high from his bite slowly dissipated. It brought me intense pleasure, but it also produced an effect so calming it was hard to care about anything. I lay there with lidded eyes, more comfortable than I'd ever been. Without thinking, I turned over and rested my head in the crook of his arm as I slid my arm around his waist.

He turned his head slightly to look at me before he pulled up the sheets to my shoulder to keep me warm.

I closed my eyes and immediately fell asleep.

———

I woke up in the same position as when I fell asleep, cuddled into his side like a lover. Repulsed by the affection, I sat up and moved away.

"That was all you, sweetheart."

I turned the other way and ignored him.

His weight suddenly pressed into me as he pinned my stomach to the mattress. His fat dick pressed between my cheeks, and his lips came to my ear. "Say you want me." He shifted his weight, and then he pressed his dick to my entrance, pushing past the lips to find the slickness. He didn't go further, choosing to hover there, taunting me.

With what little defiance I had, I said nothing.

He slid inside me, forcing me to draw breath. His mood suddenly leaped to its full height, his desire hotter than the burning sun. He wanted me to want him, but my defiance was one of his turn-ons.

"No."

He suddenly bit me, piercing my flesh with his fangs.

And that was the moment I was lost. All the addictive chemicals dumped into my blood and charred me with his fire. My legs separated slightly, and I sang the words he wanted to hear. "I want you..."

He pulled his mouth away, his fangs dripping with my blood, and fucked me so hard I had to hold myself steady with my hand pressed to the headboard. My body shook with his speed, and the friction of the sheets against my clit only added to the effect. In an embarrassingly brief amount of time, I came with tears, saying his name so many goddamn times. "Fuck, Kingsnake..."

He finished then remained on top of me, keeping me pinned in place. "Don't pull away from me again." He climbed off me then got to his feet beside the bed. He ran his fingers through his hair, his chest shiny with sweat, his dick still big even when it was spent.

I tried not to stare.

"Would you like to go on a ride today?"

I did a double take. "What?"

"You've been cooped up in here for a while."

I was surprised he cared. "I would love to."

"Then I'll be back to fetch you in an hour. Be ready."

26

LARISA

It was one of the rare times when I saw Kingsnake in something other than his uniform and armor—except when he was naked. We took the secret path underneath the floorboards to the outside of Grayson, where his black stallion waited for us.

"What about Fang?"

"Fang needs his space."

"He said that?"

He took the reins of the horse then climbed into the saddle. "Can you blame him? With all the stuff he hears..."

My cheeks tinted red. I hadn't even thought of that. Fang was in the very next room, hanging in his tree, listening to our dirty talk.

Kingsnake extended his hand.

I ignored the gesture and climbed up myself. I sat in the saddle behind him and immediately hooked my arms around his waist. It reminded me of our journey here, when we hated each other in a different way.

Kingsnake dug in his heels and directed the horse at a run.

It was as terrifying as it was last time, but I held on and didn't issue a complaint.

He left the city of Grayson and ventured into the mountains, taking a well-beaten path up the hillside and past the mighty oak trees. After an hour of solid riding, we reached the top of a mountain, a meadow of flowers in the direct sunshine, the world a picturesque image of spring.

I climbed off the horse then walked through the field, the sunshine directly on my face, the warmth moving through my clothes to my bare skin. I closed my eyes and enjoyed it —until the thought struck me.

I turned around and saw him walk the horse to the shade of a tree, totally exposed to the sunlight and unaffected by it. He secured the horse to a tree branch but left enough room to graze and drink from the water Kingsnake provided.

I continued to stare, utterly bewildered by his exposure.

He opened one of the bags attached to the saddle and pulled out a small basket before he set it on the grass. At the edge of the cliff was a stunning view of the ocean, high above the cloud bank, away from the mist that cooled my skin.

He took a seat in the shade of the tree, arms on his knees, wearing a short-sleeved shirt and pants. He stared at the ocean for a while before he met my perplexed look.

I sat beside him. "I thought you couldn't be exposed to sunlight."

"That was your assumption."

"But you only travel at night...and avoid daylight."

"That's true, but that doesn't mean I can't tolerate it." He looked out at the ocean again. "Because they only see us in the darkness, humans assume daylight will kill us. The truth is, there's only so much sunlight we can tolerate over our lifetimes, and once we reach that threshold, we'll perish."

"What's the threshold?"

"No one really knows. But our theory is light sensitivity. The more sensitive you become to it, the closer you are to overexposure. This tree is blocking a good portion of it, but not all of it entirely, so I can feel a subtle burn on my skin."

"We didn't have to come up here today."

"I knew you needed a break from your captivity. And when I was alive, I used to enjoy being outside...feeling the sun beat down on my face during a long ride." He looked at the ocean, squinting slightly because the rays were still powerful, even in the shade.

I could feel the sun on my back, and it felt divine. "Is that something you miss?"

He didn't answer for a long time. "I don't miss a lot of things...but I do miss that."

"What was your life like? Where did you live?"

"My family had farmland outside the Northern Kingdom. I built my own home from the ground up. We grew crops, raised livestock, nothing glamorous."

I tried to picture him covered in dirt from a hard day's work, and I couldn't do it. The only version of him I could accept was King of Vampires, in his uniform, his sword at his hip, power radiating from his eyes. "What happened to your mother?"

After a pause, he looked at me again. "Why do you assume anything happened to her?"

"You said your father and brothers still live. Never mentioned your mother."

He gave a slight nod. "It's a sad story."

I didn't press for more, assuming he'd shut down the question.

"My father had taken us to the Northern Kingdom to sell our harvest. She was home there alone, but we knew she could handle herself. But these raiders were no ordinary men. Not only did they take all our coin and valuables, but...they did terrible things to her...and then burned her alive."

I gave a quiet gasp, unable to believe anyone would be capable of something so heinous.

"We pleaded with the king to catch these raiders, because we weren't the only farmhouse they hit. But nothing was ever done. My father was never the same after he lost my mother. Never recovered from the guilt of leaving her behind."

"I'm so sorry..."

He turned quiet, his expression hard like always, showing nothing.

But underneath...I could feel it. Sorrow. It was the first time I'd sensed the emotion from him. It was a black shoreline in darkness, the waves low because they felt too defeated to rise. Eternal emptiness.

"We tried to find the raiders ourselves, but years passed with no vengeance. My father started to become weary in his older age, and he feared he would be too weak to challenge them. And that's how he became an Original."

"He's one of the Original vampires...?"

"He *is* the Original." He turned to look at me. "The very first. We were created later, becoming a later generation."

"Did you ever find the raiders?"

"We did—eventually."

"And?"

"Once we were done with them, we burned them alive."

Their death wouldn't return his mother, but it was still necessary. "Good."

We turned quiet and sat in comfortable silence, the warm breeze moving through our hair, the shadows slowly shifting as the sun floated across the sky.

"Is Viper one of your brothers?" I asked suddenly, making the connection at that moment.

"Yes."

"I see your relation. You have another?"

"Cobra."

"So...is he with the Cobra Vampires?"

"Correct."

"Is that who you went to see when we traveled?"

"Yes."

"You can't send a raven?"

"Cobra is the kind of man you meet face-to-face."

"You guys aren't close?"

He didn't say anything for a while. "We have different ideologies."

"Meaning?"

"We're civil to each other because of our bloodlines, but we despise each other in almost every other way."

"That's too bad."

"It's inevitable. You claim that Kingsnake Vampires are barbaric and you detest us with every fiber of your being, but if you met the Cobra Vampires, you would think of us as saints—and you would appreciate us as your neighbors."

"Why?"

He looked at me. "Are you sure you want to know?"

"I think so..."

"Their kingdom is a fortress in the mountains. It's impenetrable from the outside, but internally, it has valleys and rivers. Within their domain, they have an entire civilization of humans living there, who live ordinary lives farming and sewing...but their true purpose is to feed them. There's no escape, not unless they run directly through the mountain, which is full of vampires. You can imagine what happens to those who try."

It was so horrific it left me speechless.

"Now I'm not so bad, am I?"

I looked down at the long stalks of grass beneath me, the bright-green color reminding me of summer. Those people were born in those mountains...and they died in those mountains. They never knew life outside. Had no idea how big the world truly was. "And you just let this happen?"

"Do I look like a martyr to you?"

"Well, you can't say you're better than them if you know their crimes but do nothing about it."

He gave a slight shake of his head. "I won't intervene."

"Why not?"

"Because it'll make everything worse."

"How?"

"If I take away their food source, what do you think they'll do?"

I stared.

"They'll find food somewhere else—like Raventower. They'll come in the night and kill everyone. Your entire village would be wiped out overnight. Is that what you'd prefer?"

I looked away.

"You fix one problem but create another."

"This is why I hate vampires," I said under my breath.

He clearly heard me because his eyes narrowed in a hostile way.

"If you didn't have to eat innocent people, it wouldn't be an issue. Werewolves are bad, but they keep to themselves in the mountains. You don't bother them, they don't bother you. You can peacefully coexist. But you can't coexist with vampires."

"You can't coexist with the Ethereal either."

"Well, they haven't bothered us once, so..."

"Other than poisoning all of you," he snapped.

"You don't have proof—"

"You think this sickness just came out of nowhere? It's unprecedented. Never in our history has any kind of illness affected huge chunks of the human population. There is no other explanation."

"Unless you guys did it..."

"To what benefit?" he demanded. "Why would we poison the water we drink? You just don't want to admit the truth because you can't handle a scenario where your gods are actually evil."

I looked away.

"Let me enlighten you. Anyone with power is evil. You can't have one without the other."

I continued to avoid his stare. "Why do you care if I hate you? Once we find a solution to our problem, I go back to my life, and you go back to yours."

He remained silent.

We sat there together, neither one of us wanting to be there. It was no longer comfortable, just tense.

"If your mother and father are both gone, what's waiting for you there?"

The question made me turn back.

"A man?" His eyes were green, pumped with my blood, his body tighter than it'd been before. Whether his eyes were green or brown, they were beautiful, but the green made him look far more intense.

"No."

"Then what's the point?"

"For one, I'll be surrounded by people who don't want to eat me. And two, I could help repair our community and serve the royal family."

"Serve the royal family?" he snapped. "Let's get something straight—you don't serve anybody."

My eyes narrowed.

"A king serves his people—not the other way around. I would give my life for my kin, not hide in my castle while my people collapsed on the streets. King Elias is a joke, just like all his forefathers. Your respect is misplaced."

"You met him one time—"

"And he handed over his people without a fight. You think I would have allowed that to happen? I would have unsheathed my blade and shed my own blood for my people. He just rolled over like a dog."

"You're a vampire. He had no chance—"

"Doesn't matter."

"He never wanted to be king..."

Now his eyes narrowed. "And you know this, how?"

Flashbacks moved across my mind, the two of us sneaking through the guest rooms that no one ever used, sticking to the shadows as we continued a love affair that would get me exiled from Raventower if I were ever found. But I didn't reveal that to Kingsnake. "I used to be a maid in the castle."

His eyes were locked on my face. They didn't shift back and forth. He didn't take a break.

My cheeks suddenly felt hot from his stare. As if the words were written all over my face, I felt like he could read my story, could feel my emotions the way I felt his. When his stare became too much, I looked away, afraid he would discover my secret if he stared any longer.

Fire and wind combined together, making a storm that blew the world to pieces then set it ablaze. Anger so searing it was hot just to sense burned my skin. I felt like branded cattle, but the burn was over every inch of me. Anger so powerful, so terrifying, exploded throughout his body.

And I was actually scared.

It was a force that could destroy the entire world, and it was directed right at me.

He got to his feet and approached the horse. "We should head back." His voice was as calm as quiet raindrops, a direct contradiction to how he felt inside.

I turned to look at him, seeing him untie the horse from the tree, his face hard but not unusually so. "Why are you angry?"

He got the horse free then climbed into the saddle, still in the shade of the oak. "I'm not angry." He looked at me with an expression that gave nothing away, but the storm still raged within him like the apocalypse.

"Yes, you are." I should shut my mouth, but I couldn't help it. He replied calmly, but the forest fire that burned all around him said otherwise. It was intolerable, and I missed the intensity of his desire, the way he made me feel like the only woman who could turn his head.

He stared at me with narrowed eyes and a furrowed brow. He kept up his stare, like he was reading me just as he had a moment ago.

I forced myself to say something else to cover my tracks, in case he drew the conclusion that I feared, the secret I would take to the grave. "I can see it on your face..."

His anger disappeared instantly, leaving nothing but ash and soot behind.

Now there was nothing—and I feared what that meant.

He extended his hand. "Let's go."

———

Once I was on the back of that horse, he didn't say a word to me. We rode back to Grayson, the light slowly fading as the end of the day drew near. We returned the way we'd come, through the hidden tunnel, and one of his men took the horse back to the stables. When we were back in the palace, Kingsnake took the lead as he entered the bedchambers we shared.

His hands reached behind his back and tugged his shirt over his head, revealing a sculpted back with hard muscles. He tossed the shirt aside then kicked off his boots as he loosened his pants.

I decided to drop the previous subject, and based on his quiet mood, it seemed he had dropped it too.

Just when I passed him, my body jolted forward and hit the bed. I caught myself on my palms and bounced slightly on the mattress, releasing a quiet gasp because of the shock. When I finally looked over my shoulder, I saw him at the foot of the bed. With a maniacal look in his eyes, he tugged my bottoms right over my hips and ass.

The instant our eyes locked, the intensity began, a viciousness that filled the air. His eyes had a possessive gleam that looked utterly terrifying. I didn't get a chance to look any longer because he grabbed me by the back of the hair and jerked my head back, making my eyes face the ceiling and my back arch deeper.

Then I felt his massive dick slam into me without invitation. It was the entire thing, making me wince in pain, which was very much the point. My face started to lower as I winced between my clenched teeth, but he yanked me back again, like I was a goddamn horse.

He let his dick sit, let it hurt, observed me wince and whine before he pulled out and started his thrusts. Each one was deep and hard. Each one was vicious. Each one made me want to come and scream at the same time.

"Has anyone ever fucked you like this?"

My entire body shook, he thrust so hard. I was stuck in the same contorted position because of the grip on my hair, and my lower back ached from the arch. But it felt so good, so damn good that I didn't even feel like myself anymore.

"Answer me." He somehow picked up the speed and fucked me even harder.

I wasn't even aroused a moment ago, but now I was already on the verge. I was so damn close, and if I didn't obey, he would take it away. "Just you..."

He propped his foot on the bed beside me and deepened the angle before he shoved my face into the bed, making my ass pop into the air. He gave me his entire length over and over, grunting as he smashed my pussy.

I came with a wince, tears pouring from my eyes and soaking into the sheets.

"Damn right." He finished with a heavy groan, dumped all his essence inside me, and then he abruptly pulled out as quickly as he'd entered.

I lay there, exhausted even though I hadn't moved.

He left my body and got dressed.

I pushed myself up then sat at the edge of the bed.

He dressed in a hurry, clearly desperate to leave as quickly as possible.

I wasn't sure what made me say it, but the words came out. "What about Ellasara?"

He froze on the spot, his eyes locked on mine. Several breaths passed, and he stared without saying a word. The anger that had been there previously resumed, so his emotions were difficult to gauge.

He stormed out—and slammed the door behind him.

27

KINGSNAKE

I'd fallen asleep in my study, a glass of booze in my hand, so when Viper threw the door open, I jerked awake and spilled it all over my pant leg. "Fuck." I tossed the glass on the desk, where it rolled until it dropped on the other side and hit the rug. Then I shook out the drops on my hand and wrist. "Don't you knock?"

Viper entered the room, pale as snow. "The Ethereal approach our borders."

I turned still, shocked by this news. "How close?"

"Just a few leagues from the northern gate."

"How did the scouts not see their army much farther away?" I was on my feet now, the spilled scotch forgotten.

"Because there're only three of them."

I stilled at the revelation, finding that more sinister. My mind raced like a hawk in the sky, searching for the answer to this mystery. It didn't take long to figure it out. "They're here for Larisa."

"They're not here for war, clearly."

"Because they're here to negotiate."

Viper locked his hands together behind his back, in full general mode. "How would they know about Larisa?"

"Everyone in Raventower knew about her. It's not surprising."

Viper's eyes shifted back and forth between mine. "She's the answer to our salvation. It's no wonder they want her back. But what could they possibly offer in return?"

I didn't need to think twice. "Threats."

We faced each other for a solid minute in silence.

"This could also be a diversion," Viper said. "To draw you to the front—"

"So someone can slip in behind and take her."

"Exactly."

We stared at each other again.

"Then she'll join us at the gate," I said.

"You think that's wise? She'll be within their grasp."

"They can't take something directly from me. I made the mistake of leaving her behind when we spoke to Cobra—"

"Your mistake was not trusting me." His face tinted slightly, the anger at the surface.

There were no words to speak. She'd almost died that night, and I was the only one to blame. "An error on my part."

His color intensified further.

"I'll retrieve Larisa. Meet me at the gate."

He gave a nod before he departed, his cloak sweeping behind him.

I returned to the bedchambers, finding Larisa dead asleep under the sheets. I yanked the bedding off her naked body. "Up."

She groaned and reached for the sheets again, eyes still closed.

"I said, up."

Her eyes finally popped open with rage. "It's the middle of the night—"

"Put on your armor."

The order made her still, because there was only one reason to wear it. "What's happening?"

"Just put it on."

Fang slithered across the floor toward me. ***What'sss happened?***

A few Ethereal approach our gate.

What do they want?

No idea.

Bastardssss.

Larisa finally left the bed and dressed, wide awake now that she prepared for danger. She'd looked thoroughly fucked just minutes ago, but now she was dressed like a soldier with her hair pinned back, her sword at her hip.

I preferred her naked, but I liked her this way too.

"Are we under attack?" She kept her voice steady, but her eyes showed her fear.

"I would never let anything happen to you, sweetheart."

She forced her eyes to harden, to cover up all traces of unease. "What's happening?"

"The Ethereal are about to approach our gate."

Her eyes widened at the revelation.

"There're only three of them. No army. But I know the reason for their visit."

"What?"

"You."

She swallowed.

"I made the mistake of leaving you behind last time. I won't do that again."

"Why would they want me?" she asked quietly.

"Because you're the ticket to our salvation. If they take that away—we have no chance. I fear they've dispatched men into the city to extract you while I'm distracted, but they can't take you if you're at my side."

All she did was stare, like she needed time to understand the words.

"What do you fear?"

"I've never seen them in the flesh..."

"You've handled werewolves, orcs, and vampires. This is nothing."

"But they're gods..."

Not to me. "Come." I led the way, leaving the palace and moving through the city. It was the darkest part of the night, the stars and constellations bright overhead, the moonlight a glowing shadow. Braziers lit up the path toward the gate, the three of us approaching the border.

No one spoke.

We reached the gate, the braziers casting so much light that it nearly felt like midday. Viper was already there, along with a few of his best commanders. Archers were positioned on the walls, the strings of their bows nocked with arrows.

Viper gestured to the men above, and the gates swung open.

Three cloaked figures stood there, their blue satin hoods covering their heads. Tiny stars were woven into the fabric, made of real gold so they sparkled even in the absence of light. Together, they dropped their hoods, elegantly pulling them back to reveal fair faces. A woman was in the center, flanked by two men.

I recognized her immediately.

Ellasara.

Her eyes were blue like a shallow ocean, but possessed the unknown depths of ancient seas. Her pale cheeks were so fair they were nearly translucent, like a fresh batch of snow that had already begun to melt. Like her companions, she had a soft confidence to her expression, like this moment was insignificant when she knew all the mysteries of this world.

We stared at each other a long time, both of us thinking about the exact same thing.

She finally moved forward and approached, indifferent to the arrows trained on her neck, and stepped farther into the light.

Viper stayed back with Larisa and his men.

Fang quickly climbed up my body, circling one leg and then my torso before curling around both of my arms and propping himself on my shoulder. He was a heavy snake, but his weight was a small burden in comparison to his protection.

Ellasara stopped a few feet away, her eyes still locked on my face. Her cloak fell open slightly, revealing white armor that was so smooth it had to have been sanded for a thousand years. It deflected oncoming blades, making them slide off like a stream of water. It was understated, close to their bodies and not bulky like ours. They were too vain not to care more about protection than looks.

The stare continued, both of us refusing to speak first.

Most arrogant creatures...

Yes.

Finally, after a lifetime, she spoke. "Kingsnake." It was the same way she'd always said my name, with underlying affection.

It was a spell—but it had lost its potency a long time ago. "Why have you come to my lands uninvited?"

A glimmer of a smile moved across her soft lips. "No pleasantries, then..."

"There's nothing pleasant about you."

The corners of her lips raised farther. "You're still angry."

"Don't flatter yourself. I'm always angry."

Her lips slowly deflated.

"Answer my question. Why have you come?"

"Surely you can offer better hospitality than this—"

"I offer no kindness to my enemies. State your purpose here or leave."

A knowing smile moved across her lips as she glanced behind me, probably looking at Viper. "Very well." She looked at me again. "It's come to the attention of King Elrohir that you have a bit of an anomaly on your hands..."

Larissssssa.

Yes.

She stared at me, as if expecting me to confirm or deny it.

"Taken from Raventower, she's rumored to be the only human immune to this terrible disease..." Her blond hair shone without sunshine, so smooth there wasn't a single misplaced hair. Their entire race possessed a glow, and I could see that brightness in her skin.

"A disease you released into the world."

She had no reaction at all, as if she wasn't the least bit surprised I'd figured it out. "That's quite the accusation."

"Why else would you want her?"

"So, she is here?"

My eyes remained steady. "Whether I have her in my possession or not, I would never tell you. I'm sorry this very long journey was made in vain, but it's time for you to depart these lands and never return."

Ellasara didn't move. Didn't blink. Her stare deepened, her thoughts sharp like the edge of a blade. "You should always hear an offer before you deny it."

"Not in this case."

"Kingsnake, I know you." Her tone deepened, her impatience heavy. "I know what you crave above all else is power—"

"And power is what I have. Here I stand, denying the most benevolent race what their heart truly desires. Feels pretty damn good." I despised every single one of them, two-faced liars, making everyone believe they were good simply because they glowed like sunlight.

"What if I could give you more?"

I decided to let her make her offer. Once I rejected it, the conversation would end.

"My king has offered to make you an Ethereal, a true immortal. You would be one of us, live in our city, guaranteed to live forever without the taste of blood in your mouth. And if you so choose, you can pass on to the vault of souls."

My expression didn't change.

Her eyes shifted back and forth between mine, in anticipation of my excitement.

"If you think I would damn my people for my own self-preservation, you don't know me at all."

"*Hiiiisssssssss.*" Fang exposed his sharp fangs.

The shine started to fade from her eyes.

"I am a true immortal—and I like the taste of blood."

"Kingsnake—"

"I'd rather lose my eternal soul alongside my people than live a million lifetimes with assholes like you." I turned away.

"If you don't give her to us, there will be consequences."

I turned back around and gave her a bored look. "We've been at war with the Ethereal for centuries. This is an old threat."

"Kingsnake...you won't survive this."

I stared at her.

She stared back. "It would be wise to take my offer."

I walked back to her and got right in her face. "It would be wise to return to Evanguard and tell King Elrohir that I look forward to cutting his head clean from his shoulders in battle."

———

"Leave us." Viper and his commanders stood in the war room, but my brother was the only one in which I wished to confide. Wordlessly, they filed out of the room, and then Viper and I were alone.

Larisa and Fang had returned to my bedchambers, the windows cracked so Fang could hear every minute noise that lurked outside. Guards were posted at the doors and on the balcony, just in case the Ethereal had slipped an agent behind our borders. Cobra was successful because their kind was nearly indistinguishable from ours, but an elf would have a much harder time.

Viper dropped into one of the armchairs.

"I denied her request—and she threatened me with war."

"We've been at war." He wouldn't drop his posture, not even when he sat, so his back was rigid and straight.

"She said we won't survive it."

"We've survived their onslaught for centuries."

I stood at the table, looking at a map that was useless for the situation. "Could be an empty threat. Could be something worse. We'll find out soon enough."

"She admitted they released the sickness?"

"Indirectly."

Viper curled his fingers underneath his jaw as he propped his elbow on the armrest. "What do they want with Larisa?"

"They didn't say, but it's obvious."

"Our annihilation?"

I nodded. "She offered me the chance to be a *true immortal*." I rolled my eyes before I grabbed a drink from the bar. "Because they're so fucking righteous..." I took a sip then sat in the chair across from him. "We're just blood-sucking monsters. Well, I love being a monster, so there's that..."

Viper remained quiet.

I drank in silence, pissed off that I'd had to look at her face for several minutes. What I once found beautiful was now fucking obnoxious. The arrogance in her eyes. The preten-tiousness. The fucking bullshit.

"We need to find a cure—quickly."

I continued to drink.

"Not only will we be stronger—but we'll have more allies."

I avoided his gaze, staring at a spot on the wall.

"Kingsnake?"

I ignored his request as long as I could before I met his gaze.

"You can't identify the elements in her blood, can you?"

My hand covered my glass as it sat on the armrest.

Viper continued his piercing stare. "Kingsnake."

"It's the contrary, actually..."

Viper's stare continued like he didn't quite understand, and then he stiffened and dropped his hand from his jaw. "State your meaning."

"I know exactly why she's immune. I've known for a while."

"Then why haven't you said anything?"

"Because it's complicated."

His eyes narrowed.

"It's complicated because...I made her a promise...and now I have to break it."

Viper continued to stare, rendered speechless.

"I said I would let her go...but now I can't. Not when her blood makes me more powerful than I've ever been. Not when her blood can strengthen our armies against the Ethereal. Not when...she can read minds."

His face contorted in surprise. "What did you say?"

"I thought my suspicions were misplaced, but now I'm certain."

"That's not possible—"

"It is for her."

Viper inhaled a deep breath, his jaw tight with tension.

"She can talk to Fang."

"How? Fang told you this?"

"No, but it's the only explanation."

"Explanation for what?"

"She knew about Ellasara before she arrived in Grayson today—and I know you didn't tell her."

"No, I didn't. But Fang wouldn't betray you either."

"His affection for her runs deep."

Viper took a moment to absorb all of this. "Do you think she'd want to leave? The two of you have become...close. Perhaps she'd want to serve you and our people. Perhaps this is home to her now."

"No." I knew exactly how she felt. "She loathes our kind—including me."

28

LARISA

When Kingsnake returned, the guards abandoned their posts. The windows were closed, and Fang slithered to his branch in the other room.

I hadn't removed my armor, just in case.

He hardly looked at me as he unclasped his cloak and began the arduous process of removing every piece of protection from his body. He was careless with everything else in his life, but when it came to the plates of metal that protected his body, he was delicate with each and every piece. There was a special place in his closet where he placed everything, keeping it clean and safe from scuffs.

I watched him strip down to nothing but his black boxers, his chiseled body beautiful in the limited light, the shadow under his jawline more pronounced. His eyes looked tired, like a single evening had sucked all his energy. They were still green—but also empty.

He moved to his side of the bed and continued to ignore me.

He gave me no information so I dug for answers. "What happened?"

"The Ethereal wanted to take you—and I said no."

"Why?"

"Why did they want to take you? Or why did I say no? I think the second one is obvious."

"The first."

"Their explanation wasn't explicit, but it's to ensure there's no cure for this sickness."

"So...they admitted it was them?"

His back was to me as he spoke. "They never admitted it directly, but it was implied."

My heart sank. The people I worshipped as gods had damned us all. "They just accepted your answer and left?"

"No, there were threats. Lots of threats."

"What kinds of threats?"

"Veiled and implied." He lay against the headboard, one arm propped on his knee.

"You really think they would start a war over me?"

"Absolutely." He turned his head and looked at me head on. "But that's not your problem, so don't worry about it."

"All of this is my problem."

He stared, his green eyes still and focused, just the way Fang's were when he stared at me. The look was strange, heavy with tension, and it took me a moment to realize why.

Because he was empty.

I didn't feel anger or intensity. I didn't feel anything from him at all, and that was rare. After such an intense conversation, there should be a firestorm surrounding him, but it was just crickets.

I didn't like it. "We need to find a cure. Once we do, the Ethereal will no longer want me. Humankind will be saved. It's the best solution."

His eyes hadn't left my face. "I agree."

"Then you need to hurry..."

The corner of his lip rose in a smile, but his eyes retained their depth. A line like that should be accompanied by a flurry of desire, but there was still emptiness. "Would you like me to start now?"

I hoped the question was rhetorical, so I looked away.

He didn't press it.

We sat in silence. The room was quiet, the fire in the hearth the only noise. It was one of the rare times when my mind was empty, when it was utterly silent. I liked it when I was alone, but now that I wasn't, it forced me to realize... how uncomfortable it made me. When I knew the intentions of everyone around me, that made me feel safe.

This was the first time I truly felt afraid.

I left the bed and stepped into the closet, taking my time removing every piece of armor, thinking about the sudden change in his aura. Was it a brief drought? Or...did he know?

Not possible.

I was the only of my kind... He couldn't suspect it.

Unless I had been too careless?

When the armor and the uniform were gone, I returned to the bedroom.

He was still propped against the headboard exactly where I'd left him, and his eyes immediately shifted to my face when I returned to the room. They stayed green like the leaves in a lush forest. His chiseled jawline hardened, and his eyes suddenly looked cloudy with an oncoming storm.

Then I felt it—lightning on the horizon.

It was subtle and quiet, a nascent fire that needed more fuel, but it was there. Distinct.

I approached the edge of the bed, feeling his eyes following me, feeling them dig into my flesh. My fingers reached for the bottom of my shirt, and I slowly pulled it over my head, my strands of hair getting caught in it briefly before they fell back to my shoulders.

The fuel had been added—and the fire burned hotter.

My thumbs hooked into my panties, and I slowly pulled them down my hips, showing more skin until my sex was revealed.

Now those flames were a bonfire.

I stepped out of the panties then crawled up the bed, slowly moving toward him, seeing his eyes deepen in intensity. It was almost morning, and just last night, he'd taken me at the edge of the bed like a whore, but now we regarded each other with hunger, on the threshold of starvation.

When I reached him, my lips slowly pressed to his, a gentle landing, a toe in the water.

His eyes remained open, watching me watch him.

Then I kissed him again, parting his lips with mine, forcing my tongue into his mouth.

He unleashed an angry moan before his hand slipped into my hair.

That bonfire was now a forest fire, the kind that destroyed everything down to the soil. His intensity rivaled lightning strikes that scorched the earth. His fingers went between my legs and landed on my clit, dragging the pads of his fingers right over the sensitive skin.

I climbed into his lap and straddled his hips. I was barely situated when his hands grabbed my ass and forced me down, forced me to sheathe his big dick down to his balls. When he was turned on like this, he looked angry, every muscle in his face contracted, veins popping from his temple and his neck. He enveloped me in a blanket of possession and desire, keeping me warm from a winter storm.

His hands gripped my ass, and he lifted me up before he dragged me down again, releasing a heavy breath full of pleasure. His hands shook slightly as his fingers kneaded my ass, the desire too much for this man to contain. "You win, sweetheart." His hand dug deep into my hair before he tugged my head back with his grip. His fangs pierced my neck, and the blood immediately dripped down my chest and stomach.

I rocked my hips slowly as I gasped, having his dick so deep inside me and his bite in my flesh. The pain was gone instantly, and then I was swept away in a fog of intense pleasure unlike any I'd ever felt before.

————

When I opened my eyes, I wasn't alone in an empty bed.

His chest was my pillow, and his arm was my blanket. My hand rose and fell with his breaths. It took me a moment to digest my reality, to understand this wasn't a dream or a hoax. I snuggled with the King of Vampires—and I liked it.

I lifted my eyes and felt his stare.

"Not gonna run this time?"

I stared at my hand where it rested on his chest, rising and falling.

"Good." He rolled me onto my back as he moved with me, his thighs separating mine as he prepared my body to take his. He grabbed one of my legs and bent it, planting my foot right against his stomach as he gripped the ankle. Then he slid inside me, making himself right at home like he owned the place.

Like he owned me.

I moaned because it felt so damn good, especially when I was still half asleep. My hands reached for him, my fingers wrapping around his tight forearms, feeling veins as they pressed through the skin.

His hand went to my neck and squeezed.

My fingers dug deeper into his skin but didn't try to pull him free.

He had me bent the way he liked, my life literally in his hands, his dick erasing the memory of every man who had come before. His desire wrapped around us like a cloud of smoke that was harsh on my lungs. Without saying a word, he made his message very clear—that he was a very possessive man—and I was his possession.

———

I'd fallen back asleep at some point, because this man took everything out of me. When I woke up again, he was dressed in his armor with his sword at his hip like he had somewhere to be.

I sat up and swallowed my disappointment.

He stared at me, his eyes slightly irritated.

"What?"

"Get dressed."

"What's the occasion?" I looked at the window, seeing the light come through the curtains to tell me it was midday.

"I'm going to train you."

"Train me how?"

"In the sword."

Both of my eyebrows rose. "Really?"

He nodded toward the closet, where my armor was kept.

I was so excited I didn't ask more questions. I hopped out of bed and got ready, and we left the palace, leaving through the secret tunnel to the wildlands outside of Grayson. Fang stayed behind, making it just the two of us.

It was overcast and fog was everywhere, but the air smelled fresh and the mountains were beautiful as they stood over the fogbank.

Kingsnake unsheathed his sword and faced me in his defensive stance, ready for me to strike.

I just stood there. "Should we use real swords for this?"

"I won't hurt you."

"Well, I'm worried about hurting you..."

The corner of his lip tugged in a smile—and it tugged at my heart. "Your concern is misplaced, sweetheart."

"Why are you teaching me this? Is there something I should be worried about...?"

He spun the sword around his wrist, the dark steel giving a quick flash. "You've shown your potential. Now I think it's time we cultivate that into a skill."

"Okay...that didn't really answer the question."

He stilled, that typical annoyance in his eyes. "The Ethereal want you dead. Is that reason enough?"

I didn't grab my sword, leaving it at my hip.

"Should you come face-to-face with an adversary, I want you to kill them."

"What if it's a vampire?"

His eyes narrowed. "I don't care who it is. If someone wishes you harm, you cut them down. In the unlikely event that I'm not around to protect you, you need to protect yourself."

"But if we have our cure soon, what does it matter?" No one would want me dead. I would mean nothing to the Ethereal. Nothing to anyone.

He held the sword at his side, and the look on his face suggested I wouldn't be getting an answer to my question.

"Unless...you care about me." I didn't know what drove me to make the suggestion. It sounded ludicrous the second it left my lips.

"A long life has blessed me with exceptional swordsmanship. Instead of questioning my motive, take advantage of this opportunity to learn from one of the greatest swordsmen who walks this earth." He spun his sword again. "Unsheathe your blade and come for me." He beckoned me with his fingers.

"That's your instruction? Just go for it?"

"Experience is the best teacher."

"Alright..." I unsheathed my blade, stared him down for a moment, and then tried to strike him on the right.

His blade moved quicker than I could see. Steel hit steel. He pushed me back then beckoned me again.

"Feedback?"

"Try again."

I sighed then progressed, aiming for his right arm.

Again, he was so fast it was all a blur.

"In case you haven't noticed...this isn't going too well."

A subtle smile moved on to his lips. "Then do better."

"You're so fucking fast. How are you this fast?"

"You."

I lowered my sword to my side.

He gave me a glimpse of his fangs before they disappeared again.

"Then can we practice when you aren't high on my blood?"

"That time will never come."

I continued to grip my sword. "What's that supposed to mean?"

"I'm as addicted to you as you are to me, sweetheart." He came for me this time, swinging his sword at a much slower speed than before.

I was forced to block his attack and then the next one, shuffling backward all the while, just trying to keep my head above water.

He finally stopped. "You have to hold your guard."

"How am I supposed to do that when you're about to chop off my head?"

"Like this. Come at me."

In my frustration, I threw down my blade with more speed. His blade met my attacks, and every time his sword hit mine, he pushed, forcing me back when he was the one under attack.

"You have to force the blade back. Otherwise, they'll corral you right where they want you. Try again."

We spent the next hour going back and forth, his supreme talent humbling mine. He was fast and agile, anticipating my attacks before I made them, like he had the ability to read minds. He never gave me an opportunity to do any damage. Basically, he just kicked my ass over and over.

I stepped back, out of breath, completely discouraged. "You want to tone it down a bit?"

He stood there with his sword in hand, not the least bit tired. "No."

I reached for my pack to grab my water.

"If I go easy on you, you die," he said. "And I thought you were the kind of woman that wanted to be treated like a man—"

"Not on my first day." I moved under the shade of the tree and sat near the big roots that protruded from the base. I drank my water then reached for the snacks he had packed.

He watched me for a bit, clearly disappointed I needed a break. His sword was eventually returned to his hip, and he stood there, his hard face taking in the skyline, a gleam of sweat on his forehead. "I just want you to be prepared for what's coming."

I stopped eating, my eyes shifting back to him. "What's coming?"

His eyes remained on the horizon. "I don't know. But it's big."

———

When we returned to the palace, I rushed into the shower to get all the sweat off my body and out of my hair. The warm water hit me, and my muscles relaxed a little. I was already sore, so I knew tomorrow would be a rough day.

I suddenly felt a breeze of cold air across my ass and back. I looked over my shoulder to see Kingsnake joining me, shutting the door behind him as he squeezed into the small room with me. A foot taller than me, with a chest as strong as armor and tight arms covered in rivers of veins, he looked down at me, coming closer until we were both under the water.

I felt the rush of intensity, the overwhelming desire that had the power to move mountains.

But those weren't his feelings—but mine.

His arm hooked around the small of my back as his fingers gripped the opposite hip. He brought me closer, his green eyes were like small fires. His dick was pressed against my stomach, long and hard. He continued to stare but never kissed me.

I let his intensity wash over me in waves like the water that came from the shower head. I grew more aroused and uncomfortable at the same time, being the object of his affection but without action. All I could do was stand there and wait for this man to kiss me.

"On your knees."

My eyes stayed locked on his.

"I provided you a service this afternoon—and now it's your turn."

"I don't owe you anything."

His expression didn't change, but there was a flutter of disappointment.

"But I would love to..." I slowly lowered myself to my knees on the tile, my hands moving to his thighs for balance.

The arousal that exploded from him was one of the greatest waves I'd ever felt. It was like a hurricane, a tornado, and an earthquake, all mixed together. The surge was so great it felt like electricity between my fingertips. It made me warm everywhere, turned me on more than I'd been the moment I'd watched him step into the shower.

I grasped him by the base then directed him over my flat tongue, sliding him deep inside, deep enough to make it hurt just the way I liked. As I pulled him out, my tongue flicked over his head and tasted his desire before I took him again.

He closed his eyes, and the moan he released was audible over the falling water.

I deep-throated him over and over, and when I needed a moment to breathe, I used my hand over his enormous length, feeling the fat vein that protruded underneath the skin. I squeezed him hard and turned my hand before I put him back in my mouth.

His eyes opened, and his fingers went to my neck, holding my throat as he shifted a little closer, forcing his dick deep into my mouth like he never wanted to leave. He started to thrust his hips, fuck my mouth the way he fucked my pussy, his eyes burning with profound intensity. "You like that, sweetheart?"

I nodded, my mouth full of his cock and unable to speak.

He didn't release my neck, and his speed increased, the pleasure addictive. He gripped me hard and smashed my throat the way he did with my pussy. Tears kept streaking from my eyes, and that spurred him on more. The aggression elevated, the grip on my neck became so firm I could barely breathe, and then he halted with his dick deep in my mouth, dumping his load down my throat.

I was forced to hold my breath and wait for him to finish, listening to him moan as he dug his fingers deeper into my flesh. When he finally withdrew his dick from my throat, I was able to swallow and get everything down. Then I gasped for the air that had been taken from me, his fingers gone from my neck. I composed myself, tears still on my cheeks, my chest heaving with breaths, my knees still on the tile floor.

He grabbed my arm and pulled me to my feet, and I'd barely had the chance to stand straight before his tongue was deep in my mouth. His hand supported the back of my head as he kissed me desperately, like that blow job had just been foreplay. His hand gripped my ass cheek before he gave it a spank, his tongue in my mouth all the while.

My arms had barely made it around his neck to cradle him close when he withdrew and took a knee where I'd been a moment before. He grabbed one of my legs and threw it over his shoulder before he kissed me between the legs.

I hadn't expected it, it all happened so fast, and the moment I felt that warm kiss, my spine shivered. He put that tongue to work and manipulated that clit harder than my own fingers ever did. With heavy pressure, he swirled it and sucked, making my hips rub against his face automatically. My fingers dug into his hair, and I ground against him, watching this hot-as-fuck man kiss me on his knees like it was an honor. "Kingsnake..." I'd been so desperate for release when his dick was in my mouth, his powerful body standing above me, and now I was so close...so close I could feel the tears already.

Then it hit me, my whimpers drowned out by the falling water, my eyesight blurry with fallen tears. My hips ground into his face, and I rolled my head back, writhing in pleasure so exquisite, I feared I would never feel it again.

Searing heat erupted from him, like my climax turned him on the way his had made me wet. He continued to kiss me, now gentler as I came down from my high, his hands supporting my ass because I was slightly off-balance.

He came back to his feet, one powerful arm locking around my back, while his other hand cupped my neck. His fangs unsheathed, and then he leaned in and bit me, his sharp teeth breaking through old marks.

Held in his arms, I let it happen, let him take whatever he wanted from me and even enjoyed it. My arms circled his neck, and my fingers dug into the back of his hair. "Kingsnake..."

29

KINGSNAKE

I sat in my study, a glass of scotch for company. *I wish to speak with you.*

I'm busssy.

Busy?

Larisssa and I are playing cardsss.

Their closeness annoyed me for many reasons. *Get your ass in here, Fang.*

When I'm finished.

I said NOW.

Hiiisssssss.

I won't ask again.

Fang went silent, and I assumed that meant he would obey.

Minutes later, Fang opened the door with his long tail and slithered inside. He climbed up the other armchair and propped himself up, like a person sitting across from me. The anger was in his eyes, a small glimmer. ***Yesssss? I was winning.***

"You always win." We were alone in my study, so I spoke aloud to my closest confidant.

She's getting better.

I sat with my ankle crossed and resting on the other knee, my glass of scotch on the table beside me. "You two have become close."

She's shown her loyalty.

"And you seem to have forgotten yours."

Fang cocked his head slightly, his tongue slipping in and out.

"Why didn't you tell me?"

He remained silent. Just like a person, he searched for a tactful way to navigate the accusation.

"Fang," I pressed.

He decided to speak the truth. ***We both know you're an inherently jealous man.***

"Have I interfered in your relationship?"

His eyes were locked on mine for a long pause. ***No. But only because of your feelings for her.***

"I have no feelings."

Liessssss.

I stared.

The moment she protected me, everything was different. You were different.

I grabbed my glass and took a drink.

I see it. And so does she.

I was outsmarted by a goddamn snake.

I would never betray your trust, Kingsnake.

"Then why did you tell her about Ellasara?"

Fang stilled at the question.

"She asked me about her, and I know she didn't get her information from Viper."

Fang remained quiet, deliberating in his brilliant mind.

I waited.

She asked me if there's ever been an important woman in your life—and I said there had only been one.

I felt my anger start to bubble.

But I shared nothing else. Only her name.

"Even that was too much."

There's no shame in loving someone throughout your long life.

"All I feel is shame."

Kingsnake—

"You had no right to tell her that."

Fang went quiet.

"You betrayed me."

If she cares enough to ask about former lovers, that means this conversation will happen at some point anyway.

"And it's for me to decide what to share when that time comes."

She's asked many other questions, and I've protected your privacy.

"Then why not this one?"

I wanted to give her hope.

"Hope for what?"

***That you're capable of more than what you
show.***

My eyes burned into his, furious that he'd shared something so private. "I'm not capable of those things anymore."

You are—with Larisa.

I shook my head slightly and looked away.

***You can fool yourself, Kingsnake. But you can't
fool me.***

I ignored his words. "She's not to know that I know. You
understand me?"

Fang gave a nod.

"You're dismissed."

I'm dismissssed?

I still wouldn't look at him. "Yes."

You're angry with me.

"Immensely."

He continued to sit there and stare at me.

"I said, you're dismissed."

He continued to linger, waiting for me to look at him.

"That means get out, Fang." I looked at him again, my eyes furious.

He dropped his head slightly then gradually slid from the chair and to the door. He moved slowly, his head dropped with his mood. *I'm sorry…* He paused in front of the opening, like I might say something more.

But I didn't.

———

I entered the bedchambers quietly, Larisa asleep under the covers.

I undressed in the closet then approached the bed in my boxers, the scotch still on my breath and in my veins. Fang wasn't in the bedchambers, so he must have chosen to sleep in a tree somewhere. I pulled the covers back and got into bed.

She stirred at my entrance, her tired eyes opening to look at me beside her. Then she pressed up against me, wrapped her arm around my torso, and that was when I realized she was buck naked. Her plump tits pressed against me, her skin warm to the touch. She started to tug on me, wanting me to roll over on top of her.

I was hard at the invitation, loving the sleepy look in her eyes, the way she went to bed naked because she wanted me the moment I joined her, regardless of the time. My body moved on top of hers, my thighs separating hers before I hooked an arm behind one of her knees. I had her folded underneath me, her head on the pillow, and then I entered her, my length immediately smeared with the wetness waiting for me.

Fuck.

Her hands planted on my chest, her nails pressing into my flesh.

Every time I felt her, I needed a moment to savor it, to realize that pussy could really be this incredible. I wasn't only addicted to her blood, but her sexy body, the way she was always so goddamn wet.

I chose to keep it slow and gentle, to keep my thrusts even, to listen to her breathing as it changed from regular to heated. My eyes were locked on hers, watching her be pleased by my touch. I'd been between the fleshy thighs of lots of beautiful women, but none of them was as addictive as this spitfire.

"I'm going to come." She whispered it to me, her eyes lidded and heavy, her nails digging deeper into my flesh. "Just like that..."

I kept my pace and fought the urge to move harder. The second I heard her whisper those words to me, my dick hardened and I wanted to release. But I stayed the course, watched her eyes water, and then watched her convulse underneath me, whimpering in pleasure and whispering my name.

"Fuck." I deepened the angle and went to town, fucking her so damn hard until I came.

She grabbed me by the hip and pulled me in deeper, like she didn't want to miss a single drop.

That made me come even harder.

I dipped my head and kissed her a couple times before I started to pull out.

But she grabbed me and kept me close. "Again."

My eyes shifted back and forth between hers.

"Please..."

———

I struck my sword down and she blocked it, but she immediately gave up her ground when I swung again. "Push back, Larisa."

"Oh shit." She met my sword again and shoved me back.

But it felt like a breeze. "Harder."

"That's as hard as I can go—"

"No, it's not." I lowered my sword. "Come at me."

Covered in sweat and breathing heavily, she took a moment before she swung her sword.

I blocked it. "Grab the hilt with both hands. Plant your back foot like this. Push with your core, not your arms." I pushed her back gently so she wouldn't fly back and roll across the grass. "Come on." I came at her with a flurry of hits, moving so quickly that she would struggle to do as I told her. She slipped back farther and farther, losing ground. "Larisa."

She finally found her spot, gripped the hilt with both hands, and then pushed.

I moved back slightly, but not enough to give her much of a breather. "Not good enough." I struck her again.

"I weigh barely over a hundred pounds!"

"Doesn't matter." I slammed my sword down, met her steel, and then she did the unexpected.

She kicked me.

That made me topple backward.

"Shit, are you okay?"

I righted myself then looked at her narrowed eyes. "Good, Larisa. Do that again, but never twice on the same opponent."

"Why?"

"Because they'll grab your ankle next time." Our blades came together again, and we sparred under the shade of the oak tree, pushing her into exhaustion and soreness, forcing her to adapt to be more of a skilled fighter.

She had improved, but not by much. Despite her efforts, she simply couldn't compete with someone with my experience, at least not in the limited number of practices we'd had. For a novice, she was remarkable, but that wasn't enough.

"I need a break..." She dropped her sword to her side and walked to the tree where her pack sat on the root.

"We've just begun, Larisa."

She whipped around to look at me. "Just begun? It's been an hour."

"And we have another hour to go."

"Kingsnake, I'm not dead like you. I can't just keep going." She dropped onto the tree root and rummaged in her pack for her water and snacks.

It was another foggy day, blocking the sight of the ocean and the mountains, the mist right on the skin. To me, it was beautiful, but for a human, it was misery. Without sunlight, their moods dampened.

I used to be the same way...once upon a time.

When I turned back to her, she had finished her snack and drunk most of her water. She was in her full armor with her hair pinned back, and there was something about the way everything fit her that made it hard not to stare.

"You aren't tired?"

"I don't get tired."

"Because of my blood or..."

"It helps." She clearly wasn't ready to stand again, so I sat and leaned against a protruding tree root. It was big enough to be like the back of a chair.

"Where's Fang?" She looked at me, fatigue in her eyes. "I haven't seen him in a couple days."

"Hunting." I lied because I had no other explanation. I wondered what he'd say when she asked him about it.

"I miss him. He's my only friend."

"I'm not your friend?"

Her eyes stilled on my face and remained that way. "No... definitely not." There was a subtle blush to her cheeks, a gleam of embarrassment.

Our nights had become routine. When I returned to our bed, she was naked and waiting for me. Wet like it'd been weeks since she'd last had me rather than hours. It was unspoken, a passionate relationship without a foundation. We didn't talk much, falling into a comfortable companionship that no longer contained mistrust and mystery. It was odd, considering we hardly knew each other...but it still felt right.

I wondered if it felt right to her. "How long?"

She'd looked away during my thoughts, examining the quiet landscape before us. Now she turned back, eyebrows slightly raised.

"How long were you fucking him?" It'd been on my mind since I'd read between the lines, since I picked at the threads of her story and discovered the horrible truth. It disgusted me, made me angry beyond reason, incited a jealousy beyond my capability.

Her face immediately hardened at the question, horrified by the subject.

I needed to hear that it was a mistake, that he meant nothing to her, because he was nothing compared to her.

She looked away, the silence lingering.

I continued to stare.

"I'll answer your question—if you answer mine about Ellasara."

I felt the smoke leave my nostrils. I only wanted to take—not give.

Now it was silent.

She looked at me again, as if expecting me to agree to her terms.

I couldn't do that.

Nor would I ever.

———

When we returned to the bedchambers, the first thing she did was walk into the other room in search of Fang. He wasn't draped in his tree branches or curled up on the couch, and her disappointment was like a cloud of smoke. "I'm starting to worry." She turned back to look at me.

"He's fine, sweetheart." Instead of being irritated by their closeness, I was touched by it, touched that someone else cared for him the way I did.

"Have you spoken to him?"

"Yes." That was a lie, but if he were in trouble, he would tell me.

"He's just never been gone like this before—"

"Your worry is misplaced."

She studied my face, regarding it differently now. "There's something you aren't telling me."

"I'm not obligated to share every aspect of my life with you."

"You are when it concerns Fang. You aren't the only one who cares for him, you know."

That told me her abilities were different from mine. She couldn't communicate with him over great distances. "You think I'd ever let anything happen to him?" There was no amount of anger that could change what we've had over these past centuries.

Her eyes steadied. "No..."

"Then don't worry about it." I moved to the closet and undressed, removing my armor and tucking it away before stepping into the shower.

She followed me a moment later, tipping her head back and closing her eyes to let the water cascade down. "I'm so sore..."

I was hypnotized by her appearance, trapped under a spell she didn't cast. Her beauty was a feast for the eyes, and her blood was a feast for my power. Months had passed, and her blood hadn't grown stale. Her body hadn't either. I was just as enthralled by her now as the moment I'd first tasted her.

She opened her eyes and looked at me, as if she felt it.

My thoughts.

I did my best to guard my mind from her abilities, but when it came to moments like this, when I wanted her more than I'd ever wanted another woman, I was powerless. It was too intense to sheathe like a dagger under a cloak. The flames were too big to douse with a bucket of water. My obsession had become undeterred infatuation.

Her eyes stayed on me, as if she could read every thought like words on a page.

I decided to embrace it rather than fight it. She was the woman in my bed every night, the woman I refused to share with my people, and I wasn't ashamed to feel this desperate desire, this unbearable need. I wanted her the way the heart needed blood, the way lungs needed air. She deserved to know that she belonged to me—and only me.

My arms circled her waist, and I pulled her into me, tits against my chest, my hard dick right against her stomach. Every time I touched her, it felt like the first time, lightning between our touches. My forehead rested against hers as I considered what I wanted to do most—bite her or fuck her.

She answered for me by pulling away and tilting her neck, exposing the pale flesh for my fangs.

Just when I thought I couldn't want her more—I did. I backed her into the wall, lifted her up so her ankles locked around my waist, and then adjusted her onto my length, sliding my dick into the sheath of her tightness.

It felt like flames up my spine.

Her arms circled my neck, and she started to rock against me, turning her head to expose her neck.

I took the invitation and sank my fangs into her flesh.

Fuck.

It was oblivion, sweet and potent, tranquil.

Perfect.

————

Kingsnake.

My eyes were closed. Dreams came and went.

Kingsnake!

My eyes flashed open, and I saw my bedroom, Larisa using my body as a pillow, bed, and blanket. *What is it?*

Orcs march on Grayson.

It took me a moment to understand his words, my mind still in the throes of sleep. *How many?*

All of them.

I remained still in bed, processing all of this.

Goblinsss too.

When will they be here?

Nightfall.

That means you're far away.

I'm headed to Cobra.

Why?

**Because we have no chance of defeating them.
There are too many.**

You underestimate us.

And you underestimate them, Kingsnake.

How many march?

At least ten thousand. That's five to one.

Now I was wide awake. *This is what Ellasara spoke of.*

Yesssss.

I moved out of bed, letting Larisa slip off me and lie where
I'd been just a moment ago.

You'll need to get Larisa to safety. Grayson is no place for her.

I can't leave her unprotected.

I will come to her the moment I leave Cobra. We'll hide until the war is won...or lost.

I'd never been afraid to die—but now I was terrified. If I perished, no one would protect Larisa from the Ethereal. They would hunt her down and kill her with an arrow to the heart. *Hurry.*

I will.

I went straight into my closet and put on my uniform and armor. While I should be worried about my people and nothing else, I worried for Larisa. I couldn't possibly protect her and fight in battle at the same time.

"Kingsnake?" Her quiet voice came from the bedroom.

I lingered in the closet, not wanting to face her with this information, especially when I didn't have a plan. I eventually manned up and stepped into the bedroom, wearing my full armor, along with my two side blades and my extra blade across my back.

The peacefulness in her eyes dissipated when she saw me fully dressed, with my cloak at my back, all my weapons prepared. "What is it?" She must have sensed my mood, maybe felt my emotions from the closet.

I came to the bed and sat on the edge. "Orcs and goblins march on Grayson."

It took her a moment to understand. "Why? You're their ruler."

"The Ethereal. That's why."

Her eyes shifted back and forth between mine.

"The Ethereal sent them to do their dirty work, made them empty promises. It's their hope that they'll wipe us out—including you. Or we'll surrender, and then they can walk right in and take you."

Now she was scared. It was in her eyes. "What...what are we going to do?"

"Defeat them."

"I've fought orcs. They're massive."

My hand cupped her cheek, and all I wanted to do was take away this misery. "But we're strong."

"Well...it's a good thing you've trained me."

I didn't tell her the truth, just let the assumption sit there in the moment. "Fang is traveling to King Cobra. They'll send their armies to help us."

"Why would they help you? Because they're vampires?"

"Because we're brothers."

Her eyes softened slightly when she heard that. "Kingsnake...Viper...Cobra. I can't believe I didn't see it before."

"I need to speak with Viper immediately. I need to warn everyone what's to come."

She gave a nod.

"Stay here until I return." My fingers dug deeper into her hair, and I kissed her.

Her lips parted slightly, and she cupped my face, deepening the kiss.

I abruptly pulled away and walked out, knowing where that kiss would lead if I didn't step away right then and there.

———

"Fang said ten thousand." I stood across from Viper at the table, the commanders there as well. "It's five to one."

Viper stared at the map between us. "If they'll be here at nightfall, that means they're here." He moved one of the pawns into the Silvertongue Valley. "They'll have their respite, then arrive at dusk."

"If Cobra rides without stopping, he'll get here by morning," I said.

"We might be dead by morning," Viper said calmly. "We'll need to keep them out of Grayson for as long as possible. That means we'll need to cave in the passages in the mountains."

"We only do that in the direst of circumstances." Once those passages were closed, it would take months of manual labor to open them again.

"And this is dire," Viper said. "Some of them will still get through, but at least it'll be a fair fight at that point. We'll be able to manage. Once the others find a way around, Cobra and his army will have arrived."

I nodded in agreement. "We'll take them on in the passages when they least expect us."

"Yes," Viper said. "It'll be a good ambush. I'll take the commanders that way, but you'll need to stay in Grayson."

"Why?"

"In case they have a trick up their sleeve."

They were stupid creatures with minute thoughts, but since the Ethereal were involved, we should be prepared for anything. "They're here for Larisa, so I'll need to send her away just in case we fall."

Viper stared at me. "She won't survive long out there alone."

"She's more capable than you realize." The words tumbled out in a flourish. "Fang will protect her when he returns."

"Kingsnake."

I already held his gaze, so I knew this was important.

"You need to share her blood with your kin."

I'd been feeding on her every day, not for hunger but for pleasure. Now I was stronger than I'd ever been, and I knew that would be my greatest asset in the battle with creatures a foot taller than me. To bestow that gift on the others would be the right thing to do—for a king.

But I was more than just a king. I was her lover.

"Kingsnake." He said my name in a deeper tone, the threat obvious. "Now isn't the time to be greedy."

"It's not greed..."

"Whatever you want to call it, Kingsnake. Others need to feed if you want us to win this."

I felt the stare of the commanders, felt the stare of my brother. The hardest thing about being a king was the selflessness. I could never put myself first, could never sacrifice the many for the one, but fuck, I really wanted to. "I need to speak with Larisa."

"She's a prisoner. She doesn't get a choice—"

"Yes, she does," I snapped. "But don't worry...she'll say yes."

"Why?"

"Because I asked."

30

LARISA

I paced the room.

I was alone, my friend not here to talk to, and my lover was gone.

I guess that was what he was...my lover.

The door opened, and Kingsnake entered, his cloak swishing behind him.

I rushed to him, desperate for news, wearing my full armor that weighed at least twenty pounds. "What's happening?"

"General Viper and some of the army are going to ambush them in the passages outside the mountains. But I'll remain here in Grayson in case a second army is coming from a different direction."

"Like the sea?"

"They won't sail here, but yes."

"Alright...then we sound prepared." I'd held my own against a couple of orcs, killed a few vampires, so I believed I had some chance of surviving this attack. The well-being of the vampires that had taken me shouldn't be my concern...but Kingsnake had become my concern.

He stared at me. "You aren't staying here, Larisa."

My eyes lifted to his, the trepidation in my heart. "What...?"

"I have to send you away. There's a chance we won't win this war, and if we lose, they'll kill you."

"But leave...? Where would I go?"

"Into the wilderness. Fang will meet you there when he can."

"I...I can't leave you." My heart clenched painfully in my chest once I realized just how much I cared. I decided to cover it up, to lie to myself as well as him. "Without you, I have no chance to find a cure for my people..."

His expression didn't change, as if he didn't even hear that last part.

"This is the only way I can protect you."

"You can come with me—"

"I would never abandon my people—even if I knew defeat was guaranteed. I would die beside them, as their king, even in death."

I shouldn't have suspected anything else. "So...you think we'll lose?"

"I didn't say that."

"Then what do you think?"

He stared. "I'm not arrogant enough to assume victory is guaranteed. It never is. We're outnumbered five to one— and orcs are massive creatures."

"That doesn't make me feel better..."

"I'm not trying to make you feel better."

"I would rather stand and fight with you than flee. I know we've only trained a couple times—"

"You want to help?"

"Of course I do."

"Then there's something else you could do, something that would be much more helpful than fighting alongside us."

"What is it?"

He said nothing for a long time. "Your blood makes me stronger than I've ever been. Returns me to a youth I've long forgotten. My muscles swell...my strength increases...

my mind is quicker. It's more powerful than any armor I could wear."

My heart started to race when I realized his request.

"If you could share it with the others...they would be stronger as well."

I could feel the shock across my face. "I'm surprised you would even want me to—"

"I don't. You don't understand how deeply it burns..." He clenched his jaw, the cords popping in his neck. "But General Viper asked...and I know it would make a difference in this fight. I have to put the needs of my people first."

"So...I don't get a say in this."

"You do—that's why I'm asking."

I stared at his face, thinking about various fangs piercing my skin over and over. It had already happened to me before—and it was horrible. It didn't feel good—and it nearly killed me. When Kingsnake fed upon me, it was intimate...meaningful.

He continued to stare. "Trust me. I don't want to share you."

I could feel his pain, feel the throb of his despair. It was a different sensation, an emotion I hadn't detected from him before. It felt like a dark night without stars or clouds...just nothing.

"I don't want anyone else to have you the way I have you. It makes me sick just to think about it."

"Because they have my power?"

"No," he said. "Because they have you."

I felt the surge in his intensity, the possessiveness, the need.

"Bloodletting can just be about hunger. Predator and prey. But it can be so much more...like it is with us. Imagine if I feed on another woman...and you'll understand how I feel."

I knew I wouldn't like it, but I would never admit that out loud.

"That's how you can help us...if that's what you want."

It went against everything I believed in, to feed an army of vampires so they could annihilate their enemies. But those enemies wanted me, so perhaps it was a fair trade for their sacrifice. "I'll do it."

Disappointment radiated from him, like he'd hoped I would give a different answer. "You're certain?"

I nodded.

"Viper will be there to supervise."

"You won't be there?"

He shook his head. "I can't..."

I didn't press him for more when his message was clear. "When should we do this?"

"Now."

I was taken into my old bedroom, the place where Kingsnake had bitten me the first time. The place felt so foreign, it was like I'd never lived there at all.

Kingsnake walked in with his brother. "Only fifty of our best fighters. And only a small amount."

Viper nodded. "Can I be one of the fifty?"

Kingsnake hesitated before he granted his blessing. "Yes."

"Take her into my chambers when she's done and make sure she's fed. She'll need to sleep for a few hours before she leaves."

"Alright."

Kingsnake didn't look at me before he walked out, but I could feel his despair. It grew fainter and fainter as he walked away until it disappeared altogether.

Viper turned to me. "Are you ready?"

"You'll be here the entire time?"

"I wouldn't let anything happen to you on account of my brother."

"I know..."

"Then lie down. I'll go first."

31

KINGSNAKE

I stood in the high tower and looked over the valley, waiting for a sign of the war looming at our doorstep. I knew I wouldn't see anything before dark, but I needed to focus on something besides the horror that was occurring in that moment.

The others prepared the cannons and the gates, getting ready for the creatures that could possibly overrun our city. Orders had been given, and now there was nothing to do but wait.

Footsteps sounded behind me. "She's resting in your bed."

I didn't turn around, not prepared to see the new color in his eyes. "She's eaten?"

"Yes."

It was over, but I still felt sick. "Did you have to kill anyone?"

"They're more concerned about the army that marches on their border. Everyone is ready to serve you in this battle."

I inhaled a slow breath, relieved nobody tried to take more than their share.

"She's alright, Kingsnake."

"You don't understand..."

He came to my side and looked out over the ramparts with me. "I understand that was difficult for you, but you still chose to put your people's needs before your own. This is why I serve you—not because you're my brother, but because you're a great king."

———

I went to her bedside and watched her sleep. Color had returned to her face, and she hugged the pillow beside her like it was me.

Her neck was covered in bite marks—and none of them was mine.

My hand reached for her hair and pulled it forward to hide the evidence.

Her eyes lifted at my touch, and she stared at me for a moment as she tried to understand her reality.

"It's over."

She blinked a couple times before she sat up.

"How do you feel?"

"Fine." Her voice was raspy like she'd been sleeping all night rather than a few hours.

"Are you still hungry?"

"No..." She ran her fingers through her hair and blinked a few more times before she looked at me. "Feels like a bad dream."

More like a nightmare.

"I'd let you sleep...but you need to leave."

"Leave?"

"While you still have daylight. Once it's dark, you'll need to stay hidden until Fang joins you."

Sleep finally left her eyes when she realized her situation. "I don't think I can leave you—"

"You can."

"What if..." She couldn't bring herself to say it.

"Then that is my fate."

"You say you want to live forever...but you aren't afraid to die."

"Some things are worth dying for."

Her eyes dropped in sadness.

"Stay hidden with Fang. Once it's safe, he'll escort you east."

"What's east?"

"He'll explain everything if the time comes." I left the bed.

She pushed the covers back, still wearing her uniform without the armor.

"Get dressed. I'll take you to your horse."

She got to her feet and looked at me, like she had so much to say but didn't have the words.

I wasn't sure when this had happened. When we went from enemies sleeping together to...whatever this was. It was complicated. She cared for me when she shouldn't. I cared for her when she should only serve a purpose. But here we were.

She got dressed in her armor and cloak, took her sword and her blades, and then walked out with me. We took the secret path outside the city, where a saddled horse was tied to a tree, munching on the grass.

"Everything you need is packed. Food and water are limited, so ration them." I untied the horse from the tree and adjusted the reins for her. "You're going to head southeast, coming around the biggest mountain until you see the waterfall. You can't miss it. Stay low until Fang comes. I'll tell him where to find you."

She stared at me with emotional eyes, as if she didn't hear a word I said.

I tried to make this as clean as I could, but it was only making it worse.

"I can't leave you—"

"*You are.*" Now I raised my voice to crush this ridiculous idea. "I can't do what I need to do if I'm worried for your safety the whole time. If you want me to survive, then I can't be distracted."

She breathed deeply, a distant hint of tears in her eyes. Thankfully, she was too proud to let them fall.

I couldn't deal with that right now.

"I'm scared..."

"There's nothing to be scared of."

"You wouldn't send me away unless you feared the worst."

She was too smart for her own good. "I'm a cautious man, that's all."

"You're lying."

I did my best to close off my thoughts, but she somehow broke them down. "Don't forget what I am. King of Vampires and Lord of Darkness. You said yourself you wish we were dust on the wind."

Her eyes watered like I'd slapped her.

"That you hate me. That you hate our kind and always will."

She breathed hard.

"Perhaps you'll get your wish." I moved around the horse and prepared to help her up. "Let's go."

She stayed there, not looking at me.

"*Larisa.*"

She finally turned and faced me again.

I offered my hand to help her up.

Her eyes were fixated on mine. "Please don't die."

The searing heat flooded throughout my body, seeing the way her eyes flashed in sincerity when she spoke those words. I couldn't read minds, but right now, I could read her heart.

She moved into me and hugged me, her cheek planted against my chest.

My arms remained at my sides as she held on to me, trying to make the break as easy as possible.

But she stayed there.

Stayed there until I enveloped her in my arms and held her close, dipping my head to the top of her forehead. My fingers dug into her hair, and I felt her little chest rise and fall with emotion.

Now I didn't want to let go.

Ever.

She finally moved away and pulled herself into the saddle without my help. Without looking at me, she grabbed the reins then nudged the horse, taking off at a run. She headed southeast like I said—and didn't look back.

It was an hour before dusk.

We were as prepared as we could be for the oncoming attack. Those who drank Larisa's blood were positioned closest to the action. The cannons were loaded. The braziers were lit.

I stood beside Viper, neither one of us speaking.

King Cobra has agreed to come to your aid. He's leaving with his army now.

It'll take him too long to get here.

***He saysss he has a secret passage through the
mountains. If they don't stop, they'll arrive at
midnight.***

Thank you, Fang.

I'm on my way.

*Larisa is waiting near the waterfall in the southeast. Meet
her there.*

I want to join you in battle.

I know. But I need you to protect Larisa in my stead.

Alright.

Fang?

Yesss?

I'm sorry...about before. I hadn't seen him in several days,
and now I feared I would never see him again. The last
time we were in the same room together, I'd watched him
leave with his head bowed in shame. *I regret the way we
left things.*

Nothing changes between usss. Ever.

I absorbed his words before I turned to Viper. "Cobra will
be here at midnight."

"How is that possible?"

"He has a secret passage."

"That he's never shared with us?"

"You know he keeps his cards close to his chest..."

Viper looked straight ahead. "It's time I leave for the passages." He took a breath before he pivoted his body and looked at me head on. "I guess this is goodbye...for now."

I nodded. "For now."

His eyes said everything his lips didn't. That this might be our last moment together. And there would be no reunion beyond this...because our souls had been sacrificed long ago. Words couldn't convey the unspoken love between brothers. It couldn't convey the depth of loyalty ingrained deep in our bones.

Instead of saying more, he turned and walked off, his cloak moving in the breeze behind him.

Night deepened. The braziers lit the night in a dancing glow. The world was quiet—until the rocks fell. It was a long way away, but once the passage was detonated, the volume of debris that slid down was enough to shake the entire world.

"Good luck, Viper." I stood on the embankment at the western gate, knowing that was where the attack would come if there was another.

In the dark, I saw the scout run between the braziers, his pace at a sprint. There were supposed to be two—but it looked like only one made it back. "Open the gate."

The soldiers turned the wheel and cracked the door open so our scout could make it through. Once behind the gate, he fell to his knees and gasped for air. Someone brought him water, and he chugged it like he hadn't had anything to drink in weeks.

I made it down below and approached him. "What happened?"

He sat back on his ankles. "They got Filcon..."

"Who's they?"

"Their army. It marches not a league behind me."

So there was a second army.

Right on cue, I heard the sound of the drums.

Their forces had been divided into two, which meant we had to fight on two fronts. The sealed passages would kill some, but acted as an inconvenience for most. But they'd eventually make it to Grayson—and hopefully after Cobra had arrived.

There was a very good chance we wouldn't survive this.

But I didn't show that to my men. They all stared at me, waiting for orders, waiting for a curse or a scream.

I kept my composure. "Prepare the archers. Take down as many as you can. The rest of us will fight outside the gate. Let's go."

The men opened the gate once again, and I was the first one to walk out. The others followed me, ready to die by the sword. Up ahead, their torches were visible in the small passage between the mountains. They found a way to climb up the western side and catch us by surprise. It wasn't a way we'd anticipated to receive an army, with limited space, but that was the point.

The Ethereal had known I would never take their offer, so their true purpose had been to scope out the area and find our weakness. We were already outnumbered, so dividing us was a smart move. Pinning us against the western gate where we could be crushed up against the outer walls was an even smarter move.

Their torches grew brighter, the drums louder, and then they appeared, massive creatures with open mouths, releasing their growls into the night, doing their best to intimidate us. After I conquered this land, they'd become our subjects, but now they chose to uprise.

If we survived this, I'd kill every single one of them. No more mercy.

I turned to the men behind me. "Don't give up your ground. Otherwise, you'll be pinned against the gate with a spear in your gut. Their armor is weak near the neck and under the arm. Let them swing at you a couple times, and when they pause, go for the armpit."

Every one of them wore a stoic expression like they weren't the least bit afraid, but I knew it was a different story beneath the surface. When human men died, their souls traveled to the afterlife, where they had a new beginning. For us, it was just over, just darkness. It was the sacrifice we made to live this eternal night.

Their army came to a halt in front of us, their spears in the ground, their drums quiet.

I waited for their demands.

Kahan, chief of the orcs, stepped forward. White paint was smeared across his dark face, and he gripped his black spear with his enormous fingers. He slowly approached me, dark eyes in a terrifying face. He stopped just feet away. "Give us the girl—and your people are spared."

"How could I trust you? After our war, I pardoned your kind and allowed you to occupy my lands freely. You betrayed that mercy, and for what? A chance to live forever? Surely, you must realize that was a false promise. Their kind would never allow beasts into their eternal realm."

Kahan exposed his teeth, a quiet growl issuing from his mouth. "Give us the girl—"

"No. Withdraw your armies from my lands, and I'll pardon you once again. Or continue your war, and when you lose, I'll kill all of you—and then your women and children in the caves."

"We both know you're outnumbered, King of Vampires."

"Or so you think." Larisa's blood gave me unparalleled speed, so I swiped my blade through his neck quicker than he could anticipate the attack. It was a clean slice, severing his head from his shoulders. A second passed through his body that continued to stand there, like it didn't get the message that his brain was gone. Then it collapsed too.

I stared at the army behind him and spun my sword around my wrist. "Let's do this."

Their angry growls broke into the night, and they echoed through the mountains. Then they picked up their spears and charged.

32

LARISA

Rooooaaaaarrrrr.

I stiffened when I heard the sound. It came from far away, but it echoed through all the passages between the mountains, reaching my ears near the waterfall. My horse was secured behind a tree, and I sat near the roots in the darkness, keeping my ears strained for unwanted guests.

I'd been nervous since the moment I left, but the second I heard that noise, my stomach dropped. The battle must have begun, and Kingsnake was in the thick of it. I hoped they were able to close the passages, and I hoped the Cobra Vampires would arrive soon.

I felt like I would be sick.

Larisssssa.

Fang?

I'm almossst there.

Oh, good. I've missed you. I got to my feet and waited, hoping to see the moonlight reflecting off his scales as he slithered across the grass. Minutes later, he arrived, moving like water through the blades. When he reached me, he immediately slithered up my body and wrapped around until he was perched on my shoulder.

I swayed because he was so heavy. "Fang...you weigh a lot." I sat at the base of the tree and leaned against the trunk so my body wouldn't have to support all the weight.

I'm sssorry. He left my body and instead chose to sit beside me, his head perked up so we were eye level.

"I don't know how Kingsnake holds you all the time."

He's very strong.

"I'll say..."

I looked at his yellow eyes, watched the way they glowed in the darkness. "You don't have to stay with me. I know you belong at his side...especially right now."

He didn't say anything for a while. ***Yesss. But he said your protection is more important.***

My eyes dropped, touched by the gesture. "I'm scared..."

I'm scared too.

"Have you spoken to him?"

Not since I told him Cobra and his men were on the way.

"Check in on him and see how he's doing."

I can't.

"Why?"

He's in the middle of battle. He could lose his head if I distract him.

"You're right..."

We sat there together, neither one of us saying anything, the gentle flow of the waterfall peaceful.

"I wanted to stay...but he wouldn't let me."

War is no place for you.

"I'm decent in the sword."

But you have no experience in a battle like this.

"Still hard to leave him."

Your affection for him has deepened.

"Yes...unfortunately."

Why is that unfortunate?

"Well...he's a vampire. I've always detested their kind."

But he's a noble vampire. He keeps his word. Instead of deploying his soldiers to war while he remains hidden in safety, he fights beside them. He always put his people before himself. I know he would give his life for mine if that moment ever arose. Yes, he's a vampire...but he's so much more.

"If he's so noble, why did he choose this?"

He didn't choose it.

"What do you mean?"

Fang looked away. *I've said too much...*

I wanted to press for information, but I didn't want to compromise their relationship. "Why were you gone for so long?"

I just needed some space.

"Did something happen between you?"

He was quiet for a long time. *Yes—but that's between him and me.*

I was disappointed that he shut me out, but I let it go. "It wasn't the same when you were gone."

He turned to look at me, his tongue slipping in and out, and then he rubbed his cheek against mine, like a cat with its owner.

I smiled at his affection, even though it was strange to feel scales right against my skin.

We sat in the darkness together, neither one of us able to sleep knowing what transpired elsewhere. The man we both cared for had his life on the line, and at any moment, his head could be cut from his shoulders.

Then we heard something in the distance.

A horn.

Fang immediately sat up, perched high above the grass, looking to the ocean.

"What is it?"

We heard it again, a call coming from the south.

A battle horn.

"But it sounds close..."

Fang turned his head, catching the noise directly on his ears. *It comesss from the shore.*

"Kingsnake said that wasn't a possibility..."

Orcs and goblins wouldn't travel by sea. But the Ethereal would.

I felt my face go stark white. "Shit…"

The orcs and goblins are there to destroy them. Then the Ethereal will walk in and take what they want.

"We have to warn him."

I will try. Fang went silent, still looking out to the sea.

I stayed quiet, waiting for Fang to tell me when it was done. But minutes passed, and he said nothing.

I grew impatient. "What did he say?"

Nothing. I can't get through to him…

"What? Does that mean…?"

He could be dead—or he could be so focusssed that his mind is closed. I choose to believe the latter.

"We have to warn him."

Fang turned back to me. *His instructions were clear.*

"I don't care, Fang. We have to help."

Bringing you back is the worst thing I could do.

"Fang. We can't abandon him."

He continued to stare at me.

"I have my armor and my sword. I'm not the best fighter, but I'm not worthless either. If we stick together, we should be fine."

Fang's eyes were locked on mine. *I need you to understand how dangerousss this will be. I'll do my best to protect you, but you'll need to hold your own if you want to survive.*

"We've done it before."

He gave a slight nod. *He'll never forgive me—but that won't matter if he dies.*

33

KINGSNAKE

"Pull back!" The gate had been destroyed, and the orcs flooded into the city. The palace was the last stronghold of Grayson, so we retreated to our final stand. Cobra and his men hadn't shown up, and now I feared they would only be slaughtered once they arrived. "Man the cannons. Archers, get ready." Defeat was in everyone's eyes. They followed orders, but only halfheartedly.

"Kingsnake!" One of my men looked past me, his eyes wide with fear.

I turned around and caught the sword just in time. A pack of orcs had made it up the side of the palace, and they descended upon me with rage. They were no ordinary orcs, but the elite commanders, bigger and stronger than the rest.

I was outnumbered five to one, and Larisa's blood wouldn't be enough to overpower them. I fought them, but once they surrounded me, I was trapped. My energy wouldn't last long, and eventually, a blade would crack my armor.

The cannons fired and took down one, barely missing me.

One of them slammed their sword into my shoulder, and the momentum transferred through the armor, making me buckle to the ground.

I was on my feet instantly, swiping for his neck but missing.

Another sword hit me across the back.

I knew this was the end.

"Kingsnake!" I heard my brother's voice from afar, too far away to intervene.

I didn't lay down my arms. I didn't surrender. I kept going.

My blade was knocked out of my hand, and then I was shoved to the ground. A blade pressed against my throat, and the orc stood over me, baring all his teeth with a low growl.

My face remained stoic, looking at him like this was a civil meeting across a desk.

"Where's the girl?"

I said nothing.

He pressed the blade harder into my flesh, drawing a line of blood.

"She's not worth an eternity of darkness."

"Yes, she is."

He gave a growl before he yelled to another orc. "Bring the other one."

No.

Viper was bound by the wrists, and he was forced to the ground beside me, his face bloodied and battered, pieces of his armor missing.

The sword was still pressed to my neck, so I couldn't turn my head farther.

"What do you think, boys?" the orc said. "A clean swipe of his neck? Or burned alive in the fire?"

"Burn him so we can hear him scream."

A sneer moved over his lips. "That'll be your fate unless you tell us what we want to know."

"It'll be my fate, regardless, so get on with it."

The sneer remained. "I've been waiting for this day a long time—the end of the Kingsnake Vampires."

"The others will avenge us—and your kind will be gone from this world."

"Really? Who do you think is next on our list?" He withdrew the blade. "Grab him."

The orcs grabbed me by the arms and forced me up. I tried to fight their hold, but they were far too strong. They marched me past Viper, who tried to push himself up to help me, but an orc kicked him in the face.

They forced me to the bonfire they'd built and prepared to shove me inside. The flames were ten feet high, and the second my clothes caught fire, I would be burned to ash, dust on the wind. I'd lived a long fifteen hundred years, but I expected to live another fifteen hundred.

"Hiiisssssss."

One of the orcs dropped their hold on my arm.

Then the other roared as if something had stuck him in his side.

Chaos was unleashed. Fang appeared out of the darkness and wrapped his body around the neck of one of the monsters. *Crack.* The orc fell limp to the ground. Fang launched his body to the next one and did the same.

And then there was Larisa.

She stabbed her blade into the back of the knee of the first one, and once he dropped, she stabbed her blade deep into the back of his neck, killing him instantly.

I didn't have time to process the rescue. I snatched my blade off the ground and freed Viper before I took down the last elite orc. Once they were all dead, I saw the goblins running out of the city toward the eastern gate.

Cobra is here.

I turned to Fang, perched on top of one of the dead orcs. "I asked you to keep her safe—"

"The Ethereal march from the south." Larisa appeared at my side, strong and sexy in her armor, her sword covered in black blood from the orc she slayed. "Their ships docked on the shore. They're coming."

I stared with empty eyes, taking a moment to process what she said.

"I'm sorry, but we had to warn you."

I was so furious that my vision tinted red. But now wasn't the time or the place for this conversation.

Viper stepped forward when he heard what she said. "We need to defeat this army before they arrive. If they know we've persevered, they'll turn back. They're here to conquer—not to fight."

I turned to Fang. "How many did Cobra bring?"

Five thousand strong.

I looked at Viper. "How many orcs and goblins remain?"

"Half their forces," he answered.

"Fang says Cobra has five thousand soldiers," I said. "He should be able to defeat the rest of them on his own."

"And what about us?" Viper asked.

"Move our forces to the northern gate. They expect Grayson to be served up on a silver platter for their arrival. We'll show them how badly they underestimated us."

———

I walked into the palace, which had been vacated because every vampire had been called to serve in the war. Larisa and Fang followed behind me, and after a couple different passages, I entered the room.

I pressed my hand into the stone, and that was when the secret passage opened. It was a narrow corridor, forcing someone to move sideways between the rock. "There's a safe room at the end of this passage. Wait there for my return."

Larisa stared at me like she didn't hear a word I said.

"*Now*."

"You would be dead right now if we didn't come back."

"If that was my fate, so be it."

Her eyes withered in hurt. "You can be angry at me, but don't be angry at Fang—"

"I'll be as angry as I damn well please. Now get your ass inside."

"I talked him into it—"

"Then he's weak for listening." I felt my face flush with heat because I was so angry.

"I'm sorry, but I couldn't abandon you."

"You owe me nothing, Larisa." Not a damn thing.

"We're allies..."

It was like a blade between the ribs and into one lung. It caught my breath for an instant.

"We don't turn our backs on each other—"

"I don't have time for this."

"Well, I don't want our last conversation to be like this."

I released a quiet growl. "How did you expect me to react?"

"I—I don't know."

We stared at each other for a while.

"My life isn't worth yours," I said. "Do you understand me?"

"You're my only hope for my people."

Another blade jabbed into my side. I tasted the self-loathing on my tongue. "That was the only reason you came back?" I stared into her eyes, forgetting that Fang was in the room.

She was quiet, her eyes shifting back and forth between mine.

I waited.

"You know it wasn't..."

That made me feel better—and worse. "Get in. I have to go."

Fang obeyed and slithered inside. He didn't bother asking to join me on the front lines, knowing he shouldn't provoke my already boiling anger.

"Your eyes..."

I hadn't seen my appearance, so I didn't understand her meaning.

"They're brown again."

"Because I'm exhausted, Larisa. I've fought all night, and it's nearly dawn."

"Then take more." She came close to me and loosened her armor to expose her neckline.

My breath died in my throat the second I saw her flesh. My reserves had been depleted, and now I was starving.

"I want you to be strong."

A flood of desire hit me, that aching feeling I had whenever she was in the same room. I associated feeding with sex, and sex with feeding. I couldn't have one without wanting the other. But now wasn't the time for that, so I hugged her around the waist and pulled her into me, my fangs sliding into her flesh and locking in place.

I instantly felt better, like I'd slept all night, had a feast for breakfast.

My fingers were deep in her hair, and I hugged her to me as I took as much as I could, feeling her fingers cup the back of my neck as she kept her throat exposed. I could feel her heartbeat against my lips, feel the way it quickened at my touch.

I wanted to keep going, but I knew I'd had my fill. I forced myself to release her.

She stepped back, her eyes glowing with the same desire that I felt. Blood dripped from the little dots on her neck.

"Get inside."

She moved into me, cupping my face so she could kiss me.

I immediately stepped back. "Please get in."

Her eyes were instantly wounded by my rejection.

"*Now.*"

After a long stare, she turned sideways and began to slide down the passage.

I hit the stone again, and the door shut.

———

I stood at the southern border with our rows of soldiers, ready to greet our visitors with our blades and arrows. The sun continued to rise, and then I could see them a league away, their small army approaching. They had gifted eyesight, so they could see us long before we could see them.

Viper came to my side. "They've fled into the mountains. Cobra lost some of his own, but he's unharmed."

My eyes stayed on the Ethereal.

"Should we chase them into the mountains?"

"We'll worry about them later. Have Cobra and his men join our ranks."

Viper nodded and disappeared, his face bruised and bleeding like many others.

I watched them approach, becoming bigger and bigger, their force small, maybe several hundred. Confident that the war would be won, they'd come unprepared. If they attacked, they wouldn't win the battle—and they knew that.

Minutes later, Cobra came to my side. "This is a perfect opportunity to take advantage. With our forces against theirs, we could wipe them out."

"There would be casualties," Viper said. "But it's worth the vengeance."

And vengeance was exactly what I wanted—for a lot of reasons. "We've lost too many men tonight. They're exhausted, in no shape to do anything other than look intimidating. We need to focus on self-preservation."

Cobra gave me a cold stare like he disagreed.

"And when their army doesn't return, the Ethereal will unleash all their forces in retaliation."

"Is that your true concern?" Cobra asked. "Or are you still protecting her?"

I held my brother's gaze, wanting to smash his face with the hilt of my sword. My hand remained steady, only because he'd come to my aid and saved us all. "I'm thinking of the people who risked their lives for Grayson—and nothing else."

"I agree with Kingsnake's decision," Viper said. "He's always put his people before everything else, and I know that's what he's doing now."

Cobra ignored him. "We both know he doesn't have the balls to swipe her pretty head clean from her shoulders..."

"*Cobra.*" Viper deepened his voice.

I raised my hand to silence Viper. "I don't care what you think, Cobra. If I ever met her in battle, I wouldn't hesitate to end her life. Not only because of what she did to me, but because of the threat she poses to all vampires. If you don't trust my courage, trust my loyalty to our people."

His eyes lingered for a moment, slitted and angry, but then he looked away.

The Ethereal approached then came to a halt before us.

Ellasara stepped out, accompanied by one of her commanders. They both wore white armor with blue cloaks, their skin glowing in the morning light, their eyes reflecting distant starlight.

Her eyes were locked on mine, and instead of her typical arrogance, I saw a subtle anger.

I stepped out, flanked by my two brothers, and met her in the middle.

Her blond hair shifted in the breeze as her eyes examined my men stationed outside of Grayson, archers on the battlements, soldiers on the ground, all prepared to strike her down if they came too close. Her eyes eventually came back to mine.

"Like the cowards that they are, the orcs and goblins retreated into the mountains. They'll be pursued and anni-hilated—all because of you. You filled their heads with ridiculous nonsense—and now they'll pay the hefty price."

There was no compassion in her eyes. Not a glimmer. "I don't know what you're referring to."

"I guess you're a coward too."

A subtle flash of lightning sparked across her eyes. "I've come to see if you've reconsidered our proposition."

"Whatever you say." My eyes remained locked on hers, remembering all her tells. She couldn't contain her disap-pointment, couldn't believe that her genius plan had bitten her in the ass. "You know my answer will never change."

She stared back, her anger toward me burning underneath the surface. "Have I introduced you to Therion, the General of Ethereal, and my husband?"

I hadn't even looked at him.

She watched me, waiting to see my reaction, my jealousy.

I felt none—and I was certain that showed. "There will be consequences for this, Ellasara. You've claimed the lives of my men, good men who didn't deserve to die, all because of your need to make us suffer. The humans worship you as gods, but you would strike them down the moment it serves you."

"Empty threats don't scare me, Kingsnake."

"You'll see how empty these threats are soon."

Her eyes shifted back and forth between mine. "You mean to tell me you'll march across the world, past the humans and their armies, just to meet us on our own ground? Good luck with that."

I said nothing more, knowing she was trying to pull at the threads of my plan.

"If you're truly a man of your people, you'll hand over the girl. If you did that in the first place, your men would still be alive."

"So you can kill her and the hope for all humankind? Nice try, Ellasara." I stepped back. "I hope the next time we see each other will be in battle. Our swords will speak, and the swiftest blade will prevail." I turned away, and my brothers joined me, turning our backs on the elves who watched us go.

When we returned to the front line, Ellasara and General Therion retreated to their forces in the rear. Together, they made their way to their ships at the shore and sailed away. I remained at the gate, waiting for the scouts to come back and inform me that they had truly departed our lands.

34

LARISA

When the door opened, I knew it was over.

I breathed a sigh of relief then let Fang go through first, slowly slithering between the two walls to the other side. I turned my body and stepped sideways down the narrow path, finally reaching the other doorway so I could look Kingsnake in the eye.

But it was Viper.

Fang immediately wrapped around his legs and torso, sitting across his powerful shoulders with his head perched up. They seemed to be speaking to each other, because Viper had the same focused look that Kingsnake did sometimes.

Then he turned to me. "You saved my life and have my eternal gratitude."

I didn't know what to say. When we'd arrived, we'd seen the horror unfolding and didn't think twice before striking. "It's over?"

"Yes," he said with a nod. "It's over."

"Where is he?" I hoped his eyes would be the ones I stared into.

"The battle is over, but the grief has begun. Kingsnake is with our people, carrying bodies to their final resting places, burning the enemy, returning Grayson to its former glory."

"Can we help?"

"He asked me to escort you to your chambers." His eyes weren't green anymore, like the exhaustion had drained all my blood from his body. "He wants you to rest."

I wouldn't be able to rest until he was right beside me, but I didn't want to waste our time with a pointless argument. I agreed as I swallowed my disappointment.

He guided me back to our chambers, the palace intact, while everything outside the doors was in mayhem. Buildings burned or toppled onto the streets. One of the gates was broken into pieces. The dead lay everywhere.

Viper opened the door for me.

I stepped inside, Fang slithering in front of me.

"Larisa?"

I turned back to him.

"I underestimated you."

————

Despite the exhaustion, it took a long time to fall asleep. Flashbacks of that night came to me repeatedly, the horrible memory of Kingsnake about to be burned alive. It led to restless sleep, lots of tossing and turning, eternal discomfort.

When I heard the door click into place, I jerked awake, fearful of the worst.

"It's me."

I breathed, seeing his outline in the darkness.

"Put down the dagger, sweetheart."

It'd been on my nightstand. Hadn't thought twice before I'd grabbed it. I dropped it back on the wood.

"Go back to sleep." He walked into the closet.

I was still half asleep, so I lay back down, continuing to breathe hard because reality felt like a dream. Minutes later, the water started to run in the bathroom. Now I was wide awake, waiting for him to join me.

He eventually came to bed, in his black boxers, the cuts and bruises all over his body. He had a mark across his Adam's apple and purple bruises along his arms, like sword and shield had battered his body. He pulled back the sheets and lay beside me, releasing a heavy breath when his back hit the mattress.

I moved into his side, keeping my head on the pillow rather than his shoulder to avoid his bruises.

He flinched at my touch. "I'm still angry."

My hand remained on his stomach. "Well, you're going to be angry a long time because I'm not sorry."

He turned his head to look at me, his green eyes deep and angry.

"You fought them for me. It was the least I could do."

"We've been at war with the Ethereal for a century. This battle would have happened whether I'd found you or not. All that would have been different was the outcome."

"Then it's a good thing you found me. And it's a good thing I came back."

His anger caught the curtains on fire, and his rage filled the room with smoke. But my words had tempered it, had snuffed out most of the rage. He wanted his anger to resume, but my words had doused his fuel.

"Let it go."

He took a breath, swallowing his anger. "I've never been the type to...*let it go*."

"If you want to make love to me, you're going to have to."

Just like that, his emotions shifted, and now that yearning intensity replaced his bitterness. His green eyes looked at me like I was the loveliest jewel he wanted to add to his collection. The possession was like a heavy rain, flooding the world until it reached past my head and submerged my lungs.

In an instant, he rolled on top of me and yanked down his shorts.

I was already naked, so my legs wrapped around his waist as he sank inside me, the two of us working together perfectly, knowing each other's body like our own. He entered me fully before he kissed me, giving me a heated kiss that made me sink into the sheets underneath. His thrusts were gentle and slow, our lips locked together, our moans muffled by our searing lips.

35

KINGSNAKE

Grayson remained in tatters, homes destroyed, the sky still heavy with smoke. We'd lost a third of our population, vampires who had sacrificed more than just their lives, but their eternal salvation. They understood the risk when they became one of us, but it still stung to watch them suffer.

It was my job to protect them—and I'd failed.

I stood at the top of the stairs of the palace, watching everyone work to restore Grayson to what it was, to make our city look untouched by war. Everyone was tired and defeated, even though we'd won.

Viper came to my side. "Have you recovered?"

A single night of rest had erased my bruises and faded the cut on my neck. I knew Larisa's blood was responsible for my incredible speed of healing. It gave me a surge in battle I wouldn't have had otherwise. Kept me alive. "Yes."

"Larisa saved us all."

"I know she did." I wasn't a man of many emotions. I simply had a list of objectives that I had to meet, regardless of who it affected. But now, everything was complicated. The moment she saved me, I truly wished I were dead.

"Her affection for you runs deep."

Her affection was deeply misplaced.

"This solves all your problems."

I turned to look at him. "How? It just made everything that much more difficult."

"If she cares for you, why would she want to leave? Just ask her to stay, and she never needs to know the truth."

I looked away. "Just because she cares for me doesn't mean she wants this life."

"So you think she'd still leave if you found a cure?"

"Yes." It would hurt, but she knew there was no future for us, not when her prejudice ran so deep. "She claims we killed her father. Lured him away from Raventower with false promises. I have no knowledge of this invasion, so I told her it may have been the Cobras or the Diamond-backs, but to her, we're all the same."

Viper turned quiet.

"She'll keep asking for the cure...and I'll keep saying I don't have it...and after enough time has passed...she'll know the truth. Then she'll ask to leave—and she'll be a prisoner all over again."

"There is no alternative."

"No...there's not." I couldn't let her go, not when she'd be vulnerable to the Ethereal, not when she was so valuable to me and my people. And not when...I was utterly and hopelessly obsessed with that damn woman.

———

I sat with Cobra in my study, near the fire that warmed our blood, each of us holding a glass of scotch.

"Viper won't be joining us?" It was his last night here. He gave his people time to recuperate before they made the journey back to the mountains.

"He's chasing down the rest of the traitors."

He gave a nod in agreement. "He never takes a day off, does he?"

I drank from my glass.

"I've always admired his work ethic—but never wanted it for myself." He took a drink too, on his third glass without a hint of intoxication.

"Thank you for coming to our aid." My brother and I hadn't really had a moment alone, not when we attended to the wounded and dying, when we tried to put our broken world back together. "You saved us."

"I know—but thanks for saying it anyway."

I was used to my brother's arrogance, so it bounced right off my skin. "I'll give you a handsome payment in gold—and also scotch and wine."

"Very generous—but I'm not interested."

My body stiffened slightly because I suspected his demand. Despite our differences, Cobra would always honor our shared bloodline, would risk his life for mine without hesitation, but that didn't mean he wouldn't take whatever he could get in compensation. "That's all I have to offer."

"No, it's not." That arrogant grin came across his face. "You know exactly what I want."

I held his gaze, my fingers tight on my glass. "The answer is no."

"So Viper and the others get a taste, but I'm excluded?"

"That was out of necessity."

"If I made this demand before providing aid, you would have obliged out of necessity. It shouldn't matter that I'm asking for it after the fact. I won this battle for you and lost good men in the process. You owe me."

The anger was so potent, it felt like thunder in my blood. "She's mine, Cobra."

"Keep her. I just want to borrow her."

It made me sick. Literally. "No."

"This is the one thing I want—and you deny me?"

I looked away.

Cobra continued to stare, his look angry. "I guess she's more than just a pet."

I said nothing.

"A lot more."

"Drop it, Cobra."

"What's your plan, Kingsnake? You can't turn her. Otherwise, you'll lose the blood that makes you so powerful. You can't sustain a relationship with a mortal, because within the blink of an eye, she'll be an old hag. You can't forsake your immortality because that would just be stupid—"

"I said, drop it."

That smile returned. "You've gotten yourself into quite a predicament, haven't you?"

I ignored his stare.

He raised his glass to me. "Good luck with that, brother."

———

Days passed, and Grayson remained in upheaval. The passages would take a long time to clear, and the city itself was still stained with blood. Everyone worked to rebuild their lives, but the loss had left a permanent mark upon our city.

I didn't sit around and watch others do my bidding. I worked with the citizens to clear the debris, to pick up the pieces of the broken gate, to repair our borders in case there was another attack.

It was a long day, a day that made me sweat to the bone.

Fang appeared from behind, circling my body until he was propped on my shoulder. I'd been lifting heavy wood all day, but his weight was always welcome. ***Can I help?***

No.

I'm very ssstrong.

I know you are. I wiped the sweat from my forehead with the back of my forearm before I turned away, finished with the day. I took the long walk back to the palace, passing through the streets that would never look the same. *Cobra left.*

At least he understandsss that the vampires need to forge an alliance against the Ethereal.

Yes, but you know how my father is.

Even more stubborn than you.

Not how I would have worded it...but yes.

Have you been able to detect the elements in her blood? Larisa asksss me nearly every day.

I'd never had to keep a secret from Fang, but I'd kept my cards close to my chest. *Can I trust you?*

Of courssse.

Larisa can never know. We reached the entrance to the palace, and I entered my study where the warm fire greeted me. *Do you understand?*

Fang immediately left my shoulders and curled into a ball on the rug, right next to the fire so his blood would warm. His head remained propped, at full attention. His yellow eyes regarded me with a guarded appearance.

Fang.

I would never betray you, Kingsnake.

You did before.

Betrayal is far too harsssh a word.

I sat in the armchair. *There is no cure.*

What do you mean?

I've discovered the cause of her immunity—and it can't be replicated.

How long have you known?

A long time.

And you never told her.

No...

Fang turned to look at the fire, fully understanding the implication of my words. **When will you tell her the truth?**

I didn't answer.

Fang turned his gaze back on me, studying my face in the glow. **You won't releassse her...**

No.

Fang looked at the fire again. **What'sss your plan?**

I don't have one.

You've lied to her long enough. It can't go on.

I ignored him.

She's very attached to you, Kingsnake.

We'd fallen into domestic bliss, a routine I would normally despise. We shared our meals during the day and our bodies in the evening. Any other woman would have been replaced long ago, but with Larisa, I hadn't even scratched the surface.

Tell her the truth. Ask her to ssstay.

She'll say no.

But she may not.

Attachment isn't reason enough. There's no reason strong enough to embrace my eternal darkness. This is but a moment, a forbidden temptation, a passionate affair that will blow out the second she has another choice.

Fang said nothing for a while. **Regardless of the outcome, you must be forthcoming. You're an honorable man, Kingsnake. You always speak the truth.**

A painful smirk moved across my mouth. *We always assume we'll do the right thing even when it fails to benefit us...but we don't. We do what's best for us—always.*

If she does choose to leave, she'll be angry.

I know.

As angry as a cornered venomousss snake.

I'd expect nothing less.

36

LARISA

I looked at my hand of cards, all shit.

My eyes lifted to Fang's.

He was absolutely still as he stared at me, his tongue slipping in and out, wearing the best poker face I'd ever seen. His cards were facedown on the table as he waited for me to go first.

I sighed before I threw down the pair of blades.

The end of his tail flipped over his hand, a blade, a pair of arrows, a shield, and a dagger.

"How are you so good at this?"

Experience.

"But cards are random."

Not that random. He tossed his cards into the center of the table.

"I think I've won only once."

Yes, I felt bad and let you win.

I glared at him.

Sssorry.

The door opened, and Kingsnake entered. His mood had been grim since the battle ended, spending his days helping his people repair their fallen city. Viper hadn't returned from his voyage into the mountains. Kingsnake was distant with me most of the time, except when we were in bed together, when he came alive and burned hotter than the sun.

Fang abruptly slithered away, turning the doorknob with his tail before he glided into the hallway and left our presence. He didn't say a word to me, which told me Kingsnake had ordered him to leave.

I left the cards on the table and walked up to him. "Fang won...again."

He gave me the hardest stare I'd ever seen, his face tight with tension, his mood intense but not angry. "We need to talk."

I'd heard that phrase before, but not from him. Elias had said it to me when he'd told me he would fulfill his royal obligations and marry someone else. It hurt because I hadn't expected it, assumed his feelings for me were as genuine as mine were for him. "I know where this is going..." I'd lost my temper and shed tears last time, but I was too proud to do that now. Like all the others, Kingsnake had grown tired of me, needed another woman to replace me in his bed.

His eyes narrowed on my face. "You're my only desire, sweetheart." Now his feelings changed, turning warm and gentle like a fire in a hearth, the sunshine on green grass on a spring afternoon.

Embarrassed by my assumption, I stayed quiet.

He let the silence endure, staring at me like he wished he could read my mind.

"What did you want to discuss?"

His warmth continued a little longer before the intensity returned. "There will be no cure."

All my fears were replaced by shock. "What...?"

He held my gaze.

"What does that mean?"

"It means what I said. There is no cure."

My eyes shifted back and forth between his. "And you just realized this now?"

He held his silence.

I swallowed the lump of betrayal. "How long have you known?"

He continued to stay quiet, like he didn't want to answer. "Awhile."

My eyes shifted back and forth between his. "Why?"

His eyes were locked on mine, so still they were stone. "You know why."

I inhaled a slow breath, hurt by his treachery but also touched by it. I pushed past it. "Is there truly no cure, or were you just unable to figure it out?"

"I figured it out, but the cure no longer exists."

"I—I don't understand."

He stared at me for a long time, the emotions around him thudding like a distant drum. "The snake that bit you when you were young...was a Golden Serpent."

I never saw the scales of the serpent. My memories were fractured because of my youth. But now when I played it back, I pictured a beautiful golden snake that blended in with the stalks of wheat.

"His venom grants you the immunity—as well as your other abilities."

Shit...he knows.

"But Golden Serpents have since been eradicated."

"By whom?"

"The Originals."

"Why would they do that?"

"So they would remain the only Originals."

"But...this was just twenty years ago. They still exist."

"Maybe one or two. Maybe a couple. Not enough to ever find. We would have better odds looking for a needle in a haystack."

"But...we have to try."

"And how do you suggest we do that?" he asked coldly.

"We have all the humans search the world until we find one."

"And if they succeed, you think one or two is enough to provide the venom for all humankind? It would be given to the nobility and then hoarded. None of that would make it to the working class, and you know it."

"Maybe there are more. Maybe they've repopulated. We can't give up without even trying..."

"Golden Serpents were difficult to find, even in the beginning. They're elusive creatures, and they don't live in a single climate. They can survive all temperatures, so there's not a single section of the world where they exist in higher numbers. And what happens when the Ethereal realize what we're doing? They start their crusade against the Golden Serpents."

I didn't accept this defeat. Not without trying.

"I'm sorry."

I'd expected a very different outcome in this endeavor. I'd expected it to be easy. I'd expected it to be quick. "Well, whether you help me or not, I'm going to try. I'll return to Raventower and speak to King Elias. We'll speak to the other kingdoms and—" I stopped when I felt the rage break through his skin and bone. It was like a tornado made of fire.

It was written on his face too, his eyes murderous. "I want you to stay."

My heart started to race, both in desire and fear.

"Stay with me."

"Why?" I whispered.

His eyes shifted back and forth between mine, his anger subdued by the whisper in my voice. "For us."

My heart had grown weak for this man, but it was the same situation as it was with Elias, a relationship that had no future. "Kingsnake, you're a vampire—"

"I've proven to you that the Ethereal are your enemy, not us."

"It's more than that—"

"*Stay.*"

I was tempted to succumb to the request, but my heart had been battered before, and I didn't want to feel that again. "Kingsnake, you know I feel deeply for you. If I stay any longer…I'll fall for you. And that can't happen."

His intensity deepened, his fire burning.

"So this ends now…" I wouldn't forsake my soul to live forever. And I wouldn't spend the last of my youth with a man who couldn't age with me. With a man who couldn't give me children.

Silence spread between us. It gradually overwhelmed the room.

We stared at each other.

Neither one of us knowing what to do or say next.

After an eternity, he spoke. "I'm sorry."

"Me too—"

"I'm sorry for what I'm about to do."

My heartbreak was replaced by fear. Ice-cold fear. "What are you about to do...?"

"Break my promise to you." He looked me in the eye as he said it, his mood cold like forgotten ash. "I can't let you go, Larisa."

"We—we made a deal."

"That was before."

"Before what?"

"Before I tasted you."

My heart tightened in my chest, giving a jolt of pain down my arm.

"Before I knew you could read minds."

I swallowed.

"Before I knew what the Ethereal would do to take you."

My breathing elevated, and I couldn't control it.

"Before...I had you."

I felt it, the sorrow emitting from him in waves, the self-loathing.

"You won't survive out there. The Ethereal will hunt you. Use you."

"And how is that different from what you're doing?" I snapped.

His eyes shifted back and forth between mine.

"You only asked me so you wouldn't have to force me." His feelings weren't genuine. "I mean nothing to you." I'd risked my life against enormous orcs...for nothing. "I saved you..." I felt the fury in my eyes, imagined how red my face must have appeared.

"I never asked you to save me—"

"You're an asshole. You only want me for my blood. For my powers. I don't mean a damn thing to you."

"That's not true—"

"Yes, it is." I fought back the angry tears, but they burned.

He stepped closer to me. "I want your blood. I want your powers. But I also want you."

I automatically stepped back, not wanting him near me.

He steadied himself, the hurt in his eyes. "You know my feelings for you."

"I know you would have replaced me a long time ago if I didn't make you strong."

He stepped forward again, his eyes now angry. "I don't think that's true—"

"You didn't want me until you bit me—"

"What does it matter? You know *exactly* how I feel for you every moment we're in the same room together. Every woman who's come before you is a forgotten memory, and every woman who comes after you..." His eyes hardened. "I'll wish they were you."

I felt it, that powerful desperation he couldn't control. It was like a fog rolling in from the shore.

"I may be addicted to your blood, but you're addicted to the way I feel about you. I can see it written all over your face."

I could read emotions...but he was the one who could read minds. "Maybe that's true, but that doesn't make this real. It's just a symbiotic relationship at the moment. Nothing deep. Nothing real."

In defiance, I felt his heat surround me, felt the way he was both angered and broken by what I said. "It's the realest thing I've ever had—"

"If you turned me...you wouldn't want me anymore."

His eyes narrowed.

"Because my blood would be useless to you."

Now he was quiet.

"I would lose my eternal soul, and you would dump me." Old feelings rushed in, the way I was dismissed like old, worn-out boots. "So this isn't real, Kingsnake. And let's not pretend otherwise."

He continued to stare at me, like he didn't know what to say.

"You can lock me in a room, tie me up, and feed...but that's all. I'll never stop trying to escape. I'll hate you more than I did when I arrived here." Our passionate flame would be snuffed out in the wind.

He remained quiet, his emotions obscured.

"Let me go, Kingsnake."

His eyes focused on my face. "Please don't make me do this."

I took a deep breath.

"I don't want you to be a prisoner."

So much anger...I could feel it in my tendons.

"I don't want to lose you."

"What did you think would happen? That you would tell me the truth and I would still want you? That you would take away my freedom and we'd share the same bed later that night? You aren't the man I..." I shook my head. "I'll never stop trying to escape. I won't let you feed on me. So if you want me, you're going to have to force me...and probably kill me."

He dropped his gaze. "Sweetheart—"

"I'm not your sweetheart anymore." I couldn't believe I ever was. "So lock me up...because I don't want to be in your presence a moment longer than I have to be."

———

Nooooo... This can't be their end. But both Kingsnake and Larisa are stubborn, so who is going to win this battle? Find out in **Bite the Terror That Feeds**.

Made in the USA
Monee, IL
01 December 2023

47947328R00261